Praise for the Novels of
OPAL CAREW

"With deft attention to detail . . . and a flirtation with the forbidden . . . this pleasing love story will satisfy romance fans."
—*Publishers Weekly*

"A must-read . . . Carew definitely knows how to turn up the heat."
—*RT Book Reviews*

"Carew brings erotic romance to a whole new level . . . she sets your senses on fire!"
—*Reader to Reader*

"You might find yourself needing to turn on the air conditioner because this book is HOT! Ms. Carew just keeps getting better."
—*Romance Junkies*

"A dip in an icy pool in the winter is what I needed just to cool off a little once I finished this yummy tale!"
—*Night Owl Reviews* (5 stars)

"Whew! A curl-your-toes, hot and sweaty erotic romance. I didn't put this book down until I read it from cover to cover. . . . I highly recommend this one."
—*Fresh Fiction*

"Carew is truly a goddess of sensuality in her writing."
—*Dark Angel Reviews*

"Carew pulls off another scorcher. . . . She knows how to write a love scene that takes her reader to dizzying heights of pleasure."
—*My Romance Story*

ALSO BY OPAL CAREW

Stroke
OF Luck

OPAL CAREW

ST. MARTIN'S
GRIFFIN
NEW YORK

First published in the United States by St. Martin's Griffin, an imprint of St. Martin's Publishing Group

www.stmartins.com

Designed by Omar Chapa

Library of Congress Cataloging-in-Publication Data

Names: Carew, Opal, author.
Title: Stroke of luck / Opal Carew.
Description: First edition. | New York : St. Martin's Griffin, 2020. |
Identifiers: LCCN 2020024220 | ISBN 9781250116826 (trade paperback) |
    ISBN 9781250116833 (ebook)
Subjects: GSAFD: Erotic fiction.
Classification: LCC PR9199.4.C367 S77 2020 | DDC 813/.6—dc23
LC record available at https://lccn.loc.gov/2020024220

First Edition: 2020

10 9 8 7 6 5 4 3 2 1

This book is dedicated to
Mark, Matt, and Jason.
I love you with all my heart.
Also, to Laura and Jocelyn,
who enrich our family with love and joy.

Stroke OF Luck

Prologue

April woke up with blinding sunlight flashing across her eyelids. Her head throbbed, and she just wanted to fall back asleep so she didn't have to deal with it. She shielded her eyes with her hand and kept them closed against the onslaught.

Her head was foggy, but she knew she had to get up. For the past several months, with planning her wedding, her to-do list was always jam-packed. And the big day was . . .

Yesterday!

Her eyelids snapped open as a slew of memories fluttered through her brain. Of packing for the trip to Las Vegas. Of meeting Maurice at the hotel.

Oh, God, then the rehearsal dinner . . .

Her head ached even more as she remembered that disaster. She rubbed her temples.

As her bleary eyes focused, shock surged through her. There was a naked, masculine back facing her. Big and muscular with a small red birthmark on the right shoulder blade that looked like an eagle with its wings spread.

She sucked in a breath and realized there was an arm around

her waist, too. Strong and thick. On the wrist, there was a gold watch with the iconic Rolex crown on the black face. On the back of his hand was a small scar.

Her breath caught when she saw a wedding band on the ring finger of the hand. Oh, God, she'd gone to bed with a married man? She'd never do such a thing.

The other man's hand was draped over the covers, and she was shocked to see a wedding ring there, too.

She drew in a deep calming breath. No, she couldn't have.

Then she glanced at her own hand and . . .

Red spots flickered in front of her eyes, and if she hadn't been lying down, she probably would have fainted.

She was wearing a wedding ring, too.

She had to think, but her mind swirled in confusion.

All she knew for sure was that yesterday had been her wedding day.

And neither of these men were her fiancé, Maurice.

1

April was close to tears as she sat all alone on the cushioned bench in the elegant sitting area right outside the second-largest penthouse suite in the new luxury hotel in Las Vegas.

Today was her wedding day. An hour from now, she should be walking down the aisle wearing the designer gown her fiancé, Maurice, had bought for her, her hair coiled into an elegant updo, her face beaming with happiness.

But instead she sat here, with the head of hotel security standing a few feet behind her to ensure she didn't take off, as hotel staff went through her room packing up her stuff. She didn't know exactly what was going to happen after this, but the next stop would be the manager's office. When she explained she really had no way to pay the huge bill, she was sure she'd be thrown in jail.

She stared at the checkout statement in her hand. The penthouse suite cost more for one night than a monthly mortgage payment on her town house, and the amount for the entire rehearsal dinner was included on the bill. The final total was more than she made in a year.

Maurice had also charged some purchases from the gift shop to the room. She was sure the staff were looking for those items to return to the store. One was a very expensive diamond tennis bracelet, and there were a few other pieces of jewelry.

They wouldn't find them, though, because he hadn't bought any of that jewelry for her.

Tears prickled at her eyes as an unwelcome image rippled through her mind. Of last night when she'd gone looking for Maurice and walked into the private hospitality suite the hotel had provided near the ballroom.

She'd found him. He'd been fucking a busty blond bombshell at the time.

And the woman had been wearing a diamond tennis bracelet.

Instead of being apologetic, Maurice had snapped at her to get out. April had backed away, shocked, then turned and run to the elevator. She'd gone right to their suite.

Maurice had shown up an hour later, then banged on the bedroom door, which she'd locked. He'd said they should be adults about this. That when she was his wife he would provide for her well, and she should accept that he'd have the odd affair on the side.

She'd told him to go to hell.

He'd pounded hard on the door with his fist, terrifying her, but finally he'd left. She still quaked inside at the memory of his fury. She'd never seen him like that. It was like she didn't really know the man. Which she realized now was true. She'd never *truly* known him, despite the fact they'd dated for two years. He had always been charming and sophisticated, if a little distant, but that just seemed to be his nature. He'd always been generous with her, helping her in her career and life choices. Grooming her to be his wife.

Now she realized he wanted an appropriate wife on his arm while he fucked whatever tramp he wanted on the side.

Which told her she had never meant anything to him. It had been an act, and she'd fallen for it. All because of her need to be loved. To be the most important person in the world to someone. And she'd believed that someone was Maurice.

Her heart clenched.

She'd been such a fool.

This was the worst day of her life.

She glanced up, and her heart stopped. Oh, God, and it had just gotten worse.

Quinn left his suite and walked toward the elevator. He'd been tied up with a call, so his business partner, Austin, had gone ahead to the restaurant for lunch.

Ahead, he noticed a forlorn-looking woman in the sitting area near the other penthouse suite. The next thing he noticed was the security manager standing close by. The man wore a discreet suit, but Quinn recognized him because the hotel manager had introduced them in case he and Austin had any special security needs during this or any future stay with the hotel.

He glanced at the woman again, and his heart skipped a beat.

It couldn't be . . .

She glanced up, and her eyes widened.

Fuck, that *was* her.

April. The woman who had broken his heart in college.

He should keep walking. Just pretend he didn't recognize her.

But before her gaze had darted down to her hands, he'd seen a deep pain in her sapphire eyes. No matter what she'd done to hurt him, he couldn't ignore it.

He walked toward her, but glanced at the man behind her.

"Good afternoon, Mr. Johan," Quinn said, offering his hand.

Mr. Johan stepped forward and shook it.

"Good afternoon, Mr. Taylor. Is there something I can do for you?"

"No, I'm fine. But I know Ms. Smith and would like to know if there's a problem."

"I'm sorry, sir. It's a private matter."

He nodded. "Fair enough."

He glanced down at April, who kept her gaze averted.

"April, it's nice to see you again."

Reluctantly, she tipped up her head. "Hello, Quinn."

Her cheeks had blossomed bright red. Of course, she was embarrassed. But her eyes were puffy, and clearly she'd been crying.

Fuck, he shouldn't care. She'd callously walked away from him without a second thought. He should just walk away now.

He sat down beside her. "Are you in some kind of trouble?"

Her hand was shaking, and he realized she was holding a piece of paper.

"We're done, Mr. Johan," a woman's voice said.

Quinn glanced up to see two female staff in maid uniforms

standing beside Mr. Johan, several pieces of luggage on a cart beside them.

"Mr. Taylor, I hate to break up your conversation, but Ms. Smith needs to come with me."

Quinn raised his hand. "In a minute."

He glanced at the piece of paper, and when she realized where he was looking, she crumpled her hand around it.

"April, tell me what's going on."

"I . . ." She glanced over her shoulder at the staff standing behind her, then she bit her lip in the way he used to find so appealing.

She sighed, no doubt knowing that there would be no point in trying to avoid his question.

"I can't pay the hotel bill."

"That's all?" He hadn't known what to expect, but this was such a trivially easy thing to fix. "I'll take care of it."

"No, you don't understand. It's huge."

He plucked the paper from her hand and glanced at the amount. Without blinking, he folded the sheet of paper and slid it into his suit jacket pocket, then glanced at Mr. Johan.

"Add it to my bill."

He ignored April's wide blue eyes as she stared at him. Her jaw had fallen open, and she shook her head in disbelief.

Mr. Johan seemed just as stunned. "Mr. Taylor?"

"Is there a problem?" Quinn asked, sending the man a steely gaze.

"No. Consider it done."

"Good." He stood up. "You can take Ms. Smith's luggage to my suite for now."

"Of course, Mr. Taylor." Mr. Johan nodded to the staffers with the cart, and they rolled it away.

Quinn glanced at April, still sitting on the bench.

"Are you coming?" he asked.

She drew in a shaky breath. "Where?"

"To join my business partner and me for lunch."

April stood up, and Quinn started toward the elevator. Still shocked at what Quinn had done, she hesitated.

He glanced over his shoulder. "Come on," he said.

She hurried after him, trying not to think about the fact she had nowhere else to go. Not just because her wedding had been canceled and her life turned upside down, but she had no means by which to go home. Or anywhere else.

She didn't even have anyone to call. She had no family, and as she racked her brain to think of a friend she could call for help, she realized that all her friends were Maurice's friends first. After graduation, he'd talked her into moving to Lachelle, a large town in Massachusetts he and his family basically owned.

She caught up to Quinn and fell into step beside him, having trouble keeping up with his long-legged stride.

"Quinn, thank you for what you did back there."

She still couldn't believe it. He hadn't even blinked when he'd seen the amount.

"It's nothing." His tone was chillingly indifferent.

She glanced at him in surprise. "Not to me."

Quinn stopped at the elevator and pushed the down button.

"I don't know how I'm going to pay you back," she continued, disturbed by his silence, "but I'll find a way."

"Why didn't your fiancé help you out?" he asked.

"What?" Then she realized she'd been toying with the diamond ring again. Turning it back and forth on her finger.

She stopped and dropped her hand to her side.

"Oh." Her stomach clenched. She didn't want to tell him about her humiliation. At least, not here in the hallway. She did want to explain at some point, though, so he wouldn't think she was wildly irresponsible.

"He left me. This morning. And he canceled my credit card."

"You had a joint credit card?"

She nodded. Maurice had his own card, but he'd also set up a separate joint card for her.

Not that she'd wanted that. Maurice had insisted so she would have the exclusive perks and status of a first-tier luxury card, along with the unlimited credit and VIP treatment that came with it. He'd wanted her to become used to his wealthy lifestyle.

She would never have been able to get a card like that without his name on the account.

In truth, bringing out the gold-plated metal card made her uncomfortable, especially when paying for everyday things like lunch with her coworkers at a roadhouse. It underscored the fact she was engaged to the owner of the company and kept her a little outside the social circle.

Everyone thought she was a kept woman. She'd overheard others speculating on why she bothered working, since she clearly didn't need the income.

The truth was, however, that she'd insisted on paying her own bills every month. She didn't want to take Maurice's money. So she worked and paid her own expenses, including the mortgage on her town house, though she had accepted the low interest rate he'd arranged for her through his family's bank.

The metal door slid open with a ding, and she followed Quinn onto the elevator. She saw her face in the mirror and realized she looked like a fragile ceramic doll. Like if she fell, she'd shatter into a million pieces.

Her eyes were red and puffy, and she pulled her compact out of her purse and tried to cover the redness with powder. Quinn's eyebrow arched, and she was sure he thought her too vain, but the last thing she wanted was to walk into a crowded restaurant looking weak and defeated.

She applied some lipstick, then dropped the tube into her purse and took a final look. She still looked a wreck, but not quite as bad.

"You said we're having lunch with your business partner?" she asked as she put her compact away and snapped her purse closed.

"Yes, but don't get any ideas about replacing your rich fiancé with Austin."

Her spine stiffened as her gaze darted to his. Of course, that's what he really thought of her. That she was a gold digger. She could see it in his acid-blue eyes. She bit back a sharp retort and stared squarely at the door as the elevator glided downward.

"Or you either, I take it," she said.

"You're damn right about that."

She couldn't blame him for his attitude, since he thought she'd left him for Maurice. Quinn had been a broke grad student, just like she had been, and he'd been convinced she'd left him because Maurice was rich.

"Don't worry," she said. "The thought hadn't crossed my mind."

It was true. But even if she had thought about it, the fact that he was clearly rich himself now meant he'd be wary of her showing an interest in him. So ironically, his wealth made it impossible for her to even consider trying to turn around her mistake from the past.

"Just one question," she said. "Why did you help me by paying my bill if you're so convinced I'm just after money?"

He shrugged. "You meant something to me once. I wouldn't have felt right ignoring your predicament, especially when it was so easy to fix. The money means nothing to me." His intense gaze bored through her. "But let me be very clear. If you ever ask me for money, the answer will be no."

2

Austin leaned back in his chair sipping his imported beer. His gaze was on the man two tables over rolling a poker chip between his fingers, back and forth, as he watched the sexy blond waitress clearing dishes from another table.

The guy had been flirting with her when she'd served him his meal, and now Austin would pay odds that he'd give her that fifty-dollar chip as a tip, then invite her to his room after her shift. From her body language when she was near him, despite her warm demeanor, Austin would lay even bigger odds that she'd turn him down. Politely, of course.

She picked up the tray of dishes and carried them away. Austin couldn't help watching the gentle sway of her hips as she walked.

She had greeted Austin by name when she'd shown him to his table. It seemed the staff were made aware of the wealthier guests staying in the hotel. She'd given him the best table in the house, overlooking the stunning garden and spectacular fountain outside, and right near a trickling waterfall inside that, set among greenery and flowers, fed a small pond with water lilies.

The table's corner location, with windows on two sides, allowed him to see all the other tables while affording him a little more privacy. Which he loved because he was a people-watcher.

The waitress had flirted with Austin, and he was sure she would jump at an invitation to join him for dinner tonight. And she'd probably wind up in his bed. Seeing how she was with her customers, he was sure she'd be great company. And probably sensational in the sack.

But he didn't want someone who just wanted to be with him because of his money or status.

His gaze drifted to the couple near the opposite window. They were clearly regulars because as soon as they'd walked into the place, the waitress had nodded and brought them two slices of cheesecake and tea. She'd chatted with them for a few minutes before she'd continued on her way.

Austin smiled as he watched the two people holding hands. The look of love in their eyes was palpable.

That's what he wanted.

He and Quinn had spent the past two years thinking of nothing but building the business. Nights. Weekends. They'd had no social life at all. Except the occasional casual fling to relieve the tension. Nothing serious.

But now that the ICO had launched and the new cryptocurrency they'd put on the market had skyrocketed, propelling them to heights of wealth they'd never imagined before, it was time to start living. And not just carousing around. He wanted to find a meaningful relationship.

He wanted to fall in love.

And he knew Quinn wanted the same thing.

"Good afternoon, Mr. Taylor," the waitress said. "And Ms. Smith."

Austin glanced to the entrance of the restaurant and saw Quinn standing beside a stunning woman wearing a floral sundress in a black-and-coral print, cinched at the waist with a flowing skirt. It set off her incredible figure beautifully. Her long golden hair cascaded over her shoulders in shimmering waves, and her heart-shaped face with those full pink lips was gorgeous.

As the waitress led them to the table, Austin noted Quinn's closed expression. Also, the woman's eyes were puffy, and she clung tightly to the handle of her purse with both hands. She also wore a huge diamond ring. He'd bet she'd just broken up with her fiancé.

Austin stood up as they approached the table.

"Austin, this is April," Quinn said as he pulled out a chair for her to sit down.

She stuck out her hand, and Austin shook it.

"Nice to meet you," she said. "I hope you don't mind me joining you for lunch."

"Of course not. It's a pleasure, April."

"Thank you." She sank down on the chair as Quinn pushed it in for her.

Austin and Quinn both sat down, April across from Austin and kitty-corner to his friend.

The waitress set a third menu on the table for their unexpected guest.

"What would you like to drink?" she asked.

"I'll just have a water, please," April said.

"I'll have a Guinness," Quinn said.

"Certainly, sir." The waitress left to retrieve their drinks.

April opened the menu and glanced through it nervously. When the waitress had called her by name, he'd assumed that she was also an elite guest at the hotel, but she was behaving as if she wasn't sure if she could afford to eat here.

"How do you two know each other?" Austin asked, though he'd already begun to speculate that this might be *the* woman.

"We went out together in college," she said.

Austin's interest flared.

"We dated briefly," Quinn added. "It wasn't serious."

Aha. She *was* the woman.

Quinn's heart had been broken by someone back then, and Austin knew he'd never gotten over her, even though Quinn would deny that adamantly. That's why Quinn diminished the relationship now, because he wanted to believe it was nothing. But he could never fool Austin.

"It's nice that you two ran into each other in the hotel. What are you doing in Vegas, April?"

April gazed up from her menu and shifted uneasily.

The waitress arrived with their drinks, and he wondered why his question had made her uncomfortable.

"Are you ready to order?" the waitress asked with a smile.

Austin glanced to April, but she had her head buried in the menu.

"I'll have the prime rib sandwich," Austin said, "and the house salad."

"I'll have the same," Quinn said.

They all turned their gazes to April.

Her cheeks flushed a rosy pink as she lifted her gaze from the menu.

"I'll . . . uh . . . just have a small side salad. I'm not very hungry."

"Nonsense," Quinn said, a tad impatiently. He glanced at

the menu again. "Here, I think you'll like the seafood linguine they have on special today. Or maybe the salmon steak with dill sauce." He turned to the waitress. "By the way, put Ms. Smith's meal on our tab."

Hesitantly, she agreed to the linguine, and Quinn ordered a bottle of white wine for the table.

"I didn't expect you to pay for my lunch," April murmured to Quinn once the waitress was gone.

"I invited you. Of course I'll pay for it." Quinn glanced at Austin. "She's embarrassed because she had a slight mishap with her credit card, but I straightened things out for her."

"He paid my hotel bill," she murmured, staring at the lemon floating in her water glass.

Austin's gaze caught on Quinn's, and his friend's exasperated expression told him that Quinn had been trying to spare her that embarrassment.

"It's fortunate that you ran into each other when you did. It's nice to be able to help a friend in need." Austin sipped his beer. "So you were going to tell me why you're here in Vegas this weekend."

She compressed her lips. "I came here to get married. Today is my wedding day."

Quinn glanced her way, his eyes widening in surprise.

"Really?" Austin asked, his eyebrows arching. "Is it an evening wedding, or should I ask the waitress to put a rush on lunch?" he added in a teasing tone.

She bit her lip as she twirled the engagement ring on her finger.

"I meant it was supposed to be my wedding day. In fact, it was supposed to be happening right now. But last night . . . at the rehearsal dinner . . ." She sucked in a breath. "I caught him with another woman."

"By *with another woman*, you mean dancing? Kissing?" Quinn asked.

She shook her head. "He was . . . excuse my French . . . fucking her. I caught them doing it."

Although the situation was tragic, Austin had to stifle a chuckle at the quaintness of her excusing herself from using the word *fucking*. In fact, he found everything about her completely charming, and the devilish side of him imagined her in bed, naked, using the word *fuck* in the most imaginative ways while begging him to give her pleasure.

Whoa, what the hell am I doing? If this was Quinn's lost love, there's no way he should be thinking of her like that. No matter how delightfully attractive he found her

Even if Quinn didn't have lingering feelings for her, the fact that they'd dated meant she was totally out of bounds. Austin would never do anything to jeopardize his friendship with Quinn.

"I'm so sorry that happened to you," Austin said.

Quinn's stomach clenched. What a fucking idiot the guy was.

"Then this morning, he canceled my credit card," April said, "leaving me with the bill and no way to pay."

Quinn felt his heartstrings tug, especially seeing the sheen on her eyes. Fuck, he had to get ahold of himself or he'd convince himself that she didn't deserve to be dumped by the guy, who'd probably figured out that she was just marrying him for his money and decided to get back at her.

The guy was still a total jerk for his actions. Confronting her and breaking it off would be the appropriate thing to do.

"How did he cancel *your* credit card?" Austin asked.

"It was a joint card," she said hesitantly.

Quinn hadn't been surprised to hear that. Of course she'd be living off the guy's money.

Their lunch arrived, and conversation slowed. Quinn could tell April enjoyed her lunch. He knew she would. She'd always loved seafood, especially shellfish. Once when they'd been going out together, he'd splurged, taking a hit on his grocery bill that week so he could order her lobster bisque when he took her out for dinner on her birthday.

She'd been very thankful. He still remembered the deep, passionate kiss she'd given him when they'd gone back to his place that evening. It hadn't gone any further than that. She'd been a virgin when they were dating, and he'd respected her choice to keep her innocence until she was married, or at least knew she'd found *the one*.

His heart clenched. He'd been so fucking convinced *he* was the one. But that was before he'd realized that money meant more to her than love. Because, damn it, he'd been sure she was falling in love with him just as much as he'd been falling for her.

He watched as her cute little tongue glided over her lip to collect a drop of sauce.

Fuck, he'd love to pull her into his arms and drive his tongue deep between those soft, pouty lips. To feel her body tightly against his. To hear her beg him to fuck her.

Goddamn. Even though he knew how shallow she was, he still wanted her. With a deep desperation that scarred his soul.

She put down her fork and raised her gaze. Then froze when she saw how he was looking at her.

Fuck, he didn't want her knowing how she affected him. She'd be sure to find a way to take advantage of the situation.

She started to twirl her ring again.

"So if this guy treated you so badly, why are you still wearing his ring?" Quinn asked.

Her fingers jerked from the diamond. "Oh, I . . . shouldn't be." She slipped the ring off and stared at it with an uncertain expression.

"What are you going to do with it?" Quinn asked. Probably sell it.

"I could give it to you to help pay what I owe you."

Annoyance surged through him.

"I told you to forget that."

He certainly didn't want the fucking ring another man had given her.

"You should return it to him," Austin suggested. "Not because he deserves that consideration but to give you closure."

She nodded. "I know. You're right." She sat back in her chair, her brow furrowing. "The only thing is, I don't want to see him again, so I'm not sure how to return it. The mail doesn't seem safe enough for such an expensive thing."

"No problem," Quinn said, not letting her get away with keeping the ring based on a technical issue. "The hotel can arrange that for you. I'll go with you and make sure of it." He held out his hand. "Why not give it to me for safekeeping?"

She reluctantly dropped it into his hand, and he slipped it in his breast pocket.

The waitress asked them if they wanted dessert, and when they declined, she brought the bill for their approval. Austin signed it, then turned to April.

"What are your plans now, April? Do you need a ride to the airport?"

She drew in a deep breath. "Thank you, but I don't have an airline ticket. I flew here on Maurice's private jet."

Quinn's eyes narrowed. *Maurice Dubois.* So she'd actually been going to marry the man she'd left him for in college.

Austin nodded. "And you probably don't have money for bus fare."

She shook her head. "But that's okay. I'll figure something out."

From the anxiety in her eyes, it was clear she had no idea how. Quinn remembered that she had no family. But she must have friends.

"No matter what, I doubt you want to rush off home after all this," Austin said. "You need some time away from your normal life to let this all sink in. Why not stay with us for a few days while you figure things out? We've got a huge penthouse suite, so there's plenty of room."

Her gaze flickered to Quinn. "I don't think that's a good idea."

"Nonsense," Quinn said. "It's a great idea."

He didn't know what the hell he was thinking. Other than his cock hoping for a chance to finally sink into her.

"Your luggage is already at our place, so why not?" he continued.

"At least stay tonight, and you can keep us company at the casino," Austin insisted. "I have a feeling you're going to bring us luck."

April didn't know what to say. She had no money and no one to call for help, so having one more night to defer having to figure it out would be a godsend.

"Thank you. I appreciate your generosity."

"Good," Austin said. "Now that that's settled, I'm going back to the penthouse to check on some business. Are you two coming?"

They all stood up, and she walked with the two men to the entrance.

"Actually," Quinn said, "I think now is as good a time as any to return the ring." His eyebrow arched. "Right, April?"

"Of course."

"I'll leave you to it," Austin said. "A pleasure meeting you, April. I look forward to seeing you later."

Austin turned and walked toward the elevator. Quinn grasped her elbow firmly and guided her to the lobby. When he talked to the concierge, the man spoke with someone on the phone, then directed them to the manager's office, telling them the manager would handle their needs personally. Quinn led her down the elegant hallway paneled in contoured mahogany, then to an imposing office.

A large, very tall man stood up from behind the desk and walked toward them.

"Ah, Mr. Taylor." He offered his hand, and they shook. "So nice to see you again."

Then he turned to her, and her chest tightened.

"Ms. Smith, I'm Adrian Gunter, the hotel manager." He offered his hand, and she shook it gingerly. Then he gestured to three leather armchairs arranged around a glass table. "May I get you some coffee? A drink?"

"No, thank you. We just had lunch," Quinn said as they sat down.

"Very well." Mr. Gunter sat across from them. "First, may I say, Ms. Smith, how sorry I am about the unfortunate cancellation of your wedding."

"Thank you," she murmured, trying to keep her voice from trembling.

As polite as he might be, this man intimidated her. Especially since she knew he was the one who had arranged to have security pound on her door this morning, demand to know how she was going to pay her bill, then hustle her out of the room while they packed up her belongings.

"I understand that you would like us to arrange the safe return of the engagement ring to your ex-fiancé."

"Yes, that's right," she said.

He leaned forward, folding his hands on the tabletop. "It is most fortunate that you came in, Ms. Smith. I didn't relish putting you into another embarrassing situation."

"What do you mean?" Quinn asked, a slight edge to his voice.

Mr. Gunter leaned back in his chair. "Nothing to worry about. Mr. Dubois called me to say you have some things that belong to him. The engagement ring is one of them."

Quinn's eyebrow arched. "And the others?"

"Yes, he mentioned some jewelry, designer gowns, expensive shoes . . ." He waved his hand. "He sent a list."

Of course he had. Maurice's father and the owner of this hotel were old buddies. They would be happy to help Maurice humiliate her and, hopefully, put her in jail. They couldn't allow her to get away with rejecting him. The money wasn't of great concern to either of them, and she had no doubt that if they hadn't gotten the money from her, they would have worked it out behind the scenes.

"And what proof does he have that these are his and don't belong to April?" Quinn demanded.

She couldn't believe that Quinn was defending her. But then, he'd always been a good man.

"It's okay, Quinn," she said, resting her hand on his arm.

As soon as her fingers came in contact with him, an explosion of sensation rushed through her.

He glanced at her, and she could swear he felt it, too.

She took a calming breath. "I don't want anything from him. If he wants to take these things back, it makes it easier."

Quinn frowned, but nodded.

"Fine. You may send some of your staff to collect the items in an hour, but they will be under April's supervision. And if there's a single thing they try to take that April doesn't agree to," he glowered, "they'll have me to deal with."

"Of course, Mr. Taylor," Mr. Gunter said. "That's perfectly reasonable." He glanced at April, and a chill ran down her spine at his cool gaze. "Now. The ring, please."

Quinn reached into his pocket and pulled it out, then gave it to the man. Quinn then stood up and offered April his hand.

She rested her fingers on his and could barely breathe at the electricity surging through her at the contact.

She stood up, and he took her elbow and escorted her to the door. Having him so close, knowing she could lean on him if she had to, made it easier to hold her head up as she walked from the office.

Once the door closed behind her, her knees went weak and she slumped against him.

His arm slid around her. "Steady. You're okay."

"Thank you for standing up for me, Quinn."

When she gazed up at him, his midnight-blue eyes seemed to soften.

"I don't like to see anyone being bullied."

Even though his answer was designed to make her think he

hadn't done it for her, the gruffness in his voice and the fact he kept his arm around her as they walked made her feel cared for.

As they stepped into the hallway with the column of elevators, one of them opened, and she noticed Sarah Piner step out with her husband, Jon. They were friends of Maurice's who had come to Vegas for the wedding. Sarah's finely plucked eyebrow arched high at the sight of April with a man's arm around her.

Luckily, another elevator arrived, and Quinn guided her into it. April could see Sarah whispering in her husband's ear, staring at April with piercing disapproval as the door closed.

She leaned against Quinn. His arm tightened around her, and he didn't say a word as the elevator ascended.

She knew this wouldn't last long, but right now, she needed it. To feel supported. And cared for. It's all she'd ever wanted. Deep down in her soul.

And her heart ached as she realized she'd probably never find it.

As April walked from the elevator with Quinn toward his penthouse suite, she kept her gaze away from the door to the suite she'd been evicted from this morning.

She didn't want to think about being there with Maurice. She didn't want to think about how she'd cried herself to sleep last night, his betrayal searing through her.

She didn't want to think at all.

Quinn opened the door and led her inside. Her eyes widened as she glanced around.

The other suite had been luxurious and grand, with leather furniture, plants, flower arrangements, and beautiful décor. But this one went far beyond that. It had the same gorgeous furniture and décor, but it was much larger.

Her jaw dropped at the sight of the private swimming pool that was part indoors and part outdoors. There was a rock waterfall built into the wall that trickled into the pool. Outside the floor-to-ceiling windows, she could see a stunning garden terrace.

Maurice had been ticked off when they hadn't been able to get the best penthouse at the hotel, especially annoyed that his powerful influence did nothing to sway the hotel manager to bump the people who had booked it already. Maurice wasn't used to people saying no to him.

April had known that meant whoever had booked this suite had a larger fortune and more influence than Maurice. Never would she have imagined that person would be Quinn.

"You've come a long way from college," she said as she glanced around. "Your business must be doing well. I'm glad things worked out for you. You certainly deserve it."

He sat down on the couch, his arms stretched across the back.

"Really? And why do you say that?"

She walked to the bar and sat on one of the tall stools.

"You were extremely focused when you were in grad school. You pursued your studies nonstop, intensely determined to succeed. In school and in life."

He frowned. "Is that a comment on how I didn't spend enough time with you when we were dating?"

Her stomach tightened. "No. Of course not. I admired your dedication."

It was true. But it had also been the major reason she'd left him. She would never lay the blame on him for their breakup, though.

"But not enough to stick with me? Why take a chance on me when Maurice already had money and success?"

"I didn't care about that."

He snorted and stood up, then poured himself a drink from a crystal decanter on the bar.

"You? Didn't care about money? That's a laugh."

She stood up and walked to the window, staring out at the skyline without actually seeing it.

How could she argue with him? She knew deep inside that Maurice's money had been part of the attraction. Not because she was a gold digger but because she craved stability. Security. She'd never had that in her life.

But she would never marry a man just for his money. Maurice had been charming and attentive, and he'd made her feel special.

"Quinn, I didn't leave you because Maurice was rich."

"Then why did you leave?"

She frowned. "I loved how passionate you were about your thesis. And I understood why you put your work first. I didn't want to be a distraction."

His eyebrow arched. "A distraction? Are you kidding me?" He strolled toward her, his eyes flashing. "I cared about my work, but what I was passionate about was you. What I wanted was you."

He stood beside her now, anger and frustration blazing in his eyes, but she could see the even deeper pain beneath.

"You'd never been with a man before, and I respected that. You wanted to keep yourself for the *right* man. So I held back and gave you the time you wanted."

She could barely breathe, remembering how patient and loving he'd been.

He gaze flicked to hers, searching. "I thought I was that man." His gaze turned somber. "Did I hold back too much? Did you really not see—"

"I knew how much you wanted me," she said quickly, stopping him from finishing that thought. Not wanting him to say he'd loved her. "And I knew you didn't want to pressure me."

She could barely breathe as his gaze remained locked on hers, boring into her soul. Finally, she looked away, unable to bear the raw emotion seething between them another moment.

He drew in a deep breath, breaking the spell.

"And what about your new boyfriend? I bet you didn't make him wait. Or are you going to tell me you're still a virgin?"

She froze inside.

"That's none of your business."

But guilt washed through her because he was right. Maurice had so totally deceived her that she'd believed he was the one. That she was in love with him.

He'd been her first—and only—man. He'd known it, and it had made him even more possessive of her, which she mistook for love.

"Life isn't fucking fair sometimes." Quinn's words were a mere whisper.

The aching wistfulness in his eyes tore at her heart.

But as the moment hung between them, that wistfulness turned to a growing heat. Her skin pebbled into goose bumps as her senses heightened. As she became aware of the warmth of his body close to her. Of the breadth of his solid chest. The strength of his muscular arms. She longed to close the small distance between them, glide her hands around his neck, and give herself over to the growing desire inside her.

"Quinn, I'm so sorry—"

Frustration welled in his eyes again, and he tugged her into his arms before she could finish the thought, his lips claiming hers in a demanding kiss. He pulled her tighter to him, his arm encircling her waist. His tongue surged into her mouth and explored, taking her breath away.

Then his lips softened, becoming more persuasive. His hand glided up her back, then cupped her head. The kiss became heart-wrenchingly tender.

Oh, God, her heart ached, remembering how it had been between them.

She melted against him, a deep longing building inside her.

This feeling . . . this was why she'd had to break it off with him. She'd been worried she would fall for him, and that would have been a disaster. Because she didn't believe he could give her what she needed. To be the most important thing in his life. She had felt she would always come second to his drive for success.

So she'd broken it off with him before they could fall in love.

Except she realized that she hadn't escaped with her heart after all.

As his lips continued to move on hers, his arm tightened around her waist, and she felt his cock straining against her.

Her body ached, wanting to strip off her clothes for him. Wanting to experience what she'd always longed for. To be physically possessed by him.

As if sensing her acquiescence, his hand covered her ass, and he pulled her tighter still. His rigid cock pushing snug against her drove up her need. She arched against him.

A door off the living room opened, and Austin walked in.

"Ah, sorry to interrupt," he said.

Quinn released April and stepped back. "Not at all. We were just getting . . . reacquainted."

He sent her a sardonic smile, then walked away from her and sat on one of the high stools at the bar. He picked up his drink and took a sip.

"Want one?" he asked Austin.

"No, thanks. I'm good."

It was then that it hit her. Quinn had wanted Austin to catch them kissing. He'd warned her off going after his friend, and now that he'd established the kind of relationship he'd had with her, Austin would stay away from her.

Well, that was fine with her. She didn't intend to get involved with either one of them.

Austin got the not-so-subtle message. Quinn still wanted April, so she was off limits. Not that Austin hadn't already figured that out.

"I took April's luggage to the room off the den," Austin said.

The three suitcases had been left inside the door, so he'd taken them to one of the spare bedrooms. The suite had two large master bedrooms and two more modest-size bedrooms that were perfect for other guests or support staff traveling with their bosses.

After seeing that kiss between April and Quinn, he wondered if she might wind up sleeping in Quinn's room.

"Actually, we need to move the luggage," Quinn said.

So they were going to be open about it.

Quinn strode down the hall, and Austin followed. They walked into the room, and each grabbed a case. Quinn picked up the carry-on bag, too, then headed back to the hallway. But instead of turning into his bedroom, he continued to the shared living space.

"Are you planning on evicting her?" Austin asked.

Quinn rolled the suitcase to the couch and set it upright, then put the smaller bag on top of it.

"No. It turns out her ex-fiancé is claiming that he owns some of her belongings in the luggage and is demanding that they be returned. Some hotel staff will be arriving in a few minutes to go through the luggage."

Austin glanced at April, who sat on an armchair by the window, her face a portrait of sadness.

"I'm sorry, April," Austin said. "This guy you were with is being a total ass."

A knock sounded on the door, and Quinn strode to the entrance and opened it.

"Mr. Taylor," said the young woman in the hotel's gold blazer and black pants. Another uniformed woman stood beside her. "My name is Leslie, and this is Renee. We're here—"

"Yes, I know why you're here," Quinn said. "Come in. Let's get this over with."

The women came in, and he led them to the luggage. The one named Leslie lifted one of the cases onto the couch and unzipped it.

"Ms. Smith, would you like to see the list so you can identify the items rather than us go through your things?" Leslie asked.

Quinn walked to April's side.

"Come on, April," he said in an encouraging voice.

She glanced at him, clearly unnerved by the whole thing. But then she stood up and walked to the woman and took the list she offered.

Austin sat on the barstool and watched the whole process as

April opened the suitcase, then took out things one by one and handed them to Leslie, who set them beside the case. There were shoes, blouses, pants, and nightgowns. Renee ticked the items off the list as the suitcase emptied.

"That's all from this suitcase," April said.

"I'm sorry, but I have to check the rest," Leslie said.

April moved back as Leslie went through the remaining items, checking labels and adding to the pile.

Quinn stepped in. "If it's not on the list, why are you taking it?"

"I'm sorry, sir," Leslie said, "but Mr. Dubois said to check for anything from a list of designers."

Quinn glanced at April. She just nodded and turned away, but not before Austin saw the sheen on her eyes.

Austin hated seeing her go through this, and he could see Quinn's jaw clenching.

Once the woman was finished, all that was left were a couple of items of casual clothing, a toiletry case, and some socks. She took them out and set them on the armchair, while the other woman, Renee, started putting all the selected items back into the suitcase.

Quinn's eyebrow arched up as she zipped it up and set it down. Leslie hefted the second large case onto the couch.

"You're taking the luggage, too?" Austin asked.

"I'm sorry, sir," Leslie said. "He said he bought it. He supplied receipts for all the items."

"I'll just take out what's not on the list this time," April said as she opened the second suitcase.

She glanced at the paper as she riffled through the items, then finally just pulled out some bras and panties. Even those, the women examined, and they took most of them.

"What about your jewelry, April?" Quinn said.

The leather case was sitting atop the items in her bag.

"I don't care that he takes it back."

Quinn placed his hand on her shoulder.

"I know, sweetheart, but you need to have them inventory the items while they're here so the bastard can't come after you later for anything."

She nodded, then opened the jewelry case and set it in front of them.

While Renee went through it and ticked off the various items, Leslie opened the carry-on. Quinn watched the jewelry being sorted while April finished with the small bag.

Finally, everything was closed up, with only a few items left for April to keep.

It was a surreal experience. Austin had never seen anything like it. Someone being stripped of their belongings, and in such a methodical way. Her ex really was a bastard.

Austin had never taken his wealthy upbringing for granted. He knew how lucky he was. He'd never experienced anything like April just had, and she'd gone through it with such grace.

Renee walked to the door and rolled in a luggage cart they had waiting outside. Once all three suitcases were on it, Renee leaned in to Leslie and pointed at some unchecked items on the list. Leslie turned to April.

"There's something from the list of jewelry missing."

April's shoulders pulled back, and her eyes flared.

"If it's the tennis bracelet, he never gave that to me."

"No, ma'am. It seems to be the necklace you're wearing now. He listed it as a gold chain with a black pearl."

April's eyes widened, and her hand moved to the small pearl, covering it protectively.

"No." Her voice was shaking, but she was adamant.

Austin wanted to rush to her side. To be her support. But Quinn was close by, and Austin could see the protective gleam in his eyes.

April sucked in a deep breath. "This is *my* necklace. He had nothing to do with it."

Leslie was clearly unhappy about the position she was in.

"Of course, ma'am. I'll just mark down that there's a dispute." She made a notation on the list. Then she glanced up reluctantly. "I'm sorry, but one last thing. What you're wearing now . . ."

Anger flared in Austin, and he was on his feet.

"No," Quinn snapped. He drew April to his side and angled in front of her as if shielding her. "You're not taking the clothes off her back. Tell Mr. Dubois he can send *me* the bill."

"Yes, sir."

"And tell him I happen to know that Ms. Smith had this necklace long before she ever met him, so if he harasses Ms. Smith about this or the clothes, he'll be hearing from my lawyer."

"Of course, sir."

The two women turned and pushed the cart to the entrance, then disappeared out the door as quickly as they could.

Quinn slid his arm around April and drew her close to him. He guided her to the other couch and sat down beside her. Austin poured a drink and brought it to her.

She sipped it. He noticed she still clung to the necklace.

It was simple and understated, and on her gracefully curved

neck it looked classy. But it wasn't an expensive piece of jewelry. Why would her ex-fiancé want to take it?

Clearly, he just wanted to hurt her.

"That necklace is obvisously important to you," Austin said as he sat on her other side. "He had no right to try to take it. I'm sorry this man is putting you through such a terrible ordeal."

She nodded, tears now swelling from her eyes. "It's all I have of my mother." Her voice shook.

"Did she . . . pass away?" Austin asked.

She raised her gaze to Austin. "I don't know."

The words hung in the air between them. How could she not know?

She lowered her gaze. When she lifted it again, she seemed surprised he was still looking at her expectantly. He got the impression she wasn't used to people taking an interest in what she had to say.

"I hope you're not going to leave it there," he said, hoping to encourage her to open up.

She sucked in a breath. "I was abandoned at the hospital right after I was born. My mother left me there. It turns out she used false insurance papers, so they had no way to track her down. She'd been wearing this necklace when she arrived at the hospital, and she'd left it on her bedside table. The hospital staff made sure it was passed on to the orphanage with me."

"I didn't know that you were abandoned," Quinn said. "Why didn't you ever tell me?"

She bit her lip. "I don't like to talk about it."

"Yet you just told Austin."

She glanced to Quinn. "He asked," she said simply.

Quinn frowned, and Austin knew he needed to have a discussion with Quinn about this later.

"Why do you want to keep a necklace from a woman who abandoned you?" Austin asked.

She held the pearl between her fingertips.

"Because it's all I have in the world that's truly mine."

Her words tore at Austin's heart.

3

Quinn had hated watching that whole thing. The pain in April's sapphire eyes tugged at his heartstrings and made him want to pull her into his arms and promise to take care of her forever.

But he couldn't let himself feel that way. If he went down that path, he might start caring for her again . . . wanting her to be a part of his life. And that would be foolhardy.

She would probably be all too happy to start dating him again. Marry him. Because he had a big enough bank account now.

He watched her walk to the small pile of clothing that was left, along with her bag of toiletries, and gather them up.

"Where do I sleep?" She didn't look to him or to Austin. Just kept her gaze cast downward.

Austin sent a querying glance at Quinn, and he realized his friend thought Quinn might be considering having her in his room.

"I'll show you," Quinn said.

He pressed his hand to the small of her back and guided her down the hall to the guest room where Austin had put her luggage earlier. She dumped her stuff on the bed, then started sorting the clothing items.

"I have an idea," said Austin, who was leaning against the doorjamb. "Why don't we all go for a swim? We have this great pool right in the suite, so we should enjoy it."

Quinn knew that April loved the water, so it was a great idea to cheer her up.

"Sorry. I don't have a swimsuit," she mumbled.

She had pulled several bikinis out of her luggage, but Leslie and Renee had claimed them all as part of the list. They must have been designer pieces. Not that Quinn would know the difference.

He did know that the sight of one of them, made up of a couple of triangles of fabric held together by strings, had sent his imagination running wild with erotic images of her practically naked body, setting his groin on fire. And his cock started to swell now as the images returned to haunt him.

He never would have believed that April would wear a thing like that. But then, had he ever really known her?

"We can figure out something," Quinn said. He walked to the bed and picked up a simple black bra and panties. "Here, wear these."

She frowned. "You want me to swim in my underwear?"

He examined the bra. "Why not? You can't see through it. It covers all the necessities. In fact, it covers more than the bathing suits you owned, from what I saw."

She gazed at him doubtfully.

"Come on, April," Quinn said. "Don't spite yourself. I know you'd love to go in that pool. We're all adults here. What does it matter if you're wearing black panties and a bra instead of a black bathing suit?"

She tugged the bra and panties from his hand. "Okay."

"Good." Quinn turned and joined Austin at the door.

"We'll see you out there," Quinn said, then closed the door.

April stripped off her dress, then her lacy coral bra and panty set trimmed with black ribbon. She picked up the black panties and pulled them on, then the bra. Once she had it fastened, she looked at herself in the mirror.

The lingerie wasn't very revealing. The panties had a low-rise waistline and flattering high-cut legs. The bra had smooth cups and only showed a slight swell of her breasts. Both were a simple black satin finish with no lace. What she wore could easily pass as a modest two-piece bathing suit.

But the thought of walking out there in front of the men in this . . . her underwear . . . made her uncomfortable.

She stared at the rest of her clothes still spread out on the bed. She'd been trying to sort it into piles, but there were only a couple of T-shirts, a pair of jeans, and a sweater. She scooped up everything but the cardigan and dropped it in the drawer of the dresser. She frowned. There was plenty of room to spare. Everything she had left fit in the one drawer.

She pulled the cardigan on and glanced in the mirror. She looked ridiculous wearing a wool sweater over what was supposed to be a bathing suit. She tossed it in the drawer and grabbed a red T-shirt and pulled that on instead. Then she turned and left the room.

As she walked across the living room, she saw Austin through the glass wall surrounding the indoor portion of the pool. He was sitting on the side, his legs hanging in the water.

The sight of his half-naked body sent heat shimmering through her. Good heavens, the man was godlike. He clearly worked out regularly with weights. His chest was broad and sculpted, his arms bulging with muscles, and his waist trim.

As she opened the glass door, he glanced her way.

"Hey, there. The water's great." Austin pushed himself to his feet. "Why don't we go outside?"

He picked up a stack of three towels from a shelf, and April followed him through another glass door. The dazzling sunshine warmed her arms and legs as they walked across the large patio to a couple of lounge chairs at the far end of the curved pool.

As Austin tossed the towels on the chair, April glanced at the view below. She spotted the replica of the Eiffel Tower at the Paris Las Vegas right away, then her gaze drifted to the Bellagio fountains. Sunlight glittered on the dancing water, and she knew it would be an absolutely stunning sight after dark.

She turned to the pool again and walked to the lounge chair. Austin dove into the water, and she couldn't help admiring the smooth line of his body as he broke the water's surface.

His head popped back up, and he shook it, then sent her a brilliant smile.

"Are you coming in?"

"Yes, of course," she said hesitantly.

The glittering blue water called to her. She reached for the hem of her T-shirt and pulled it over her head. As soon as she tossed it aside and saw Austin's heated gaze on her body, she remembered she wore only a bra and panties.

Damn, wearing the T-shirt for modesty had been a really bad idea. It was one thing walking out here in the black bra and panties, because she could have convinced herself it was the same as a bathing suit, but taking off her shirt to reveal her lingerie made her feel like she was stripping in front of him.

Austin pushed himself up on the side of the pool as she

walked to the diving board. His muscular torso glistening with droplets of water was a sight to behold.

She dove in and glided through the water. She loved the feel of it sluicing along her body. When her head broke the surface, she saw Austin watching her with a smile.

She swam from one end of the free-form pool to the other several times, wanting to get some exercise. The longest path took her inside the penthouse. When she finally popped her head up, she realized Austin had gone inside and was sitting on the pool's edge by the stone waterfall.

"You want something to drink?" he asked.

There was a bar near the waterfall.

"Sure, a lemonade would be nice." She swam to the steps and walked up to the terra-cotta-tiled floor.

"Be careful, it's—"

Before Austin could finish his sentence, April's foot slipped out from under her. Austin lurched forward and caught her before she fell face-first onto the hard tile floor. She found herself firmly in his arms, her body pressed tightly to his.

She sucked in a breath and gazed into his dark teal eyes.

"Slippery," he finished.

She couldn't think straight with her breasts crushed tightly to his strong, hard chest, his muscular arms around her. And that amazing smile of his, so full of warmth that it took her breath away.

"What?" she asked, her eyes wide.

"I was saying it's slippery." His words came out low and husky.

The moment seemed to hang between them as though they were suspended in time. She was intensely aware of their bare skin touching, his hot and hard. Her heart pounded in her chest, and a powerful longing to feel his lips on hers, to sink into his embrace and give herself to him completely, surged through her. The need threatened to overwhelm her.

And worse, she could see the same need reflected in his glowing eyes.

The only time she'd ever felt anything like this before was with Quinn.

"What the hell are you two doing?"

At the sound of Quinn's voice, she tried to jerk back, but Austin's arm around her waist held her firmly, though she did lose her footing on the slippery tile and dropped against him again.

"If you don't watch it, you'll wind up flat on your back," Austin said.

"Really?" Quinn said in an even voice. "Are you propositioning her?"

"Not at all," Austin replied.

He turned April until she was pressed against his side, his arm around her, and guided her to a teak table, then eased her into one of the chairs around it.

"April slipped on the wet tiles when she stepped out of the pool. I caught her before she fell." He turned to April. "Did you hurt your ankle?"

"No, I'm fine." She couldn't bring herself to look at Quinn, not wanting to see the disapproval in his eyes. Knowing he thought she was making a move on his friend.

Austin crouched down and wrapped his hand around her left ankle. His touch was so gentle she forgot to protest.

"It doesn't feel swollen," Austin said. "Let me see the other one."

Before she could move, his big hand was wrapped around her right ankle. His touch continued to make her quiver inside.

"I'm sure she's fine," Quinn said through gritted teeth.

Austin released her ankle. "I'll get some ice."

She rested her hand on his forearm. "Really, Austin. I didn't hurt anything."

He nodded and smiled. "Okay. That's good."

He walked to the bar and grabbed a can of lemonade from the small fridge, then poured it into a glass and gave it to her.

"I thought we were going to spend some time in the water," Quinn said.

"I'm game to go back in." Austin glanced at April. "How about you?"

"Sure," she said and started to stand up, but Austin rushed to her side and slid his arm around her.

"I don't want you to fall again," Austin said.

Water was still dripping from her hair, leaving the tiles around her wet.

"How about I give her a hand?" Quinn said as he stepped to her other side.

"Of course." Austin waited while Quinn slid his arm around her, then relinquished his hold and eased away.

April felt more than a little overwhelmed by the whole thing.

As Quinn guided her toward the door to the patio, she started to feel dizzy. Being pressed against Quinn's warm, masculine body made her senses go haywire. It was wonderfully familiar and welcome. She wanted so much to lean against him. To accept the support he was offering.

But she knew better. He didn't want her. He would never be hers to rely on.

To love.

When they got outside and onto the hot stone patio, Quinn loosened his arm.

"You okay on your own now?" he asked.

"Yes, thank you."

She slid away from his warm body and walked to the wide steps ascending from the long curve of the pool. She sat on one of the lower steps so she was immersed in the warm water to her waist.

She glanced at Quinn for the first time, and her breath caught at the sight of his ripped, broad-shouldered body. He walked toward the end of the pool, and she watched his leg muscles ripple as he stepped up on the diving board. Then he dove into the pool, his body breaking the water's surface in a graceful, streamlined arc.

"Don't worry. I'll make sure Quinn understands what happened," Austin said.

She glanced around, not realizing he'd followed her down the steps and now sat beside her.

"Good. I don't want to cause any problems between you. You seem very close."

"We are. We met two years ago at a mutual friend's birthday party. We got to talking, and I could see the man was brilliant. And driven. Then he told me his innovative idea for a new cryptocurrency, and I knew it was going to be wildly successful."

Austin smiled as Quinn swam past them, doing laps just like she had done.

"I have an instinct about people and about good ideas," Austin said. "And I'm rarely wrong. Since I was sure his idea would make us both a ton of money, I backed him. Even learned enough about blockchain programming to roll up my sleeves and get involved. I believe for a good partnership to work, you both need to get your hands dirty."

"And you did?"

"You mean get dirty?" he asked, a teasing gleam in his dark, periwinkle-blue eyes.

"No, make all the money you'd hoped for."

He smiled in satisfaction. "And then some."

He stood and walked up the steps, then returned with a bright blue floatable lounge chair. He put it in the water and scooped her up, then set her on it. She laughed, exhilarated by being swept up in his arms.

"Let's enjoy the water and this gorgeous sunshine," he said, then set her adrift.

As the chair floated toward the center of the pool, she noticed that Quinn had stopped swimming and was hanging on one side of the pool, watching her with a frown on his face.

Quinn walked into the living room with Austin. Their time in the pool had been cut short when Austin had received a text from an old friend who wanted to meet for a drink to discuss some business. He was passing through Vegas on a business trip, so he only had a few hours.

"The idea is sound, and I'm sure it'll be quite successful," Quinn said, "but I still prefer not to take on a new project right now. After working so many hours for such a long time—"

"Don't worry about it," Austin said. "I already told you, I feel the same way."

Relief washed through Quinn. They'd discussed this when Austin's friend had first approached them a few weeks ago about partnering up to start another cryptocurrency, but Quinn wasn't sure if Austin had reconsidered.

"Since he's a good friend of yours," Quinn said, "I'd be happy to give him technical advice along the way."

Quinn knew Austin would do the same with offering information about the organizational details he'd be facing.

Austin smiled and patted Quinn on the back. "I know I can
always count on you, buddy."

Austin headed to his bedroom to change, and Quinn walked
to the bar and poured a drink. His gaze flickered to the window
and April floating on the pool lounge chair. The sight of her
curved, sexy body, sunlight glistening on the water droplets on
her skin, had his groin tightening.

But anger simmered through him. Austin counted on him,
but he was letting down his friend where April was concerned.
He could plainly see that Austin was being pulled into her co-
quettish spell, and he'd be damned if he'd let her take advantage
of Austin.

Austin, dressed in a suit, walked back into the room.

"How about I text you when I'm done, and we can get on
with the evening we'd planned?" he asked.

Austin had been looking forward to a couple of hours in the
casino followed by a very exclusive poker game that had been arranged for a handful of the more prestigious guests of the hotel.

"Sure thing."

Austin walked out the door, and Quinn turned back to the
window. April was out of the pool now and drying herself off.
Patting the fluffy towel over her breasts, then her taut stomach,
and finally down the long expanse of her legs. His cock ached at
the sight of her nearly naked body as she draped the towel over
her arm and headed to the door.

Fuck, no wonder Austin was falling for her. She had the
body of a goddess. On top of that, she had a way of bringing out
a man's protective instincts. It was a killer combination.

She proceeded through the glassed-in area around the pool, then into the living room.

"You certainly were making a play for Austin out there," Quinn said.

April's head spun toward him. "I'm not after Austin."

"Then why were you all over him when I walked in here?"

"He told you. It was all innocent. I slipped."

"Right into his arms. How convenient."

April ached inside. She had done this to Quinn. Made him this angry, untrusting man. At least, untrusting of her.

"Look, Quinn, I want to apologize. I know what I did in college hurt you and caused this mistrust between us, and I'm so sorry for that."

His eyes flared, then his expression turned to one of indifference.

"I got over it. Once I realized what kind of woman you are— that all you really care about is money—I realized that nothing between us had been real. You couldn't really love me. Or anyone, for that matter."

He swirled his drink, the ice cubes tinkling against the glass.

"Tell me," he said. "Why did you go out with me at all?"

She sucked in a breath, trying not to wilt under his withering glare.

"I really liked you, Quinn." Her heart ached at the words. "Being with you. Spending time with you."

"You *liked* me?" He shook his head. "But you knew I was falling for you."

Anger blazed in his eyes, but she could also see flickers of pain.

Then he set his drink down and stepped closer, a dark aura emanating from him. Her heart thundered in her chest as she took a step back.

He stepped forward again. When she tried to step back, she bumped against the wall.

He grasped her arms. "Well, baby, I'm immune to you now. But watch yourself around Austin. He sees the best in people, and I won't have him hurt by someone like you."

"Let go of me, please," she murmured. "I want to get dressed."

At her words, his gaze dropped to her bra, reminding both of them that she was standing there in only her bra and panties. Goose bumps danced across her entire body as heat flared in his eyes.

"Really? That sounds like a good idea. Why don't I help you?"

He curled his arms around her body, and she felt his fingers playing over the back of her bra. She placed her hand flat on his chest and pressed against the solid wall of muscle.

"No, I can manage, thanks," she said in as even a voice as she could muster, but it still came out a squeak.

The hooks on her bra released.

He looked like he was under a spell as he dropped first one bra strap from her shoulder, then the other. He eased back, his gaze dropping to her breasts. She clung to the front of her bra, holding it in place.

He slid his fingers along her shoulders, then down her sides, his thumbs dragging along her ribs.

"I've wanted you for so long." The heat in his words seared her.

Then he pulled her against him and captured her mouth. His tongue pushed inside and explored thoroughly.

Her heart was pounding, and she could hardly breathe. Oh, God, she longed to be with him.

But right now, his intensity overwhelmed her.

Then everything changed. His lips moved more gently, and his tongue glided on hers in sweet, teasing strokes. Her insides melted, and she slid her arms around him.

This was how he used to kiss her. Her heart ached as the love she'd buried so deep inside swelled to the surface.

He suckled her tongue, drawing it into his mouth. His lips moved tenderly on hers, awakening needs inside her she couldn't restrain.

Oh, God, she wanted this so badly. She wanted to give herself to him.

Heat rippled through her and turned to blazing desire. Her breasts swelled, and she could feel the melting heat between her legs. She could feel his cock growing hard against her, and she wanted to reach down and stroke it. Then to feel it glide inside her.

Her arms curled around his neck, and she clung to him.

Then his mouth tore away from her.

"Fuck, this is a spectacularly bad idea," he muttered.

As he pulled back, the bra started to slip away. He grabbed the straps and pushed them back in place, then fastened it again.

"You said you were going to get dressed." He stepped back, then turned and strode away.

4

April closed the door to the guest bedroom and leaned against it, catching her breath.

Her pulse still raced at the memory of Quinn holding her tightly to his body, her breasts crushed against his naked, muscular chest. And his cock thick and solid against her belly.

She tingled at the thought of welcoming it inside her. Longed to feel it fill her completely.

She sucked in a breath and pushed away from the door. She unhooked her damp bra as she walked across the room to the en suite bathroom, then stripped off the panties. She hung the lingerie on a towel rack to dry, then showered.

Afterward, she combed her long hair, then blow-dried it. Once it was cascading in shiny waves over her shoulders, she walked back into the bedroom and pulled on the coral bra and panty set and the sundress she'd been wearing earlier.

As she turned toward the door, she suddenly felt overwhelmed. So much had happened today. Her emotions were frayed. She sank down on the bed and stared at herself in the mirror.

What was she going to do? Austin had invited her to stay

here, and she would tonight, but what would she do after that? She didn't have money for a bus ticket back to Lachelle. And the thought of going back there right now after what had happened with Maurice . . .

She dropped her face into her hands. No, she couldn't deal with that. Not yet.

She had four weeks before she had to return to work.

But she had nowhere else to go. No one who could help her.

Her phone beeped. She walked to the side table by the couch and picked it up. Who would be texting her?

Her heart skipped a beat when she saw the display.

Maurice.

What could he possibly want?

She opened the text app and saw a number of texts from him.

He couldn't possibly be apologizing and trying to get her back after all that he'd done. Could he?

Not that she'd take him back.

As she started reading the texts, her chest tightened.

Don't bother coming back to work. You're fired.

Maurice owned the company she worked for. She shouldn't be surprised that he wouldn't let her continue working there.

And don't bother looking for a job elsewhere in town. You won't get one.

Her heart sank. That was no idle threat. He had enough clout in Lachelle to ensure no one hired her. No one wanted to be in Maurice's or his family's bad graces. They essentially owned the town.

BTW, the bank is calling in the loan on your town house. If you can't pay off the remaining balance, they'll foreclose.

Shock surged through her. Could he really be that vindictive?

His family owned the bank that held the mortgage on her home. The only way she could get the money to repay the loan would be to sell the town house, and she was absolutely certain Maurice could arrange it so no one would buy it. No real estate agent in town would list it, she was sure, and trying to sell it on her own would be futile.

It felt like her insides had been ripped out of her body and shredded.

She sat on the bed staring at the phone, her hand trembling.

Oh, God, what was she going to do now?

Quinn raked his hand through his hair as he paced the bedroom, anger flooding through him.

What the hell was wrong with him?

That wasn't the kind of man he was. Bullying a woman. Almost stripping off her bra. All because his emotions were totally out of control.

Anger. Anxiety. Lust.

His cock wanted April, but his brain knew better. The battle taking place between the two was throwing him wildly off balance.

Fuck, he realized that with the position she was in, he could easily persuade her into his bed. But he would never take advantage of her vulnerable position. And no matter what, winding up in bed with her was too dangerous a game, given his past feelings for her.

He strode to the shower and washed off the chlorine from the pool, then toweled off. As he walked back into the bedroom, he heard his cell vibrate on the dresser.

I'm ready for some gambling. Bring April and meet me in the casino in 30m.

Quinn grinned. Austin loved to gamble, and he was good at it. He had an instinct, and it usually paid off.

Quinn walked into the living room. April was still in her bedroom, and he was worried that after what had happened, she might stay in there to avoid him. He frowned. Austin wouldn't like it if Quinn left April here, even if she wanted to stay. Austin would probably insist on coming up to get her.

He walked down the hall and tapped on the door.

"April, Austin is in the casino. He wants us to join him."

She didn't answer, so he knocked harder this time.

"April?"

She still didn't respond.

"April, if you don't answer, I'm coming in."

After two seconds, he pushed open the door. He glanced around to see April staring out the window, dressed in the same lovely sundress she'd had on earlier. Of course, it was the only appropriate thing she had left for going out.

"I'm sorry. I won't be very good company tonight," she said softly, not turning around. "Why don't you go without me?"

He strode toward her until he stood a foot away.

"Look, Austin wants you down there, and it's the least you can do to thank him for his hospitality."

"His hospitality?" she asked evenly, still staring outside. "And yours, too?"

"Sure. Mine, too. Austin loves to gamble, and he's looking forward to your company this evening."

"All right," she said simply. "I'll need a minute to fix my makeup."

"I'm sure it's fine."

But when she turned around, even though she kept her head down, he saw her eyes were puffy and red. She'd been crying.

"I'll only be a few minutes." Her voice sounded so empty.

His heart ached. He hated seeing her like this.

As she walked to the dresser where her makeup bag sat, he knew he couldn't leave it at that.

"Wait," he said.

She stopped walking, but didn't turn.

"April, are you upset about how I acted earlier? Because I'm sorry about the way I behaved."

She shook her head. "That's not it."

"Then what is it? Has something new happened?"

She drew in a shaky breath and nodded.

"Then come here and tell me."

"No, I don't think—"

"I said come and tell me," he said firmly. He walked toward her and took her hand, then led her to the couch facing the window. He sat down beside her.

"I want you to understand, I'm not trying to get sympathy," she said. "I'm not trying to get anything."

"Noted."

She gazed at him with wide, sorrowful eyes, still gleaming from her tears. Every protective instinct he had surged forward. She bit her lip, and his heart ached. God, he'd always loved how that made her look so sweet and innocent.

He squeezed her soft, delicate hand. "Just tell me."

"It would be easier to show you."

She drew her hand from his, and he hated feeling it slip away. She picked up her cell phone from the side table and flicked it on, then handed it to him.

As he read the series of texts, his chest constricted.

Hell, her ex was a fucking asshole.

He glanced at her again. "I take it he can follow through on these threats?"

She nodded.

"What about friends? Do you have anyone who can help you?"

She shook her head. "I moved straight to Lachelle when we graduated. My friends are *his* friends. They're loyal to him. And I didn't really make any of my own friends during college."

He remembered. She'd been painfully shy. He'd had a devil of a time getting to know her himself. Then after she'd left him, whenever he saw her, she'd always been hanging out with Maurice's friends.

"And I don't have any family." Her voice wavered.

Goddamn, he couldn't help himself. He slid his arm around her and pulled her to him. She rested her head on his chest, and, fuck, feeling her close to him like this made him want so many things. Stupid things he shouldn't let himself want. Like keeping her in his arms forever. Like marrying her and being with her for the rest of his life.

She drew in a breath, then straightened her back, easing away from him.

"But it's okay. I'll be fine. I'll figure something out."

Part of him wanted to convince himself she was playing the martyr to see if he'd jump in and rescue her. But he couldn't quite manage it.

"How?" he demanded gently.

She stood up and paced. "I don't know. Not yet. Maybe I'll get a job at the hotel."

"I'm not sure they need a graphic designer. Maybe you could get a job waiting tables or cleaning rooms, but only if you've done it before. This is a high-end hotel. They want someone with experience. And even if you do get a job," he said gently, "how will you find somewhere to live without first and last month's rent?"

Her expression crumpled. She stopped pacing and faced him.

"Quinn, what do you expect me to say? I'm trying to stay positive, and you're not making that easy."

"I'm not trying to make it easy. I just want you to understand the reality of your situation."

Which was pretty dismal right now.

Anger flared in her blue eyes. "You don't think I know? Not only do I have no money, no job, and nowhere to live, I also have to figure out how to pay you back for my hotel bill."

He frowned. "I keep telling you, that's not an issue. I don't want you to pay me back."

"What you want and what I want are in complete opposition," she said, her eyes blazing. "You don't necessarily win."

Why the hell did she cling to the pipe dream of paying him back? Unless she assumed she'd find a rich husband and pay Quinn with that sucker's money.

That thought triggered the emotional upheaval simmering below the surface.

Anger flared. More likely, she was just trying to convince him that she was reliable and honest so she could get under his skin again. She'd been doing an amazingly good job of that.

His jaw clenched. "Get this straight," he said between gritted teeth. "I don't want your money."

April's eyes widened at the cold glint in Quinn's eyes.

She had dropped her guard because he'd been so compassionate. When he'd held her in his arms, she'd felt cared for. Protected.

It had felt wonderful.

Until he'd poked at her precarious attempt to remain optimistic. Then everything had collapsed around her, leaving her stomach in a total state of chaos. And now he'd made it crystal clear that he would not allow her to repay her debt to him.

Her stomach coiled tighter. She needed to pay him back. Somehow, she had to find a way. She had to be able to stand on her own two feet, or how could she ever make it on her own?

She dragged her gaze from his and sighed. Right now, though, she had to worry about the immediate future. She had somewhere to sleep tonight, but tomorrow would come all too soon.

She stared at her hands. In his harshly spoken words, he'd told her he didn't want anything from her, but she knew that wasn't quite true, and that gave her an idea. One she didn't savor, but it might be her only way out.

She moved closer to him, standing facing him while he sat gazing up at her.

"Fine. You want me to face facts," she said, trying to keep her voice even. "The fact is I'm in trouble, and I have no one to turn to." She shifted her gaze to his again. "Except you."

He raised an eyebrow and waited.

"I need to ask for your help. I hate it, but I don't know what else to do. I don't want to be out on the street tomorrow, and I really need to pay you back somehow. If you won't discuss money, then I have another idea that might appeal to you."

"And what's that?"

"One thing I know you want from me is sex. What if I give you that?"

His eyebrows shot up. "You're suggesting you pay me back by fucking me?"

His coarse wording made her uncomfortable, but she shrugged.

"Why not? You don't have to worry about any romantic entanglements. It'll be just a straightforward physical relationship."

His eyebrow arched up. "You don't find this kind of arrangement a bit demeaning?"

She shrugged. "Why? It's not like I'm being forced into it. And with the strong attraction there's always been between us, it's the same as if we just decided to have a fling."

"And you think a few fucks with you is worth over a hundred grand?"

She flinched inside, but kept her head held high. "It can be as many *fucks* as you want. You call the shots. And before you continue insulting me, I wanted to pay you in cash."

Fuck. Quinn stood up and raked his hand through his hair. He was being an asshole again.

But damn it, her suggestion had thrown him totally off balance. He could barely think straight at the thought of finally having her in his bed.

And to tell the truth, the prospect terrified him.

If he finally got what he'd dreamed of for so long . . . If he finally felt her naked body beneath him . . . surrendering to him . . .

Fuck, he might fall for her all over again.

"I told you I don't want you to pay me back."

Her eyes glittered as she stared at him, and her back slumped in defeat.

"Fine. I'll have to find another way."

She started to turn away from him, but he knew he couldn't let this opportunity slip away. He slid his arm around her waist and pulled her tightly against him. The feel of her soft breasts crushed against his chest sent need churning through him.

"But I do want to take you up on that offer."

Her eyes widened again.

"I'll even throw in enough cash to get you started again."

"That's not necessary."

"You don't dictate the terms. I do."

He waited for her to protest, but she didn't.

"You'll stay with me for a month. I'll expect you to be totally cooperative. You'll do whatever I tell you to do. Fuck me whenever and however I want. Agreed?"

She nodded, her cheeks flushing a deep rose.

He released her and stepped back.

"Good. At least it's an honest proposition," he continued. "We both know what we're getting out of it. No one's being taken advantage of. And there'll be no messy ending. When the time is up, you'll just leave."

"Yes, of course. Now that that's settled, I'll go fix my makeup so we can go down and join Austin."

"Wait. There's one more thing."

"What's that?" she asked.

"I'll be sharing you with Austin."

"What?" April's heart raced. He couldn't be serious. Being with two men at the same time? How could she do that?

She'd only ever been with Maurice, and she'd believed she loved him at the time. And being with Quinn . . . she'd never stopped wanting him. But she hardly knew Austin.

"It's nonnegotiable," he stated flatly.

"I thought you didn't want me to go after Austin."

He smiled. "That's the beauty of it. If we're sharing you—and I've always wanted to share a woman with Austin—then there's no way he'll fall for you. Sharing a woman means we can fuck you all we want, but there's no way it'll go any further."

She compressed her lips. What choice did she have?

"All right."

His eyes glittered, and his lips turned up in a ghost of a smile. "Good. This should prove very interesting."

His phone vibrated. He pulled it from his pocket and glanced at it, then tapped on the screen for a few seconds as a turmoil of emotions fluttered though her.

Oh, God, had she really agreed to this?

"Is that Austin?" she asked.

He slipped his phone back into his pocket. "Yeah. He's wondering where we are."

She stood up. "Okay, I'll go and get ready."

He grabbed her hand again.

"Not yet."

5

Quinn felt April's fingers tremble in his hand as he drew her back to him. Now that he knew he would finally have his wish fulfilled, to have her in his bed, the hunger threatened to overwhelm him. Even just the feel of her hand in his had his cock pulsing.

Her gaze flicked to his, then her cheeks blossomed a deep rose. She knew exactly what he had in mind.

"I thought Austin was waiting for us." Her voice quivered.

"I told him we'd be down in twenty minutes."

"Why?" she almost squeaked.

He chuckled. "Well, because you and I just made an interesting agreement, and I think we should seal the deal."

"You want to . . . uh . . . do it . . . right now?"

"If by *it*, you mean fuck, then no. I'd want more than twenty minutes for that."

He led her into the living room, then walked to the bar and picked up his drink.

"First, let's discuss safe sex. Austin and I both had physicals recently and were tested for STDs. With how busy we've been preparing the ICO launch, neither of us has had a sexual partner for several months before or since. What about you?"

"I . . . uh . . . yeah, I had a physical about a month ago so I could be added to Maurice's health insurance."

"But learning about his recent infidelities must have you worried."

She bit her lip. "Not for health reasons. He hasn't touched me in about six months. Now I understand why."

Fuck, the guy was a total idiot.

"So if you're on birth control, we could dispense with condoms if you agree," Quinn said.

"Yes, we can do that."

"Good."

He sat down on the barstool and took a sip, watching her biting her lip. After the shocking offer she'd just made, and the thought of what he and Austin would be doing with her later this evening, the sight no longer made him think she looked sweet and innocent. Now all he could think of was the warmth of that mouth. How it would feel to be inside it, her lips wrapped around his hard cock.

His gaze lingered on her lip as her teeth teased over it, pulling on it. His cock twitched, and he took another sip, then set his drink down.

"Before we make the deal official, I want to ensure that you'll be sufficiently cooperative."

"I told you I would be. Don't you believe me?"

"It's not that. I want to make sure you understand what I mean by *cooperative*."

"You want me to be enthusiastic? Creative?"

"Yes. And yes. But more than that. I want you to follow orders and treat me with proper respect. For instance, you'll also call me *sir*."

"*Sir?* You want me to call you that all the time?"

He tipped his head as if considering, watching the nervous tremor of her lip.

"For now, just when I tell you."

He poured another drink and held it out to her. She stepped toward him and took it, then tipped it back for a sip.

He turned on the bar stool until he faced away from the bar.

"Take another sip, then come stand in front of me."

She swallowed another mouthful, then walked to him and deposited the glass beside his.

"Good. Now take off your dress."

Her cheeks flushed a beautiful shade of rose again.

His eyebrow arched as she hesitated.

"Is there a problem?" he asked.

"No. Of course not." She took a step back, then reached around behind her and tugged down the zipper.

"This isn't a big deal, baby," he said. "I already saw you in a bra and panties when we went swimming." A sudden thought occurred to him. "Unless you don't have a bra on under the dress."

The very thought sent his already swelling cock twitching.

"I do," she said as she slipped the sleeves of the sundress from her shoulders, keeping her gaze averted.

Then the dress fluttered to the floor, landing in a heap around her feet.

But his gaze was locked on her body. She did wear a bra and panties, but the superbly cut coral lingerie trimmed with thin black ribbon was incredibly erotic. Not like the simple black set she'd worn in the pool earlier, which had still been the sexiest thing he'd ever seen. Until now.

The bra lifted her breasts and pressed them together,

presenting him with a heart-stopping display. The way the flesh swelled from the lace made his groin ache. The bikini panties were cut high on her legs, making them look sensationally long.

His focus settled on the small triangle of lace in front, and he longed to tear the garment from her so he could see her sweet, tempting pussy. He hadn't intended to fuck her right now—that's why he'd purposely given Austin a short time frame—but at the sight of her like this, he was wavering.

"Very good. Now come closer."

She stepped closer, and he had to stop himself from reaching out and stroking her soft breasts.

"Kneel down in front of me and say something that will turn me on. And remember to call me *sir.*"

She knelt down and tipped her head up. Her wide sapphire eyes looked so innocent.

"Please, sir. May I take your cock in my mouth?"

An image of her soft, pink lips wrapping around him, then his cock gliding inside her sweet mouth, made his cock throb.

He chuckled. "Yes, well, that will do it. But let's start a little slower."

She sucked on her lower lip, then nodded. "Please, sir. I would love to touch you."

"Would you?" He smiled. "Then go ahead."

Her delicate fingers glided the length of the growing bulge in his pants. Adrenaline surged through him. Then she pulled the zipper down. Her fingers glided inside and stroked over the bulge in his boxers.

Heat pulsed through him.

"I like you touching me like that," he murmured.

Fuck, it was incredible.

Her fingers wrapped around him through the cloth.

"May I look at you, sir?" she asked as she squeezed lightly.

"Yes," he nearly hissed as his groin tightened.

She drew his cock out through the flap. Her gaze locked on his long column.

The sight of her looking at him, hunger in her eyes, took his breath away.

"Oh, sir. It's so massive."

"Is it too massive for your small mouth?" he asked. The thought of her taking him inside made his cock ache.

She licked his tip, sending excruciating need radiating through every part of him.

"I don't know, sir. I'll do my best."

When she pressed her lips to his tip, he stifled a groan. She opened and her mouth glided over his crown. Widening. Covering him in warmth.

He rested his hand on her head, her hair silky under his palm. As she stretched her jaw wider, his cockhead slid all the way into her mouth. She squeezed around him, and if he'd been standing, he was sure his knees would have buckled.

"That's right, baby," he said gruffly. "You're doing great."

She pushed forward, slowly taking his shaft into her mouth, her lips tight around him.

God, it was like being caressed by an angel.

She kept going until she was halfway down, then she wrapped her hand snugly around the exposed part.

Fuck, the warmth from her body felt unbelievable.

Then she began to move, gliding her head forward and back. Pleasure quivered through him at the sweetness of the sensation. After a few strokes, she slid back and swirled her tongue over his crown, round and round, then dragged it under the ridge. She teased that sensitive spot just under the front, setting his blood boiling.

When she sucked, deep and hard, he moaned.

Then she went back to gliding his length.

His fingers twined through her long hair, and he wound it around his hand. As she moved, he guided her head, setting the rhythm he liked. She followed his lead perfectly. The tension in his groin coiled tighter as pleasure rippled through him. He urged her to move faster.

"Oh, fuck, baby, I'm so close. Do you want me to come in your mouth?"

He knew he could just order her to do it, but . . . he wanted her to want it.

Her gaze tipped up to his and she nodded, her head continuing to move. Taking him deep into her warmth. In fact, he realized she'd pressed her hand tightly to his root and was taking him almost all the way in.

Back. Then forward.

Fuck, he was all the way inside her now.

The tight control he was keeping on his body to make this last as long as possible began to fray. She slid back, and he pulled her forward in a quick swoop. All the way again.

"Ohhh, fuck, baby."

Then she started to surge forward and back, taking his full length every time. His breathing was erratic, and he knew he was clinging to the edge.

She squeezed him with her lips. When she slid back, she paused to suck his cockhead, then slipped off.

"Please come in my mouth, sir." Her beautiful blue eyes peered up at him, pleading.

How did she do that? Look so sincere about giving him pleasure?

Then she glided deep again, and he lost it.

The tension in his groin coiled tight, then released. He groaned as pleasure erupted through him, his cock pulsing. Hot liquid filled her mouth, surrounding his cock. He jerked forward, filling her deeper, as the orgasm consumed him.

Oh, God, the intensity of it blew his mind.

He slumped back against the bar, sucking in short, deep breaths.

After a moment, he turned his attention to her, still on her knees in front of him, and met her blue-eyed gaze. His cock still sprouted from her full lips, her hand wrapped firmly around it. Slowly she glided back, swirling her tongue around his shaft as she moved, then over the cockhead. Her tongue lapped over every part of the crown before she finally slipped off the end of him.

Then she swallowed.

Fuck, he wanted to pull her into his arms and take that pretty little mouth of hers. To drive his tongue inside and taste his essence on her tongue.

"Thank you, sir," she said softly, then bowed her head as if awaiting further orders.

At the sight, a grim melancholy washed over him.

Now he felt like a total jerk. His first time with the woman he loved had been a cheap, tawdry blow job. For his pleasure only.

Fuck, he wanted to drag her to the couch and go down on her right now. To rip away the tiny lace panties so he could see her pussy for the first time, then drive his tongue into her so far . . . to tease her clit so intensely . . . that she'd scream his name.

But he pulled the reins tight on that overwhelming desire

as he realized what he'd just admitted to himself. Goddamn, he could *not* allow himself to love her.

He *didn't* love her.

It was just residual sexual frustration from so many years of wanting her.

Fuck, he had to get the hell out of this suite.

"Now go and get ready," he commanded sharply.

"So what took you two so long?" Austin asked as Quinn and April joined him at the table.

He'd texted Quinn to meet here so they could have dinner before they started their evening in the casino.

Austin hoped it was because they'd finally started talking and chipped away at their issues enough to allow themselves to get caught up in the obvious attraction between them. The way April stared down at her folded hands sitting on the table, her cheeks flushing a soft rose, might have convinced him, but Quinn's expression was solemn.

"April got some bad news."

Austin frowned as he glanced at April. "I'm sorry to hear that, April. I hope it's not as bad as what's already happened."

April raised her face, and the despair emanating from her was like a punch to the gut.

Quinn's gaze locked on his. "It's worse."

"What happened?"

"Her jerk of an ex had her fired and is ensuring that no one else in that town will hire her. He also arranged to foreclose on her mortgage, so she's lost her home and the equity she's built up."

Austin's chest tightened. "The guy is a vindictive bastard. It sounds like going back to that town wasn't really going to work for you if your ex has that kind of pull. But as for your town house, there's no way he should be able to get away with that. What's the address of the property?"

April raised her gaze. "Why?"

Austin pulled out his cell phone. "Just humor me."

"It's 1260 Apricot Lane in Lachelle, Massachusetts."

Austin tapped in the address and emailed it to his lawyer with a note.

"If you can pay off the mortgage, they can't take the town house. They're betting that you can't sell it fast enough. So I propose that I buy the town house. Then you have the money to pay off the outstanding amount on the mortgage and you keep your equity."

Her gaze turned to his, and he was happy to see hope gleaming in her lovely sapphire eyes.

"Why would you do that? You don't even know me."

He smiled warmly. "Of course I do. We met earlier today. Remember?" he teased.

Her cheeks flushed. "Thank you, Austin. It's very kind of you."

He rested his hand on hers and squeezed. "I don't like to see anyone bullied."

Goddamn, touching her had an effect on him he hadn't anticipated. He meant his attention to be friendly. And a little protective. But there was a need that simmered below the surface. A need that flared when he touched her. It had happened in the pool. Fuck, his cock had lurched to attention when her soft, almost naked body and fallen against his.

"We should order dinner," Quinn said, picking up one of the menus from the table.

Austin released her hand, his gaze darting to Quinn. He'd expected to see jealousy, or suppressed anger, but none of that flickered in Quinn's eyes.

The waiter came by and took their orders, and soon they were eating their entrées and making small talk.

Austin had just pushed aside his plate when his cell vibrated in his pocket. He pulled it out for a quick glance, and when he saw there was a message from his lawyer, he opened it.

"Damn it," he said when he scanned the message.

"What is it?" Quinn queried.

6

Austin compressed his lips. He hated to be the bearer of bad news, especially after April had already been through so much today.

"It seems that they've already sold your town house."

"That's awfully fast. But isn't that good news?" April asked, her sweet blue eyes wide as she gazed at him.

"No, because they essentially sold it to your ex at a rock-bottom price. So low that you make nothing on the deal."

"Can they do that?" Quinn asked.

"April, my lawyer said your ex cosigned the loan."

"Yes. I'd just started my job and didn't have much of a credit history. Maurice pushed me to buy right away, saying it would be better for me in the long run. He negotiated the mortgage so that I didn't need much of a down payment, and he got me a low interest rate, but the bank required that he cosign." She frowned. "But *I* paid the bills. Every month without fail."

"It seems he had a clause worked in so that if you defaulted on a payment, or the bank decided to call in the loan, he had the option to buy the property for the amount of the outstanding portion of the loan. It would have been in the small print. He probably had his lawyer go over the contract for you, right?"

She nodded. The color had drained from her face. "I trusted him."

"Can he get away with this?" Quinn asked, anger flaring in his eyes.

Austin shrugged. "It looks like he did." He turned back to April and took her hand. "April, I'm sorry I got your hopes up."

"It's okay," she said. "You tried. Thank you for that."

The waiter came and took away their plates, then brought by a cart covered with tempting desserts. April chose a blueberry custard tart, and Austin took a slice of decadent chocolate cake. Quinn chose mocha cheesecake. The waiter poured them each a cup of the restaurant's special blend of coffee.

"Let's do something to lighten the mood," Austin said.

"Like what?" Quinn sipped his coffee.

"Something that will get us in the right frame of mind for the rest of the evening." Austin nodded toward a table with a couple sitting together. "Do you see that couple?"

Quinn glanced at the couple who were holding hands and gazing lovingly into each other's eyes in the secluded booth in a corner of the restaurant.

"Yeah."

"I bet you a hundred bucks they leave separately."

Quinn shrugged. "That doesn't seem likely, since they look like they're ready to race off to the bedroom together, so sure."

They watched as the waiter placed a bill on the couple's table. The man glanced at it, then dropped a pile of cash on top. He slid his arm around her and kissed her, their lips lingering. Then he stood up and walked out of the restaurant. The woman settled back in her seat and sipped her drink.

Quinn pulled out his wallet and snagged a hundred-dollar bill from inside, then handed it to Austin.

"How do you always do that?" Quinn slid his wallet back into his pocket.

"In this case, research, my friend. I saw that he was wearing a wedding ring, and she wasn't."

Quinn nodded. "Okay, but that's still luck. They could be staying at the hotel on a clandestine romantic weekend, so they would have gone back to the room together."

"True, but I also saw the man at breakfast this morning with his wife. They were sitting at the next table, and I overheard them making plans to meet for a show in"—he glanced at his watch—"about ten minutes from now."

Quinn shook his head. "You and your crazy memory and attention to details."

Austin chuckled. "Which is one of the things you love about me."

Quinn smiled. "So true."

"April," Austin said, "now it's your turn. I bet you the same amount that—"

"No, I can't," she broke in. "I don't have any money. Remember?"

He smiled. "No problem. We don't both have to wager money."

Quinn's eyebrows arched. "What exactly do you have in mind?"

Austin's gaze shifted to Quinn, and he expected to see sparks flaring in his eyes, but instead his friend seemed amused.

"Nothing untoward, I assure you." He turned back to April. "Here's the deal. If you win, I give you a hundred dollars. If you lose, then you . . ." He shrugged. "I don't know . . . how about you answer a question?"

"Something personal, you mean?"

"Sure, it wouldn't be much fun otherwise. But not *intimate* personal. I'm not going to try to embarrass you. Just something that'll help us get to know each other better."

"That sounds like a great idea," Quinn said. "I like the idea of you and Austin getting to know each other better."

The look Quinn and April exchanged confused Austin, and he wasn't used to the feeling. Usually, he could read people pretty well.

April's cheeks flushed again, which confused him more. If he didn't know that Quinn had it bad for her, he'd almost think Quinn was trying to push Austin and April together.

"So what's the bet?" she asked.

"How about that the last two digits on our dinner bill—and to be clear, I mean the cents—are thirty-seven?"

Quinn leaned in close and whispered in her ear, then she gazed at Austin.

"So if it's thirty-seven, you win and I lose?" she asked.

"That's right."

She smiled. "How about I accept the bet, but only if we turn it around? *I* win if it's thirty-seven."

He kept his expression even. "I don't know."

Just as he'd thought. Quinn had told her that Austin probably knew the amount, since he could do quick calculations in his head. His friend figured he'd set her up to lose.

The fact was he hadn't even bothered to look at the prices.

"Maybe we should choose another bet," Austin said.

He actually wanted her to win, and she was practically guaranteed to win the other way around.

"Come on, buddy," Quinn said. "Give her a chance to win some money."

Austin shrugged. "That's what I'm trying to do, but okay. You're on."

Quinn flagged the waiter and asked for the bill.

"I'm sorry, sir. I didn't realize you're in a rush," he said.

"No rush. We just have a wager on the final amount," Quinn said.

The waiter grinned. "Of course, sir."

The man had probably seen a lot stranger bets than that. He returned moments later and handed them the bill.

Austin glanced at the amount. The final two digits were sixty-eight.

He smiled. "I'm afraid you lose, April."

Even though he had tried to set it up for her to win, and the bet got turned around so it was wildly in his favor, he still got a rush from winning.

April sighed. "Okay. So what's the question?"

"We all know that your ex is an ass," Austin said, "but you thought you loved him once. What about him or your relationship made you think you were in love?"

April's eyes widened. "Wow. You don't pull any punches, do you?"

"I think that examining the bad things that happen to us—the good things, too—helps us understand ourselves better and helps us make better decisions going forward."

"Not repeating history, you mean," she said.

"It's more than that. You believed you loved this guy. There were things about him you were blind to. There's a reason. There was something in the relationship that fed something inside you. If you understand what you wanted, then you're better equipped to see the next relationship more clearly."

She pursed her lips. "You're right, but I'm not sure I could avoid the same pitfalls again."

She turned her gaze to his, and in her wide sapphire eyes he saw a deep sadness and loneliness that tore at his soul.

"Then tell me about it." At her hesitation, he smiled. "You did lose the bet. And it'll just stay between the three of us."

She glanced to Quinn, who simply sat in his chair observing.

She sighed. "It helps if you understand a bit about my past. I didn't tell you that the reason my name is April is because that's the month I was born. My last name is Smith because . . . well, the person who named me didn't have much imagination. You remember that I told you my mother abandoned me at the hospital. The insurance she'd used was someone else's. They didn't want to give me that person's name. After that, I was put in foster care."

"I'm surprised you weren't adopted," Austin said. "There are so many couples looking for an infant to adopt."

"I was. But my luck has never been good. My adopted parents weren't . . . well, as caring as they should have been. I was pulled from their home when I was about two years old. A neighbor reported a problem, and the authorities checked in and found that the parents were practically starving the child. She was suffering from malnutrition, and it took a lot of hospital visits, therapy, and patience by one kind woman to get the child back to a normal weight."

Austin was confused at first when April started talking about *the child* and *she,* but he suddenly realized she was referring to herself in the third person. He didn't think she even realized she was doing it.

"That woman couldn't adopt her, though," she continued, "and the child went to another home. Now labeled as a difficult child for care, she didn't stay in any foster home for very long."

She was staring at her glass and started tracing lines on the surface.

"I could go on and on about the problems of being in the system . . . the heartbreaks . . . but . . ." She drew in a deep breath. "When I met Maurice . . . The attention he paid me . . . I felt wanted for the first time in my life."

Austin noticed Quinn's compressed lips, and even though his expression was closed, Austin could tell that her statement was a kick in the gut.

"I saw what I wanted to see," she continued. "He took care of me. He said he loved me."

"So you mistook things like him cosigning your mortgage, getting you a job in his company, keeping you within his group of friends as his looking out for you?" Austin asked.

She bit her lip. "Yes, that's right."

"And his money," Quinn said. "I'm sure that played a big part in your *love* for him."

She winced a little.

After a brief hesitation, she said softly, "I'm not going to deny it."

Austin could feel the pain in her words. Her gaze turned to Austin, her eyes begging him to understand.

"When you're in the system," she said, "you know that you're out on your own at eighteen. No fallback. No safety net. I was lucky to get a scholarship for college so I had a hope of a better future, but the uncertainty I'd lived with all my life left me craving security. I believed he loved me. And he had money. I'd never have to worry."

Austin could see that she hated herself for having to admit that. He could also see that Quinn couldn't see anything past her admission, which would exacerbate his belief that she was a gold digger.

Damn, but their relationship history was fraught with pain and misunderstanding.

He'd asked this question not to torture her but to get her to open up about what she wanted in a relationship. About what love was to her. He'd hoped that her answers would help Quinn see that she wanted more from a romantic relationship than money. And he'd hoped it would give him some insight into why she hadn't found what she'd needed with Quinn. Austin was sure she hadn't left Quinn just because he'd been broke at the time. He'd hoped to find some clue that might help bring them together again.

Because it was so clear to him—it had been all along—that Quinn loved this woman.

"Okay, so we get that he made you feel secure," Austin said. "But as a man, what did he do? How did he behave to make you think he loved you?"

She glanced at him in surprise—as if amazed he would even talk to her now that she'd made her admission.

"As I said, he paid attention to me. He made me feel special."

Austin could feel Quinn seething behind his indifferent expression. Austin was sure he was thinking that he had done the same thing. From what Quinn had mentioned of her, he had showered her with attention.

"What specifically did he do?"

"I don't know. He listened to what I said. One time, he surprised me with a scarf I'd seen in a store window the night before when we'd gone out for a walk. I hadn't even realized he'd noticed my interest. He knew I loved breakfast more than any other meal, so he'd often take me out to a pancake house in the evening so I could have breakfast for dinner. But mostly, he just always made time for me."

"It sounds like you wish you were back with the guy," Quinn said, his voice devoid of emotion, but Austin could hear a tinge of bitterness.

She shook her head. "Of course not. I realize how superficial those things are in the long run. And he didn't really care. He just put on a good show."

"But it gives a clue as to what you need in a relationship," Austin said. "With your past, it's important that you have someone who makes time for you. Who listens. Who shows that he cares. Because all of that has been wholly missing from your life."

Quinn looked at his watch. "As fun as this conversation is," he said dryly, "we should get moving. We have the poker game scheduled in about two hours and, Austin, you said you want to hit the casino first."

Austin added a generous tip to the bill and signed it, then turned to April.

"You deserve to find a man who is everything you've dreamed of." Then he took her hand and kissed it.

April stood up and accepted the arm Austin offered, curling her fingers around his elbow. A quick glance at Quinn's cold stare made her want to shrivel into a ball. What did he want from her? He'd already told her he wanted to share her with his friend. Why would he care about such a trivial intimacy as her holding his arm?

Unless it was because he hadn't given his permission.

She walked alongside Austin, and the heat of him so close set her stomach fluttering, his strong, muscular arm making her feel protected.

Austin was a good, sensitive man. The questions he'd asked, although uncomfortable, showed his insight and compassion.

They stepped from the relative quiet of the restaurant into the din of the crowds. As they walked along the carpeted floor, video screens blared with bright lights and flashing displays. The continuous sound of the machines and people's voices bombarded her.

Quinn pulled his cell from his pocket and stared at the screen.

"That's Johan," he said. "He's having a PR issue. Carl Veron is trashing the company all over the internet, and Johan is taking some interviews to set things straight. He wants to go over a few things with me before his first one in half an hour."

"Do you need me to help?" Austin asked.

"No. You go ahead to the tables, and I'll meet you there. The usual?"

Austin nodded, and Quinn hurried away toward the nearest elevator in his long-legged stride.

"Johan is our PR person," Austin said.

"I gathered," April responded.

As she walked by Austin's side, passing people playing slots, blackjack, and other games she had no clue about, she wondered how people could stand sitting at these machines in the midst of the pedestrian traffic flowing around them. He led her past the machines, showing no interest in the crowded tables they were passing by.

"Where's *the usual*?" she asked.

"There are VIP areas that are less crowded. Quinn and I have one we favor."

They followed the flow of the crowd for a while, then he turned down a wide corridor. There were columns and plants and even a lovely fountain ahead. They passed by designer shops and restaurants as they walked. As they got closer to the fountain, which took up a long portion of the center space, a distinctive blond head caught April's eye.

Oh, God, that was Sarah Piner and her husband, Jon, stepping out of Cartier's. Just her luck that she would run into them twice in the same afternoon.

April's body stiffened, and she slowed down. Sarah hadn't seen her yet.

Austin tipped his head. "What's wrong?"

She turned her head away from Sarah. "That couple. I don't want them to see me."

Austin stopped, turning toward her. His big body blocked Sarah's view of April, but that wouldn't last when she and Jon got closer.

"Really?" His lips turned up in a grin. "There's an easy solution to that."

The flare in his eyes caught her off guard, then she found herself pulled against his broad chest, his arms gliding around her. His mouth captured hers. His hand slid up to cup her head, and he drew her closer as his lips moved persuasively on hers. His tongue nudged her lips, and she parted them without thinking.

Her heart stammered at the sweetness of his tongue invading her mouth. Of his muscular body wrapped around her. Of melting into his arms and giving herself over to his passionate kiss.

It seemed to last an eternity. Her arms were around his neck, her breasts snugly pressed against the heat of him.

Then he drew back. His grin was gone, and he looked as dazed as she felt.

"I think they're gone," Austin said.

"What?" She had trouble drawing in air.

"That couple you were avoiding. They're gone."

"Oh." Her cheeks flushed, and she eased away, sliding her hands from his neck to his shoulders, but his arms were still around her.

Good thing, or she might have melted to the floor.

"Uh . . . look," he said. "I know you and Quinn have a thing. I'm not making a move on you."

"Good to know," she said, finding it hard to think while pressed so close to his warm, masculine body, his strong arms around her.

"He's my best friend, and I wouldn't jeopardize that."

"Of course. But . . ."

"But what?"

"Is there a reason you're not letting me go?"

His expression changed, his eyes glittering as a slow smile spread across his face.

"I guess because I'm enjoying having you so close. I know I shouldn't indulge myself, but"—he shrugged—"there's really no harm done since it's all innocent."

He released her, and she stepped back, immediately missing his warm arms around her. People walked by totally ignoring them. He offered his elbow, and she curled her fingers around it. He rested his hand over hers, and the comfort of the gesture made her feel protected and cherished.

"So are you going to tell me why you were avoiding those people?" he asked.

"They're good friends of Maurice's. My ex. They came here for the wedding."

They started to walk again.

"That's awkward. There'll probably be quite a few of your wedding guests who decided to stay over for the weekend even though the wedding was canceled." He grinned. "It sounds like I might have several opportunities to"—he winked—"help you hide out."

Her heartbeat raced at the thought of being swept into his arms again.

"I . . . uh . . . no. It's not like that. It's just . . . Sarah isn't shy about asking questions. Or stating her opinion. And doesn't much care if it cuts to the bone." She flicked her gaze to his. "I really appreciate what you did."

He squeezed her hand again. "I was glad to be of service."

7

April followed Austin around another corner, and after a few moments, they approached a wide, ornately decorated gold door with *VIP Lounge* written on it. Maurice had taken her here yesterday afternoon before everything had gone wrong.

Austin opened the door, and she accompanied him inside. A hostess greeted them with a tray of champagne-filled flutes. Austin picked up a glass and handed it to April, then took a sip of his own. He continued across the lounge to another door and pushed a button. The door slid open, and she realized it was an elevator. When Maurice had brought her here, they'd sat in the lounge and talked with some of his friends, then left for the rehearsal dinner afterward.

Austin pressed the eleven button, and the elevator moved upward. When the door opened, they stepped into a casino that was quite different from what they'd left downstairs. It was wood paneled and more elegant. Unlike the casino downstairs, the video machines were isolated to a section off to the right. The main casino was mostly filled with gaming tables. Lots of different kinds. All with several people around them.

There were women in glittering gowns and simple cocktail dresses, men in everything from casual suits to tuxedos. Austin fit right in with his well-tailored designer suit. Her sundress, in black with coral flowers, was borderline acceptable, but she felt a little out of place. Not that she had a choice. This was now the dressiest thing she owned as of this afternoon.

"This way," Austin said as he led her past several tables to a craps table. "I've had a lot of luck at this one."

As they approached the table, she glanced at the people surrounding it. Her heart stuttered. Oh, God, three couples who were supposed to be at the wedding today were standing at that table. She stiffened, slowing down a little.

"Something wrong?" Austin asked as he slowed to a stop.

She knew how gamblers were. The fact he'd had luck at that table would be important to him. She couldn't ask him not to go there.

"No, nothing." She tried to urge him to keep moving, but he stared at her face, reading her anxiety.

He frowned then glanced at the table. "You know, it's probably a good idea to try a different table. Stale luck and all," he said.

"But—"

He interrupted her protest by turning her forty-five degrees. He glanced around, and all the other craps tables she could see were full except one.

He led her to that table. As they approached, someone threw the dice, and then there was a groan and the chips were cleared away. Austin guided her to the table's edge and slid his arm around her waist, tucking her close to his side.

"New shooter," the uniformed man hovering around the table called.

The man slid the dice to an attractive brunette in a green

dress. She picked them up and tossed them across the table. They bounced jauntily on the table, then rolled to a halt. Twelve. More groans, and the chips were swept away.

"Do you know how to play craps?" Austin asked as he laid a large stack of bills on the table and a casino staffer slid a large stack of chips toward him.

"Not really," she said, glancing at the complicated pattern of numbers, grids, and words on the red felt of the table. It didn't help that she was pressed to his hard, masculine body, sending a warm flush through her.

"It can sound a bit complicated, but—"

"It's okay. Why don't I watch for a bit to see if I get the hang of it?"

He smiled. "Sure. But feel free to ask questions."

She nodded. He set three red chips on a strip labeled *Pass Line*. Several of the other players did the same, including the woman with the dice. She tossed them across the table again, and they bounced to a stop with a three and a six. A staff member slid a white disc labeled *On* to the nine in a strip of numbers at the top of the table.

Austin placed blue chips on five and six on that same strip.

The woman rolled a few times. On the second roll, a five came up and Austin won. The chips on the other numbers weren't cleared away, though. April was confused by the goings-on, with people adding chips, winning chips, then suddenly, all the chips were cleared away, and the man who'd been calling out the rolled numbers in a humorous banter called, "New shooter!" again.

April lost track of what was going on as the dice rounded the table.

She glanced around as someone stepped up beside her. It was Quinn.

"What's going on? I expected to find you at your favorite table," he said to Austin.

"I decided to go for a change," Austin said, placing another bet.

"But this table . . . you haven't had great luck here."

"No one has, but I believe that's about to change."

"Are you up?"

Austin shook his head. "No, down about a third. But I've got a feeling."

"It's your money," Quinn said with a good-natured smile as he settled in beside April.

After a few more rolls, Quinn started betting, too. Finally, the dice wound up in front of Austin. Austin's stack of chips had gone down a little more. He picked up the dice, then turned to April.

"I want you to roll. You're going to bring me luck." He smiled encouragingly as he placed the white dice in her hand.

"I don't know what I'm doing," she protested.

Austin placed six red chips on the pass line. Quinn also set several chips down, as did other players.

"You don't have to. Just throw the dice so they bounce off the other side of the table. That's it."

She bit her lip, aware of everyone watching her. She tossed the dice and watched them hit the side, then bounce back across the table. They rolled to a stop. Six and five.

Murmurs of approval rippled around the table, and everyone who had chips on the pass line received more chips. Austin got his original five reds plus five more reds.

He tightened his arm around her and smiled. "You're doing great."

He pushed all ten reds back in place. Quinn also kept all his chips, including winnings, on the table.

"Roll again," Quinn said.

She picked up the dice and tossed them again. They bounced to a stop with a three and a six. The staffer behind her slid a white disc labeled *On* to the nine in the strip of numbers at the top of the table.

"April, pick a number from those ones at the top. Other than the nine."

"Um . . . eight," she said.

Austin pushed a stack of chips onto the eight. Her stomach fluttered at the thought he could lose all that if she'd picked a bad number. Quinn placed chips on eight, and also on five and six. Other players placed chips on various places on the table.

She rolled the dice, praying for an eight to come up. But instead a four and a one appeared. She glanced at Austin, stricken.

He chuckled. "Don't worry about it. I didn't lose anything. And Quinn won."

Quinn slid his arm around her waist above Austin's and squeezed her lightly.

"Thanks, baby," Quinn said with a smile, then drew his arm away again.

He pushed his winnings onto ten. Other players added bets.

No one had called for a new shooter, so she picked up the dice and tossed them again. She had to admit, this was kind of fun.

The dice rolled to a stop. Two fours.

She watched wide-eyed as a big stack of chips was pushed Austin's way. Quinn also won quite a bit.

"Nice, sweetheart," Austin said. He pushed all his chips onto eight again.

Quinn pushed a tall stack of blues onto it, too. Several other players also jumped in.

She rolled again, worried that everyone would lose because of her. This time, a six and a four came up. Quinn was a winner again. He grinned and leaned in to give her a kiss on the cheek. The light pressure of his lips on her skin sent quivers dancing down her spine. He then turned back to the table.

"You know, I'm feeling really lucky," Austin said.

To April's horror, Austin pushed all his chips onto eight. Quinn laughed, then pushed all his chips there, too. There were a few whispers around the table, but as if everyone's confidence in her was boosted by Austin's bold gesture, several more stacks of chips were pushed into place on the eight.

April's hand was trembling as she picked up the dice. She tossed them across the table, holding her breath as she watched. After the seemingly endless rolling of the small cubes, they landed in double ones, which she knew were called *snake eyes*. That couldn't be good.

She glanced around the table in trepidation, but everyone just sat calmly.

She leaned in to Quinn. "I don't understand what's going on," she whispered to him.

He gazed at her and squeezed her hand.

"It's okay, baby. You keep rolling until you roll a seven. If you roll any of the numbers along the top there, that number wins. If you roll an eight, we win *big*."

"So don't roll a seven. I can keep rolling as long as I don't roll a seven." She kept repeating the words under her breath as she tossed the dice again.

The dice rolled and rolled. One landed as a four.

Please, please be a four.

But her gut clenched, fearing it would be a three. The extra seconds it took for the second die to stop seemed to take an eternity.

Then it came up two.

April sucked in a breath, staring at the huge pile of chips on eight.

"I don't think I can do this," she murmured to Quinn, her lip trembling.

He turned to her, his gaze warm and reassuring. "Baby, no matter what happens, it'll be fine."

She bit her lip. It was nice of him to say that. And, of course, he wanted her to be confident. But it wouldn't be all right. If they lost all that money, she would feel responsible.

She shook the dice in her hand, the feel of the cool cubes jostling against her skin strangely soothing. Then she drew back her hand and tossed them hard. They bounced and ricocheted in opposite directions across the table in a lively dance.

One die turned up as a five. She jerked her head around to catch sight of the other die, but people were already gasping. Her stomach clenched.

Then a whoop went up, and she realized . . .

Oh, God! She'd actually rolled an eight!

Austin, with his face beaming, grabbed her and pulled her into his arms, lifting her off her feet. Elated, she clung to him, a smile spreading across her face. He squeezed her tightly, then spun around in a circle. She began to laugh in sheer exhilaration.

Then as he slowed and set her on her feet again, she became intensely conscious of her breasts pressed tightly against his hard chest and his thick, muscular arms tight around her.

Austin released her, but their gazes caught, and she saw heat blazing in his teal eyes. Her cheeks flushed, and she turned to the table again.

Then she realized Quinn was watching her, his expression unreadable.

"I won, too, you know," he murmured, then pulled her into his arms in a hug that was less energetic, but far more intense. In his embrace, she felt completely owned by him. And not in a bad way.

Her heart stammered, and all she could think of was him kissing her. Taking her lips with his confident, possessive mouth. Then him dragging her to his bed and stripping off her clothes . . .

He drew back, and she eased away, tugging her gaze from his before he could see the need in her eyes.

Then it landed straight on Sarah Piner's, who was standing in the crowd watching the excitement around their table. Her disapproving stare cut right through April. April's cheeks blazed with a fiery heat.

She felt Austin's hand rest on her lower back, then he leaned in close.

"Don't worry about her," Austin murmured. "Just finish rolling, and we'll get out of here."

April nodded and lifted the dice, tearing her gaze from Sarah's. April rolled three more times before getting a seven, then the dice moved to someone else.

"What's going on?" Quinn asked as Austin led April from the table.

"Just an old friend of her fiancé's that has her spooked." Austin led her to the bar along the side of the room and ordered her a drink.

Quinn glanced around. "We saw that woman after we left the manager's office this afternoon."

April grasped the drink the bartender handed her and took a deep sip. She hadn't realized Quinn had even noticed.

The crowd dispersed from around the table they'd just left, and Sarah was nowhere to be seen. April sucked in a deep breath, then took another sip of her drink. She didn't know what it was, but it was cold, fruity . . . and strong. Just what she needed.

Austin guided her to some armchairs circling a round table, and the three of them sat down.

"Why does this woman have you so agitated?" Quinn asked.

"It's just . . . her husband is Maurice's best friend, and I know that she'll tell Maurice everything she saw."

"So what? The guy cheated on you," Quinn said. "What do you care what she tells him?"

"She'll also tell all my friends and . . ." She shook her head as she stared at the glittering droplets of condensation on the side of her glass, misery seeping through every part of her.

Austin rested his hand on her arm. "Forget about it, sweetheart. None of that matters. You're moving on."

She nodded, but it was hard to hold back the tears threatening to spill.

She set down her drink. "It looks like there's an outdoor patio over there," she said, spotting a glass door leading outside. "I'm going out to get a breath of fresh air."

Quinn watched April walk away, her delightful ass swaying.

"I'm going with her," he said. "She's pretty shaky right now."

"That's a good idea," Austin agreed.

Quinn stood up and followed her to the door. As he stepped out into the warm night air, he glanced around to see where

April had gone. There were several people outside, but the foliage from the large flowering plants offered a level of privacy to the sitting areas scattered around the outdoor garden.

He caught sight of April's back as she strolled to the far corner. He followed. As he approached, he saw her sit in one of the comfortable upholstered chairs.

"Did you see that slut?" a woman said, her voice carrying from beyond the thick plants beside April.

April's eyes widened, and she turned her head in the direction of the voice. She must have seen him approashing, but she didn't acknowledge it.

"She was throwing herself at not one but *two* men. And I saw her with one of them earlier today, too."

"I was a little surprised," said another woman, "when Maurice told us that the wedding was off. And it was because she cheated on him. And on the night before their wedding. That's so awful."

Quinn stopped dead. What the hell?

April had said the asshole had cheated on her, but was she lying?

That would explain why the guy was being so vindictive. If Quinn caught the woman he loved cheating on him, especially right before their wedding, his heart would be torn in two. He didn't agree with the guy's ruthless actions, but he could understand him lashing out at her.

"I know. But now . . . well, I always thought she was a gold digger, and now it's very clear she is. Jon recognized one of the men as Austin Wright. He's from big money. And it seems he just made a huge fortune with crypto-something-or-other, so now he's got to be the wealthiest man in the country. It seems clear that she's going after bigger fish."

At that moment, April's gaze shifted and locked onto Quinn's. He was standing only a few feet away from her. Her jaw tensed, and her cheeks blossomed crimson. She stood up, her arms stiff at her sides, and marched past him. He turned and followed her, not wanting to start a conversation here where those women could overhear. He was sure April had the same idea.

She pulled open the glass door and strode back into the casino, then turned right and continued marching toward the exit. Quinn followed. Austin stood up from the table, watching what was going on, then headed toward them.

April had stepped into the atrium before Quinn could catch up to her.

"April, wait."

She ignored him and kept walking.

"Where are you going? You don't have a key card for the suite."

A few people glanced around at them, but he ignored them as he kept moving. April slowed, and he finally caught up to her. He moved to face her.

"I don't want to talk about this here," she murmured, her voice swelling with emotion.

"What's going on?" Austin said as he hurried to them.

April stared at him, her chest rising and falling with her agitated breathing.

"April overheard that woman talking about her. It *was* the same woman, wasn't it, April?"

She nodded in one curt movement of her head.

"Nothing good, I take it?" Austin said.

April's hands were balled into fists, and Quinn knew she wasn't upset just because of what the two women had said. She was also upset because she'd seen Quinn's face and the doubt that had lingered there.

"Please. I just want to go up to the suite," April said through gritted teeth.

Quinn glanced at his watch. "The poker game starts in a few minutes, so we don't have time. We'll just put this on hold for now."

Her blue eyes were like acid, but she didn't argue. He'd already made it very clear that he expected her to attend the game. He knew it would ruin it for Austin if she went and hid out in the room. As much as Austin had looked forward to the game, he'd give it up rather than leave her alone and depressed. That's the kind of guy he was.

Austin had glanced from one to the other of them. Quinn knew his perceptive friend could tell how upset she was and that he understood that something new had been unleashed into the mix. The anger rippling through April was obvious, but Austin would see past that to the deeper pain within.

Quinn wished he had his friend's keen instincts about people, because he couldn't tell if April was angry because the woman had exposed the truth about their breakup, or if it was a lie and she was upset and hurt because she had seen in Quinn's eyes that he might believe it.

And, fuck, right now he had no idea what he actually believed about April.

Austin rested his hand on April's shoulder. "Sweetheart, if you want to go back to the penthouse, that's fine. If you want to talk, or if you'd rather be alone, that's all fine." He squeezed lightly. "But you've had such a rough day, why not kick loose and put it all behind you? At least for tonight. I say, let's forget about that stuffy poker game and do something wild and fun? Totally take your mind off your troubles."

April frowned. "But I thought you really wanted to play poker."

Austin grinned. "Okay, I tell you what. How about we start with a private poker game? Just the three of us."

Quinn gazed at April, whose cheeks were flushing. He could think of a lot of interesting possibilities.

"I think that's a marvelous idea," Quinn agreed.

8

April found it hard to breathe as Quinn called the concierge and arranged a private poker suite for the three of them.

The insinuation of a poker game—a *private* one—made her imagine stripping off her clothes in front of these two men as she lost each hand. Then once her clothes were gone, the two of them demanding special favors at each loss.

But it was Austin who'd suggested the game, not Quinn. She couldn't believe that's what Austin had in mind.

She ran her hand through her hair, knowing she wasn't quite thinking straight. She'd downed that last drink a little fast, and on top of the wine at dinner, her head was a little fuzzy.

Quinn shoved his phone back in his pocket.

"It's all set. They didn't have anything available here in the hotel, but they arranged something at a place a few doors down."

She drew in a deep breath as she followed the two men. It was only a short walk to the other hotel, and soon they were in an elevator gliding upward. When the doors whooshed open, they stepped out to see a man in a tuxedo waiting for them.

"Mr. Taylor. My name is Alan Bellamy. I'm here to take you to your private poker suite."

As they followed him down the wide hallway, several staff hurried out of a room, a couple pushing empty carts. That was the door Mr. Bellamy led them to.

"We have everything set up for you," he said as he opened the door. "There's a full bar and a selection of food if you're hungry. If you'd like something more substantial, just dial zero and you'll be put straight through to me."

April stepped into the room and glanced around. The walls of the suite were paneled with dark-stained wood, and it wasn't just a room with a table for playing cards. It was a huge suite with a large sitting area on one side, facing the floor-to-ceiling windows overlooking the street below.

Along one wall was a bar glittering with different types of glasses neatly arranged on a tray on the mahogany counter. Behind that, liquor and wine bottles were on display on a shelf, and several fancy bottles sat on the counter beside the glasses.

On a table near the window was a layout of food—appetizers, small fancy sandwiches, and desserts. The poker table was on the other side of the room, set up with several decks of cards and three stacks of chips all ready for them to sit down and start playing.

"Would you like staff to manage the bar and food service?" Mr. Bellamy asked. "Or a dealer to oversee the game? Or anything else at all?"

"No, we're fine," Quinn said.

"Very good, sir. Enjoy your game." Mr. Bellamy walked to the door, then closed it behind him.

As soon as the door clicked shut, April's stomach clenched. She was alone with the two of them, and she wasn't quite sure what Quinn had in mind. Would he tell Austin about their arrangement right here and now?

She and Austin walked to the food, and she admired the decadent-looking desserts—tall chocolate mousse cake, thick New York cheesecake, blueberry tarts, and many other tempting treats. The small sandwiches, cut into crustless triangles, were arranged beautifully on a plate right beside a cheese and pâté platter. She picked up one and nibbled. Smoked salmon with dill. She finished the tiny sandwich in two bites, then grabbed another.

She walked to the bar, where Quinn opened a circular-shaped bottle with a gold cap and poured the amber liquid into a glass.

"Would you like something?" he asked.

"I think so. I'll just take a look."

"Pour me what you're having, will you, Quinn?" Austin asked as he headed over to join them.

April found herself drawn to the fancy bottles. One was shaped like a faceted crystal, another with a seductive curve and tall teardrop-shaped stopper. The one that grabbed her attention was a tall, slender, tapered bottle with a liquid inside that was a lovely rosy red. She removed the crystal cap and poured some into a stemmed liqueur glass.

Quinn raised an eyebrow. "You're being adventurous."

She took a sip. It had a citrus flavor. "Why do you say that?"

"It's quite strong."

She shrugged. "I could use something strong."

Austin chuckled. "Couldn't we all?"

"Cheers," Quinn said as he raised his glass.

April and Austin both clinked against it, then sipped. She finished hers, then poured another.

"Let's play poker," she said and walked toward the game table.

Austin and Quinn joined her, and soon Austin was dealing out the cards. All her anxiety about what would happen during the game seemed unfounded. They simply bet chips and played their hands, though the men carried on a good-natured banter.

April wasn't giving them much of a challenge. She hadn't played poker much and kept losing. Austin could read her face too well for her to bluff. She played with gusto, though, betting them up in hopes that her two kings or three tens would win, only to find Austin had a full house, or Quinn four of a kind. Her stack of chips had dwindled to about a quarter.

"I'm going to run out of chips soon," she said as she tossed in her ante. "I don't want to leave you without a third player, so should we ask for some more?"

"Sure. No problem," Quinn said. He walked to the house phone and dialed. "Alan, would you send up some more chips? Yes, a hundred should be fine."

"He's sending a hundred chips?" April asked Austin.

"No, that's the dollar value of the chips."

A thought spiked through her alcohol-muddled mind.

"Dollar amount? Are you paying for the chips?" A hundred dollars seemed excessive for a stack of chips. Even these lovely, high-quality ones.

"Not exactly," Quinn said as he returned to the table and sat down. "The casino takes a percentage of all gambling that officially takes place in the hotel. Since this is a private game, and the players settle up between each other, the casino takes a percentage of the chips delivered to the private game rooms."

Her stomach twisted. "So I'm guessing the hundred you referred to isn't a hundred dollars."

Austin smiled and shook his head. "No. We each started with a stack that represented a hundred grand."

"And so we've been betting real money." Her stomach coiled so tightly she thought she'd throw up.

"Don't worry about it," Quinn said. "We never expected you to pay your losses. That's why we didn't mention it."

She leaned back in her chair, chewing her lower lip. She stared at the chips she had left. A quick calculation told her she'd lost the equivalent of about $70,000.

Oh, God.

"April, it's not a problem," Austin said. "We wanted you to be part of the game, and we understand your circumstances. It's not like either Quinn or I are worried about money."

She frowned and turned her gaze to him. "Let me ask you this. If I had come away from the game with more chips than I'd started with, would you have given me the winnings?"

"Of course," Austin said.

"Then I was playing with real money."

A knock sounded at the door. Austin got up to answer it.

"Oh, God, that'll be the new chips. That's going to cost you even more money. Austin, just tell them we don't need them."

But Austin was already signing the paper the man handed him. He returned with a new stack that he placed in front of her.

"Look, we're not going to force you to be in further debt because of a casual poker game," Quinn said firmly. "So just relax and enjoy the game."

"I can't." Her hands were trembling now. Her head was foggy, and she had trouble thinking. All she knew was that she wasn't comfortable with them just forgiving her debt.

"I have to find a way to pay back my losses, but . . ." She shook her head, feeling panicky. "I don't know how."

"Sweetheart," Quinn said softly, "take a deep breath."

She drew in a lungful of air, then released it slowly.

"Now, just think about it. We didn't tell you that we were playing for real money. That means you shouldn't be held accountable for the debt you racked up. If you were, we would feel that we'd taken advantage of you. And all this for an amount of money that means nothing to us. So please . . ."

He slid his hand across the table to hers and squeezed it. She glanced at him, and his eyes glowed with compassion.

"Let it go. We'll forget the debt and move forward."

The panic faded. What he said made sense.

She nodded. "Okay. But I can't play anymore."

"That's unfortunate. I don't think any of us wants the game to end yet." Quinn leaned back. "Let's think about this a different way. We all have different resources. Austin and I have a lot of money, so we're happy to risk that. What are you willing to risk?"

"What do you mean?" She'd already made a deal to give him what he wanted. Sex. And Austin, too, even though he didn't know it yet.

"Keep in mind that the money isn't a big risk for us. I'm not asking more from you. All I had in mind is something like you granting the winner a request when you lose." He smiled. "And if you think about it, that might even help with the previous arrangement we discussed."

"What arrangement?" Austin asked.

April's gaze darted to Austin, then back to Quinn. He was going to tell him now. Butterflies fluttered through her stomach.

"April and I have a special agreement, but I'll tell you about that a little later. What do you think, April?"

She nodded. She didn't want to end the game for Austin, and if this is what Quinn wanted, then she wouldn't say no.

"Does this work for you, Austin?" Quinn asked.

"I'm happy with keeping April in the game. But what do you mean by requests?" Austin asked.

Quinn shrugged. "Anything you want. You might dare her to down a shot, or ask her a question like you did over dinner. It's pretty open-ended."

Austin chuckled. "I was worried you meant something like strip poker. With her luck, the girl would be freezing in no time."

April bit her lower lip as her cheeks heated. She wasn't sure where Quinn was going to take this, but clearly Austin had no idea that's exactly what might happen.

Austin was a little uncomfortable with the idea of April paying off her losses by granting requests, since he had no idea what Quinn had in mind. But Quinn was protective of April, so he wouldn't have her do anything sexual in front of Austin.

Quinn dealt out the next hand of cards. After a few rounds of betting, Austin won with three fives.

Quinn leaned back in his chair with a smile as Austin raked in his chips.

"So, what's it going to be?" Quinn asked.

Austin glanced at April speculatively. She stared at the table, probably nervous about what he'd ask her to do. He thought back to truth-or-dare questions from college, grasping for something.

"Tell us about your first kiss," he said finally. "Set the scene for us. Tell us things like where it happened. What it was like. How you felt about it."

April's gaze flickered to Quinn, then to Austin. She leaned back in her chair, and her hands curled around the armrests.

"He was walking me home after a party. There was a full moon, and we were holding hands. We took a shortcut through the park, and halfway through, he stopped and pulled me to him. He slid his arms around me and drew me close."

Her gaze had drifted, and she now stared into space. It was as though she were reliving that moment. Her voice grew soft.

"He didn't rush it. He kissed me gently at first, moving slowly on my lips, his fingers gliding through my hair. Then it turned more passionate."

Her eyes had grown wistful, and she drew in a slow, almost quivering breath. Then she shook her head as if dragging herself from the memory.

"This was in college?" Quinn asked, his eyes narrowed.

She nodded.

So Quinn was the first man to kiss her?

Austin's gaze turned to his friend's face and could see that clearly he hadn't realized it. And the thought disturbed Quinn.

"It sounds like you'd rate that kiss pretty high," Austin said.

"Of all the kisses I've had in my life, that is the most special."

Silence hung over the room. Finally, Quinn sat forward.

"Let's get on to the next hand."

Damn, Quinn hadn't known that he'd been April's first kiss. She'd been in college, for God's sake. Who knew she'd never kissed a man before that?

He sat back in his chair and watched as Austin dealt the cards.

But thinking about it now, with all he'd learned about her background, it made some sense. She'd been abandoned by her own mother. She'd never had anyone in her life to take care of her. To love her. It made sense that she might have kept men at a distance, her lack of trust in others making her believe, even if only at a subconscious level, that she would probably get hurt.

Why the hell had she let him kiss her, then? Especially only hours after meeting him?

"Quinn, your ante," Austin said, dragging Quinn's attention back to the table.

Both of them had thrown in their chips. Quinn grabbed one from his stack and tossed it in with the others, then picked up his hand. He had two fours with a king high. He tossed the other two cards and got back another four and a king. Exhilaration rushed through him, but he kept a tight rein on his expression.

After a quick round of bets, Quinn laid down his full house with a smile.

He didn't want to push Austin into this too fast. Austin had challenged April with a truth or dare that any college student might have tried. Quinn could work with that.

"Describe the bra you're wearing, April." He gave her a slow smile. "And I want details."

He'd already seen it, and they both knew that, so it would be clear to her that he was doing this for Austin's benefit.

"Um . . . it's a coral color and has thin black ribbon woven into the edges."

When she didn't continue, Quinn prompted her. "Is that

all? Is it underwire so it lifts your breasts nice and high? Is it a three-quarter cup? Or maybe a half cup so it reveals most of your breasts?"

Quinn saw Austin lean forward in his chair. His friend was obviously envisioning April's round, firm breasts in a half bra, her hard nipples exposed and peaking forward.

"No," she said quickly. "It's not . . . uh . . . it's three-quarter."

"So if you showed it to us now, we'd see a nice swell of your breasts."

"Uh . . . yes."

"What else?"

"Um . . . it's made of lace. And I think there's a little bow on the front."

"Show us."

April's gaze darted to his.

Austin jumped in with, "Isn't that going a little too far? That sounds like strip poker to me."

"Not at all." Quinn smiled. "She doesn't have to take off her dress to show it to us."

She could take off the bra and slide it out from underneath her dress. It always amazed him when women did that.

"It's all right, Austin," April said.

She then surprised Quinn when she slid her fingers into the deep V of her dress and tugged a bit of the bra forward, exposing the coral lace and a small bow in black satin ribbon. The sight of that small amount of lacy undergarment, which was supposed to be hidden, along with her breasts swelling from the widened neckline, made his cock tighten.

From the hunger in Austin's eyes, it was having the same effect on him.

April dealt the next hand. Quinn had three aces, but decided to toss two of them. He wanted Austin to win next to see what he would do.

Austin won the hand and gazed at Quinn speculatively. Then he gestured for April to lean in close and whispered in her ear. She nodded, then stood up and approached Quinn. When she was beside him, she rested her hand on his shoulder and leaned in slowly.

Had Austin told her to kiss him? He waited in anticipation as her lips moved closer, but they stopped by his ear.

She whispered, "Austin wants you to tell me the color of your underwear."

The softness of her breath against his ear made him long for her lips to nuzzle against him. Fuck, he wanted to get on to having sex with her. To watching Austin have sex with her.

But he knew he had to ease Austin into this. He wasn't sure quite how to tell him about the arrangement, so ramping things up seemed the best approach.

Quinn laughed and nodded. "All right. Sit on my lap and I'll tell you."

He rolled his chair back, and she sat on his thighs. He curled his arm around her waist, his body reacting to the feel of her warm body so close.

He turned her sideways on his lap and leaned in, nuzzling her temple.

"My underwear are charcoal black," he whispered, "and are snug boxers. So snug that when my cock swells like it is right now, since I find it so sexy when you're on my lap, that it stretches the thin cotton."

He brushed his lips against her ear, noting her quickening breath.

"Now," he whispered, "go back to Austin and sit on his lap just like this, and tell him exactly what I just told you."

As she stood up, Quinn knew that on his next win, he was going to push Austin to the limit.

9

April stood up, her knees a little shaky, and walked toward Austin. He gazed at her with curiosity, probably wondering why she wasn't just relaying the information out loud.

When she reached his chair, she stopped. How was she going to get on his lap with his chair facing the table?

"Help the girl out and push back your chair, Austin," Quinn said.

Austin rolled back from the table, and April timidly sat down on his lap and curled her hands around his neck.

Austin's arm circled her waist, just as Quinn's had done. Being so close to him sent a quivering awareness through her.

"Quinn wants me to whisper it to you." She leaned close to his ear and lowered her voice. "He says that his underwear is charcoal black and they're . . . um . . . tight. So tight that when his cock hardens like it did when I was sitting on his lap, that it . . . uh . . . stretches the fabric."

April could feel Austin's cock swell against her thigh.

"Okay," he said a bit stiffly. "More information than what I asked for, but Quinn is always very thorough."

Quinn laughed. "I could show them to you if you like."

Austin raised a hand. "No. I'm good."

Austin's cock was still hard and pressed tightly against her. Her insides ached at the thought of touching it. Of gliding her fingers along its length, then squeezing gently.

She stood up and walked back to her chair.

Austin drew in a deep breath. After Quinn had made this crazy suggestion to have April perform requests for them, Austin had decided to use this opportunity to tear down Quinn's barriers so that he'd realize how much he wanted April and act on those feelings. Unfortunately, Quinn had decided to tease Austin by having her do things to excite him.

And it was fucking working.

Why was Quinn playing with him like this?

Austin tried to will his aching cock to calm down. Fuck, if this kept up, he would fall prey to the potent desire building up inside him and turn this game around to get what his body wanted.

But he couldn't do that. It wouldn't be right, and it would screw up his friendship—and his partnership—with Quinn.

It was Quinn's turn to deal, so he picked up the deck and distributed five cards to each of them, then tossed in his ante. Austin and April followed suit.

After distributing additional cards and a quick round of bets, Quinn laid down four kings. He ignored the pile of chips he'd just won and turned his gaze to April, his eyes gleaming like a predator's.

"April, come over here," he said.

April stood up and walked toward him. Austin watched as Quinn gestured for her to lean closer and whispered in her ear.

April nodded.

"Austin, I'd like you to stand up for this," Quinn said.

"Okay." Austin stood up, wondering what Quinn was up to.

April drew her shoulders back, and her gaze shifted to Austin's. A transformation came over her as her stance seemed to soften and her eyes grew sultry. She glided her hands down her body slowly. His heart pounded as her fingertips brushed the sides of her breasts. She continued following the gentle curve of her waist and down until her hands disappeared in the fullness of her skirt. Then she walked toward him.

Actually, it was more like she floated in a billowy cloud of soft fabric swaying around her hips and glistening blond hair cascading over her shoulders. Her movement was fluid and graceful, but oozing with sexual allure.

As she got close, her hands glided up her sides again. He held his breath, watching her fingers. Would they glide over her full breasts? Would she lift them? Squeeze the two mounds together, showing him more of a swell in her deep neckline?

Would she tweak the nipples so they visibly pushed against the fabric?

He sucked in a deep breath. Fuck, his imagination was running wild.

She stopped in front of him. Her sapphire eyes turned up to his.

She rested her hands on his shoulders and tipped up her face. They were close, but the difference in their heights, even with her high spike heels, left a good six inches between their lips. The scent of her apple blossom shampoo wafted through him. His body, already tight with need, ached to taste her.

She ran her hands down his lapels, then her fingertips glided over his shirt, caressing his chest. The warmth of her . . . the delicate feel of her touching him . . . set him ablaze. Then she wrapped one hand around the knot of his necktie and drew him toward her. Slowly.

His breath caught as their faces moved closer. His gaze locked on her lips, so full and pouty. He longed to feel them against his. Her tongue flicked out and glided over those full lips, making them glisten.

Oh, God, his cock swelled at the sight.

Then she stopped, their mouths a hairbreadth apart. He could feel the blood pulsing through him. A potent need settled deep in his gut. Time slowed as seconds—or was it minutes?—ticked by. All he knew was he was desperate to feel her mouth on his.

But instead of closing the distance, her tongue glided from her luscious lips and brushed his. He groaned at the delicate caress. His lips parted, and her tongue slid inside.

Oh, fuck! He pulled her against him, one arm around her waist, the other cupping the back of her head. Their lips were crushed together now, her tongue inside his mouth. She teased and flicked, driving him wild. He drove his tongue deep into her, needing to taste her.

Needing to possess her.

She whimpered, then melted into him. Her soft breasts pressed tightly against his chest, and the sharp contrast of her bead-hard nipples pushing into him drove him insane with need.

If Quinn weren't sitting in the same room watching them—a fact Austin had to cling to with all his might—he would cup one of those soft mounds and caress it until she sighed in delight and begged him for more.

Then he'd give her what they both craved. Relieving her of the sexy sundress hiding her tempting curves, he'd bury himself in her soft, inviting body. He'd drive into her again and again, watching her face fill with blissful abandon as he took her to ecstatic heights.

His hands glided up and down her back as their mouths moved together. Her breath was erratic, and he could feel her staccato heartbeat against this chest.

Fuck, she was definitely affected as much as he was.

His cock ached, and the urge to pull her tightly to his groin and arch against her was overwhelming.

He tore his mouth from hers and stared at her. Her eyelids blinked open, and she returned his gaze, clearly unsettled by what had just happened.

"You two seemed to enjoy that," Quinn said in a much calmer voice than Austin would have expected.

Austin pulled his gaze from April's sweet face and turned to Quinn, expecting to see jealousy in his eyes. But instead he saw his friend staring back with a half smile on his face.

"What's the hell's going on?" Austin demanded. "Were you testing me? Seeing if I'd resist the temptation of kissing your woman?"

The thought angered him, even as he realized if it had been a test, he'd failed miserably.

Quinn leaned back in his chair. "April, get us all another drink."

"Yes, sir," she murmured, then walked to the bar.

Quinn gestured for Austin to come closer, then he leaned in.

"April insists on paying me back," Quinn said in a lowered voice. "Knowing how much I've wanted her for such a long time, she made a suggestion I found very intriguing."

"Are you telling me she agreed to have sex with you for

money?" Austin said in the same hushed tone. He didn't like the sound of that. The poor woman was in need, and he didn't want her to prostitute herself out of desperation.

"Let's just say that she and I will finally consummate the relationship we started so long ago . . . something that should have happened anyway. And when she leaves, I'll ensure she has enough money to start again in a new town. It's a much cheaper proposition than if I wound up married to her . . . and more honest."

Austin scowled. "Fine. Whatever you want to do is between the two of you. But what the hell was the point of that kiss?"

"Well, you see, I haven't told you the best part. She's agreed to be with both of us. We're going to share her."

Austin stared at him blankly. "What?"

He glanced over his shoulder to see April pouring the last of the drinks. His gaze moved over her. Her angelic face, still flushed from their kiss. Her full breasts filling out the dress so seductively. The soft curve of her hips.

He remembered her breasts pressed tightly against him. Those soft, full lips of hers moving on his. His cock swelled. The thought of being with her—with Quinn's blessing—sent need rocketing through him.

"This is crazy. I can't . . ."

Quinn chuckled softly. "Are you sure?"

Fuck, no. That was the problem. He wanted this woman with an intensity he'd never felt before. But his head told him it was wrong. He'd be taking advantage of her.

"At least give it a chance. We'll ease into it slowly, so no one's uncomfortable," Quinn suggested.

The tinkling of ice in glasses signaled April's return. She set the three drinks on the table.

"Come over here, baby," Quinn said.

She walked to his chair and stood beside it.

"How did you feel when Austin was kissing you?" Quinn asked. "Were you getting turned on?"

Austin watched closely as she bit her lip. She had to know how turned on she'd made him. His cock had hardened and pushed against her belly. And he knew it had affected her, too.

"Yes," she murmured softly, gazing down at her hands.

"Good," Quinn responded. "I told Austin about our deal, and he's on board."

She glanced at Austin, her cheeks blazing with color, and Austin couldn't help but wonder why she'd agreed to the threesome part of the deal. Of course, Quinn could be very persuasive when he wanted something and may have given her little choice.

But still . . . she'd admitted that the kiss between them had turned her on. His cock twitched.

Fuck, he was so turned on now he could barely think straight.

"Shall we continue the game?" Quinn asked, and Austin hesitated, wondering if grabbing April's hand and dragging her back to the suite was an option.

He drew in a deep breath. But Quinn was in charge of this deal, so Austin would settle back and finish the game.

April walked to her chair and sat down again. Austin dealt out the cards, and April won. Then she won the next hand, too. He couldn't help but smile when her eyes lit up and she pulled the chips toward her. She was obviously inexperienced at poker and feeling out of her depth playing with him and Quinn.

Quinn dealt this time. Austin had three queens, but Quinn beat him with a flush.

Austin was filled with a mix of apprehension and excitement. What was Quinn going to have April do?

Quinn's gaze locked on Austin's, then a slow smile spread across his face. He pulled out a pen and one of the small black notebooks he always carried from his jacket pocket and jotted something down. He tore out the page and slid it across the table to April.

April read it, then her gaze flickered to Austin's and back to the paper. She nodded, then stood up and disappeared through a door inside the suite. Austin raised an eyebrow at Quinn.

"Don't worry. She won't be long," Quinn said, his lips still turned up in a grin.

April returned to the room and walked straight to Austin.

"Hold out your hand, please," she requested demurely.

He held it out as if ready to take her hand, not sure what she had in mind.

"Palm upward," she clarified.

He complied, and she placed her closed fist on his hand. The brush of her soft skin sent awareness prickling along his arm. She pressed something against his palm, then with her other hand urged his fingers to close around it.

Whatever she'd given him was soft and warm. She stepped back and walked toward her chair. He opened his hand and looked down at her gift.

He saw a small bunched-up ball of coral lace and thin black ribbon.

Fuck, it was her panties. Still warm from her body.

That meant she wasn't wearing anything under that flowing skirt.

His cock surged to life again. He couldn't help watching her as she rounded the table to sit down again. Watching the sway of her hips, imagining her naked ass under the fabric. When she sat down, he couldn't stop thinking of her naked pussy with only the thin cotton of her dress between her and the chair.

He sipped his drink, then picked up the cards and dealt them.

As they continued playing, every time she moved, shifting or leaning forward to toss in a chip, his groin tightened at the thought of her naked pussy moving on the chair.

10

Quinn could tell this was having the intended effect on Austin. This would push things up a notch. Austin's gaze had been glued to April's ass as she walked back to her chair. Probably imagining her sweet pussy.

Quinn's gaze shifted to her, and his cock tightened at the thought of her naked pussy under that flowing sundress.

April won again, probably because both he and Austin were more than a little distracted. It was her turn to deal, but as she reached for the deck, Quinn decided to push things a little more.

"April, I think I'd like something to eat. Would you bring us a plate of sandwiches?"

"Yes, of course." She put down the cards and stood up, then walked to the table with the food.

Quinn was aware of Austin watching her, but that didn't steal his own focus, especially as he imagined her thighs brushing together as she walked. Her pussy cozy between the warmth of those thighs. Maybe it was even getting wet.

She picked up a dinner plate and placed a collection of the tiny sandwiches on it. She added some crackers and cheese, then turned and walked back to the table. Quinn's cock was growing as he stared at her skirt, wishing he could see through the flowing cotton fabric to her intimate flesh below.

He shifted in his chair, adjusting his straining cock.

As she stood beside him to place the plate on the center of the table, he wanted to pull her onto his lap and glide his hand up her thigh, then under her skirt. To seek out that warm, velvety place he'd yearned to touch for so long.

She started to walk away.

"Baby, come here."

When she came to him, he pulled her onto his lap and his arms slid around her.

The feel of her warm body in his arms was driving him crazy with need. She shifted on his lap, and his cock lurched. Fuck, there was almost nothing between her naked pussy and his cock.

"Why don't you feed me one of those sandwiches?"

"Yes, sir."

She picked one up and brought it to his lips. He opened, and she delicately pressed it into his mouth, her fingers brushing his lips. He had to stop himself from nibbling her fingers as he closed his mouth around it. He watched her with a smile as he chewed and swallowed it. Smoked salmon. He was sure she'd chosen that one because she knew he liked it.

Because she wanted to make him happy.

Hunger blazed through him, but not for another sandwich.

Fuck, he had to get himself under control.

Once back in her chair, April picked up the deck and dealt. During the betting, Austin tossed in chips with confidence. Quinn was sure that Austin was not only confident he'd win but was looking forward to it. Good. Maybe he'd make an interesting move with April.

The thought that his friend might order April to do something sexual, that Austin might touch her intimately or have her pleasure him in some way, had Quinn's heart pounding. He could imagine Austin holding her close, his hand freely exploring her breast, then gliding down her hip and tugging up her skirt. A pang of jealousy seared through him at the same time as a blaze of excitement made his cock throb.

Austin raked in his winnings with a huge smile on his face, and Quinn realized he'd zoned out. He picked up his drink and took a sip while his gaze turned to Quinn.

"April," Austin said, "I want you to kiss Quinn. But not just a kiss. I want you to reenact that first kiss you told us about."

Quinn's stomach clenched. Damn, Austin. He must have figured out that Quinn was the one she'd been talking about.

Fuck, he didn't want to be reminded of what it was like to kiss her back then. When their budding relationship was full of such promise.

When he'd already known he was well on his way to falling in love.

April stood up and moved a few feet from the table. She didn't look at him as he stood and approached her. He took April's hand, trying to ignore the tingles of awareness dancing through him at the feel of her soft fingers curled in his.

"You said you were walking through the park with this man?" Quinn asked.

"Yes," she murmured.

He drew her farther across the room to give them space to set the stage, then he started to walk, her falling into stride beside him.

He remembered the sound of the amber leaves crunching underfoot as they'd walked along the paved path. The smoky smell of wood burning in fireplaces wafting from chimneys on the houses surrounding the park. A nostalgia settled deep in his belly, along with a craving he remembered all too well.

After a few steps, he stopped, and she turned and gazed up at him. He drew her close, just like he had on that crisp fall evening. When he looked into her eyes, he was overwhelmed by the same feelings he'd had that night.

He'd met this sweet, wonderful woman at a party and been enchanted by her. She was in several of his classes, and he'd already developed a crush on her, but it had no foundation other than her alluring yet understated beauty. He'd made a point of meeting her at the party and found her to be a little shy, but intelligent and sweet-natured.

The last thought before his lips brushed hers was that this was dangerous territory, and he resolved to stay immune to her. But when their lips met, all constraint flickered away. She was so soft and warm in his arms. His heart pounded in his chest as adrenaline rushed through him, making him feel almost giddy.

Her arms came around his neck, and her lips pressed tighter to his. He slid his hand down her back and drew her closer. She sighed against his mouth as he deepened the kiss.

He breathed her in. She smelled like apple blossoms and vanilla. He stroked her face and threaded his fingers through her silken hair. His tongue nudged her lips, and she opened for him, allowing him to sweep his tongue inside her mouth.

He plunged deep, stroking his tongue over hers. She whimpered softly, melting against him.

Oh, God, he was going to lose himself in her. This was too sweet. This is what he wanted so badly.

Slowly, he drew back, forcing himself to pull away. His groin was tight and his cock hard, but worse, his heart ached in need.

Damn, he was still in fucking love with this woman.

He didn't want to be. He knew how incredibly foolhardy it was. But he had no control over his heart.

He did, however, have control over his head.

He walked back to his chair and tossed back his drink, then grabbed his jacket.

"I have to check on something," he said, then strode from the room.

Austin stared at the door. Well, that hadn't worked out quite the way he'd hoped.

April still stood in a daze, staring after Quinn. Austin stood up and walked to her side.

"Do you think we should go after him?" she asked.

"No, he'll work it out. How about you? Are you doing okay?"

She glanced his way. "Yes, of course."

He smiled, not believing her. That kiss had rocked both of them.

"Good." He nudged his head toward the sitting area. "Why don't we sit down and relax until he comes back?"

"Sure." She walked to the couch while he poured them both another drink, then settled down beside her.

He swirled his drink, watching her. "It was Quinn, wasn't it? The first man who kissed you?" he asked.

"Yes."

"So tell me about your relationship with Quinn back then."

She turned her gaze to him, her lips pursed. "You ask a lot of questions, Austin."

Austin grinned. "Yeah, I know. It's my most endearing quality."

She laughed, but even though he'd been joking, he knew

that to her it probably was. She wasn't used to people taking an interest in her.

"But I hope you'll answer," he continued. "Quinn's my best friend, and I want to understand."

She sighed and kicked off her shoes, then curled her legs beside her on the couch. Unfortunately, the move reminded him of her lack of panties.

The arousal that had been raging through him ever since Quinn had told him about this special arrangement had finally settled to a slow simmer, but now it flared back to life again. His cock strained uncomfortably in his pants.

He urged his body to relax.

"What do you want to know?" she asked.

He wanted to know what it would feel like to stroke his hand along her soft thigh . . . then up under her skirt . . .

Calm down, man.

"What was it like when you were with him?"

"It was . . . wonderful. Quinn really saw me. Really listened to me. I was important to him, and that made me feel important."

He took her hand and squeezed it. "You are important, April."

Her lips pursed, and she nodded. "That's very nice of you to say. It's what we always say."

Her gaze turned to his, and the depth of pain in her shimmering blue eyes tore at his heart.

"But when you don't feel it inside yourself, it doesn't matter how much someone tells you it's true. When everyone in your life who is supposed to care has abandoned you without a thought, it's hard to believe otherwise."

She leaned forward and picked up her drink, then took a sip.

"But with Quinn, I could feel it."

She stared silently at the contents of her glass. At her long hesitation, Austin leaned forward, watching her teeth tug on her lower lip.

"What are you not saying, April?"

She sucked in a deep breath. "Just that it also made me afraid. If I let myself believe I was special to him, that he really cared, and then he left . . ." She frowned. "I didn't know how I would deal with that." Her words were hushed, as if she didn't want to say them out loud.

He wanted to pull her into his arms and tell her he cared about her. That he would never leave her if she wanted to be by his side.

Fuck, what the hell was he thinking?

"So you pulled away?" he asked.

"No. I loved being with him. I loved how it made me feel. Especially at the beginning when he was very attentive. Spending every day with me. Calling or texting when we were apart. But then life kicked in again, and he turned his attention back to his work. I mean, it makes sense. We'd both fallen behind on our academic deadlines with being so focused on this wonderful new relationship. I totally understood Quinn jumping back into his work. His dedication to what he's passionate about was one of the things I loved about him. But once I'd experienced what it was like to have someone put me first, not seeing him for a week or more at a time made me miserable."

"You didn't tell him?"

"No. When we were together, everything was great." She gazed wistfully into space. "Better than great."

She set her drink down and leaned back with a sigh.

"I finally realized that it was just the way he is. It wasn't his fault that I had issues. And I wasn't going to put that on him. It was my flaw."

"So you broke up with him."

She gazed at Austin, her eyes pleading for understanding.

"I had to. Losing my heart to him would have been a disaster."

Austin saw the pain in her eyes and squeezed her hand. Maybe it was a disaster she hadn't actually avoided.

"But, April, if you had told him—"

"No," she interrupted. "Telling him about the problem would have been the same as asking him to choose me over his work, and I would never do that."

He settled back on the couch and swirled his drink.

"So I'm curious. Why did you agree to this arrangement with Quinn?" he asked.

"It's really important to me to pay back my debt to him," she said, "and this is the only way I have to do that. This arrangement allows me to give him something he wants. I still intend to find a way to give him the money, but as he keeps reminding me, I'm not in a position to do that right now."

Austin nodded. It's too bad that Quinn's emotional turmoil didn't allow him to see the April that Austin saw. A woman who wanted to live up to her responsibilities. Who cared about others. And who just wanted to be loved.

"And why did you agree to me being part of it?"

A soft blush blossomed across her cheeks, and she stared at her fingers.

"When he suggested it, it caught me off guard, but it's what Quinn wants."

"I see." He didn't like the idea that she felt like she had no choice.

She glanced his way, and her eyes widened at his frown.

"I didn't mean that to sound like it did. I'm not doing it because Quinn's forcing me. I wouldn't have agreed if I didn't feel an attraction to you."

He smiled. "Good to know."

The moment hung between them, their gazes still locked. Then an awareness prickled through him. They were alone together. They shared a very strong mutual attraction to each other.

And she wore no panties.

His groin tightened, and he wanted to lean in and capture her full, pink lips. To slide his tongue inside her warmth, then draw her close to his body.

She seemed mesmerized as he leaned in closer. He wanted her, and the agreement between her and Quinn gave him permission to have sex with her. Quinn might have decided to go walk off his emotions, but did that mean Austin had to hold back?

The door opened, and Quinn strode into the room.

Austin eased back and in his head let loose a string of expletives. He'd almost made a reckless move that could have ruined his friendship with Quinn. Because, of course, it wasn't all right for Austin to put moves on Quinn's woman. Not unless Quinn was a part of it.

11

When Quinn had strode out of the room, he'd had no idea where he was going. He'd just needed space. After walking for a while, he'd found himself in a courtyard staring at the moon.

He'd had feelings for April once, but that was done. Now she was just a woman from his past that he'd helped out this morning. She wanted to pay him back and made an interesting proposition that meant he could finally act on their mutual attraction. They would both enjoy it, so it was good for her, and it was definitely good for him.

It was a win-win situation. Actually, win-win-win since Austin would be a part of it.

This arrangement between them was just about sex. Any feelings he had for her were squarely in the past.

So what the hell was he doing out here? He should be back in that room doing what he'd longed to do for years.

He walked into the lounge and approached the bar.

"Good evening, Mr. Taylor," the bartender said.

"Good evening. Give me a bottle of the best champagne you have. On ice with three glasses."

"Would you like it sent to your gaming suite?"

"No, I'll take it up myself."

"Very good, sir."

The bartender signaled another staff member, then disappeared in the back. Five minutes later, he appeared with a bottle in a silver ice bucket and three finely cut crystal glasses.

Quinn signed the bill, giving the bartender a 20 percent tip, which was in the three digits. Quinn didn't care how much it cost. Tonight was going to be a very special night.

He tucked the bucket against his body and curled his fingers around the delicate stems of the glasses. Moments later, he was at the suite door. He pushed it open and strode inside.

Austin and April were sitting on the couch and . . .

"What the hell's going on?"

The two of them had been sitting close together, leaning in as if they were about to kiss. Then Austin had pulled away when he saw Quinn.

"We were just talking," Austin said.

Quinn knew damn well they weren't just talking, and jealousy trickled through him that April was so comfortable with Austin. But he pushed it aside. It was actually a good thing. That meant that she was fully on board with what they were about to do.

"Actually, I think you were about to kiss."

April stood up. "Quinn, you're not really going to be mad at Austin, given the situation, are you?"

He laughed. "Not at all. I just didn't want you starting without me."

He walked toward them, the cold bottle of champagne tucked under his arm. He set it on the low table and popped the cork. As he poured, the liquid tumbled into the glasses, frothing with bubbles. He handed a glass to each of them, then sat down in one of the armchairs and leaned back.

He lifted his glass. "To a night none of us will ever forget."

April watched Quinn tip back his glass as she took a sip of hers. Her stomach quivered, and she barely tasted it, both nervous and excited at the prospect of what was about to happen.

Quinn turned his gaze to her, then patted his thigh.

"Come here, April, and sit on my lap," Quinn instructed.

Her stomach fluttered as she walked to him. As she got closer, his gaze darkened. Gone was the tenderness she'd seen in his eyes when he'd kissed her like he had that first time. It was replaced with a lustful hunger.

She sat on his lap. His thighs were hard and muscular beneath her. He turned her to face him and pulled her tightly to his chest.

"No more reminiscing and sentiment. This is about straight-up sex." Quinn stared straight at her, a predatory hunger shining in the depths of his midnight-blue eyes.

His mouth swooped down on hers, and his hand slid down her back, pulling her closer still. Her heart thundered, and heat blossomed inside her. He caressed her ass and then squeezed. Her skirt pulled up a bit, reminding her that she was naked under the fabric.

His lips were firm and demanding, taking her breath away. Then they turned coaxing, and she found herself melting against him, conscious of her breasts crushed against his chest, her nipples spiking forward. As he continued to stroke her ass, his fingers sometimes brushed over her intimate flesh through the thin cotton. Her inner muscles contracted, and she could feel dampness forming.

Finally, he drew his mouth away and smiled at her.

"Now turn around and face Austin."

She turned on Quinn's lap. Austin was on the couch watching them, his teal eyes dark and glittering with desire.

"Show Austin how you'd like him to touch you," Quinn murmured in her ear, his breath sending tingles along her neck.

She pressed her hands to her breasts and stroked, aware of Austin following her movements. Thinking about his fingers moving over her. Electric heat surged through her as her nipples blossomed to hard buds.

"Mmm, I love watching you touch yourself like that," Quinn murmured softly. "Are your nipples growing hard?"

"Yes, sir." Her words came out a hoarse whisper.

His fingers curled around her waist, and he stroked up and down. Then one hand glided over her stomach and pulled her tighter to him. The feel of Quinn's cock, hard and thick, pressing against her back, almost made her gasp. Her heart pounded as heat washed through her.

Austin sat mesmerized, his gaze locked on the two of them. She could see a bulge forming in his pants. She longed to go and touch it. To wrap her fingers around it through the fabric. To hear his breathing accelerate as she stroked him.

She reached around behind her and found Quinn's cock, then squeezed it. The feel of his thick column in her hand made her quiver with need. But he drew her hand away and placed it back on her breast.

"Baby, if you want to feel a cock in your hand, I want it

to be Austin's first. Austin, do you want her to stroke your cock?"

From his flushed cheeks and the yearning in his eyes, clearly he did. But he hesitated.

"Come on, buddy," Quinn urged. "April's really okay with it. Right, baby?"

"Yes, sir," she murmured.

"I might believe you more," Austin said, "if she didn't sound like she was following orders."

Quinn chuckled. "But she is following orders. Part of the arrangement is that she follows my commands. And she calls me *sir*. But that doesn't mean she's doing anything she doesn't want to do. Right, baby?"

Staring straight into Austin's eyes, she nodded. "That's right, sir."

Quinn grabbed a handful of her skirt and drew it upward. Austin's gaze locked on her rising hem. April shifted a little on Quinn's lap, wondering if he was going to expose her intimate flesh to Austin. Her cheeks flushed at the thought.

But when the hem of her skirt hovered over her upper thighs, he stopped pulling it, and she felt his hand glide over her inner thigh. Goose bumps danced across her sensitive flesh. His hand slid higher, disappearing under her skirt.

"You remember she has no panties on?" Quinn asked.

Austin's gaze was riveted on her skirt. "How could I fucking forget?"

Quinn laughed again. His fingers grazed her intimate folds, and she sucked in a breath. He stroked over them. His quickening breath whispered across her neck, sending wisps of hair fluttering over her skin. Then he slid deeper into her folds, finding the dampness just inside.

"Fuck, man," Quinn said. "She's wet. This is definitely turning her on."

Pleasure quivered through her as Quinn stroked a few times. When his fingers slipped away, she stifled a murmur of protest. Quinn held up his fingers, and they were glistening with her dewy arousal. Austin licked his lips as if longing to taste her.

"I think Austin might be ready for you now, baby. Go over and pull out his cock, then show him how much you want him."

"Yes, sir." She stood up and walked toward Austin.

Austin watched her approach and kneel in front of him. She pressed her hand against his chest, loving the feel of the solid wall of muscle beneath her fingertips. She dragged her fingers down his taut stomach, then lightly over his cock. It twitched at her touch. He still seemed tentative, but didn't stop her.

She stroked him with a firmer pressure. He was thick and hard beneath her hand. She stared at the growing bulge, longing to bring it out where she could see it. Oh, God, she wanted to feel his shaft, hot and naked, in her hands. She unzipped his pants, then shifted her gaze to his.

"May I touch your big cock, sir?" she asked in as seductive a voice as she could.

His jaw twitched, but he nodded.

She slid her hand inside his pants and found the hot, hard rod. She drew it out and stared at it. The head was purple and as big as a plum. Veins pulsed along the side of the shaft.

"God, it's so hard and thick," she said, stroking it in awe.

The feel of it throbbing in her hand delighted her. She loved that he was so aroused by her.

"I want to take it in my mouth. May I do that, Mr. Wright, sir?" Her gaze was locked with his.

"Just call me *Austin*," he said, his voice tense with need. "Not *sir*."

"Of course. May I take it in my mouth, Austin? I really want to suck on it," she said persuasively.

"Fuck," he said tightly, his need overcoming his reluctance. "Just do it."

She leaned forward and pressed her lips to his tip. He groaned at the contact. She slid out her tongue and lapped at him. She swirled it around the ridge at the base of the crown.

His fingers slid into her hair, tangling in the long strands. She opened her mouth and glided her lips down his cockhead. Taking him in slowly.

"Fuck, sweetheart, you're torturing me."

She smiled, then opened wider and swallowed his whole cockhead. She suckled, and he groaned, slumping back on the couch. She glided downward, taking him deeper. His fingers tightened around her head, but he didn't guide her. Just followed her movement.

She slid back, then glided down again. Going even deeper.

She continued pumping his cock with her hand and mouth. Moving up and down. His already heavy breathing accelerated. She glided to his tip and sucked on his cockhead again, while her hand continued to squeeze and pump.

"Oh, yeah," he groaned. "I'm getting fucking close."

She slid off the top. "Don't hold back. I want you to come in my mouth, Austin."

She covered him again and bobbed up and down.

"Fuck, sweetheart." His fingers tightened around her head, urging her a little faster. "That is so fucking sexy."

Then she felt his groin tense. He groaned, and his hot seed

erupted into her mouth. She kept moving, wanting to give him as much pleasure as she could.

Quinn watched April's head move up and down on Austin's cock. Quinn's hand was already around his own cock, stroking up and down. The sight was an intense turn-on. A little jealousy flickered through him, but the sight of her sucking off his friend . . . knowing that Austin was coming in her mouth . . . overrode his possessiveness.

April was not Quinn's woman. This was just an erotic interlude. He would enjoy fucking her, and watching Austin fuck her, for a month. Then it would end.

Exactly as he wanted.

But watching the two of them together, he couldn't help but be envious of the easy way they enjoyed each other.

April drew back, still holding Austin's now flaccid cock in her hand. She kissed it, then stood up, but Austin grabbed her hand.

"Wait a second," Austin said. "You don't think you're getting away that easily, do you?"

He tugged, pulling her onto his lap. His arms slid around her, and he kissed her passionately. Finally, he released her lips, but didn't let her go.

"That was incredible." Austin smiled, his eyes twinkling. "Now it's your turn."

April's gaze jerked to Quinn as if seeking his permission, but Austin gave her no chance to protest. He twisted, rolling her onto her back on the couch, then he knelt on the floor. His smile broadened as he glided her skirt up her thighs, then lifted.

Once it was around her waist, Austin's smile faded, and his

eyes glittered in awe. Quinn's gaze locked on her fully shaven pussy. Fuck, his cock jumped at the sight, need burning through his groin.

As soon as April felt herself tumbling backward, she knew Austin's intent. The look in his eyes as he stared at her nakedness made her feel intensely desirable.

He rested his hands on her lower thighs and slowly glided upward. Goose bumps danced across her skin, and she ached with need. His thumbs brushed her inner thighs as he drew closer to her intimate flesh. Then when his fingers were almost at her folds . . . he stopped.

She whimpered.

He smiled and leaned forward to kiss her. The delicate brush of their lips set a fire blazing inside her. She rocked her hips, wanting him to touch her. He drew back and chuckled softly.

"You're beautiful."

His finger grazed one of her petals, and she groaned softly.

"Tell me, April. Do you want me to touch your pretty pussy?"

"Yes, Austin. Please." The words came out a hoarse whisper.

His eyes glittered in delight, and he stroked the length of her intimate flesh, right along the damp seam.

"Oh, yes," she murmured.

She couldn't believe how incredibly aroused she was. His touch was barely perceptible, but it had her practically panting.

He drew her folds apart with his thumbs. The coolness of the air washed over the newly exposed flesh, but heat flared through her. He smiled as he leaned in closer. When she felt his lips touch her, she moaned.

His tongue dragged over her folds, driving her wild. She curled her fingers through his sandy-brown hair and held him to her. His tongue flicked over her clit. Pleasure flashed through her. When his fingers found her opening, she widened her legs, welcoming his thick digits as two slid inside her slick passage.

"Oh, God, Austin, that feels so good."

They glided inside her again and again as he lapped at her clit. Pleasure spiraled through her, higher and higher. His tongue vibrated for several seconds, then he suckled. Blissful sensations quivered through her, and she moaned.

His mouth drew away, but his fingers stroked deeply inside her.

"I'm going to make you come, sweetheart. I want you to say my name when you do."

She arched against his hand, needing him deeper. Wanting his mouth back.

She nodded. She'd do anything for the release he promised.

He chuckled and swooped down on her again. His tongue teased, then he began to suckle her little button again.

"Yes," she groaned. "That's so good."

He suckled harder, and she felt a tidal wave of pleasure sweep through her. It rose higher and higher.

"Oh, I'm going to . . ." She gasped as ecstasy claimed her.

Through the haze of delight, she cried, "Austin, you're making me come."

His fingers glided into her faster. She rode the wave . . . on and on. When it started to subside, he stroked her clit with his finger, his others still moving inside her.

"Oh, God," she squeaked as the pleasure rose even more.

The orgasm flowed through her with ease, a fast and steady stream of pure euphoria.

After a long time, his fingers slowed, and her body relaxed.

When he finally settled on the couch beside her, she was sucking in air.

Then Austin leaned in and kissed her. She wrapped her arms around his neck and kissed him passionately.

"Thank you," she murmured against his ear.

He drew back, his eyes glowing. "The pleasure was totally mutual."

Austin shifted back onto the couch. She smiled, then sat up, smoothing down her dress. Then she saw Quinn and froze.

How had she forgotten he was watching?

12

At the sight of April's enormous eyes, Quinn chuckled.

"Don't worry, baby. That was the hottest fucking thing I've ever seen."

So hot he'd almost come watching, pumping his cock at the incredible sight of her face in blissful surrender. But he'd forced himself to slow down, anticipating when he could plunge inside her and take her to ecstasy all over again. He'd tucked away his cock when Austin had leaned in to kiss her.

It bothered him that Austin was getting so close to her, but it shouldn't. Austin wouldn't do anything to jeopardize their friendship.

April chewed on her lip as she picked up her champagne flute and sipped. Her eyes lit up.

"This is delicious." She tipped back the glass again.

Quinn sipped his, appreciating the floral and fruity components with a light and elegant finish. He wouldn't tell her the champagne cost more than his first car.

Austin picked up the bottle and refilled all their glasses, then held his up.

"To what's shaping up to be a fabulous month together," Austin said.

April and Quinn lifted their glasses, too, and they all clinked together. April drank, then set down her empty glass. Austin picked up the almost empty bottle and refilled her glass almost to the rim, draining the last of the bottle.

She picked it up and took a couple of sips. Then she giggled. "This really is good champagne."

"Be careful," Quinn said. "It'll go straight to your head."

They'd all been drinking steadily this evening, and April had had a couple of glasses of the rose absinthe. He wanted her alert and cognizant when he finally took her to heaven. He wanted her to be swept away into exquisite ecstasy and to know it was him who was giving her such intense pleasure.

April turned to him, and with a flash of defiance in her eyes, tipped the half-full glass back and drained it.

He was tempted to call her out for it. To order her to come over and lie across his lap so he could spank her. The thought of pulling up her skirt and revealing her naked ass had his cock swelling. He could imagine her smooth, round cheek under his hand, the skin silky smooth. Then the feel of it heating up as he smacked it until it glowed red.

He sipped his champagne, resisting adjusting his aching cock as it strained against his pants.

He could just walk over there right now and pull up her dress, then drive into her. He'd enjoy the warmth of her soft body around him as he pumped deep, filling her over and over until her face glowed in ecstasy. She would call out his name, like she had with Austin. And when she did, he'd explode deep inside her, coming so hard she'd never forget it.

But he didn't want their first time to be on the couch in a

gaming suite, no matter how luxurious. And especially not right where she'd just given his best friend a blow job and been pleasured by him in return.

"Why don't we take this party back to our suite?" Quinn said.

As soon as they stepped outside and breathed in the night air, Quinn's head started to spin. Whoa, and he'd been worried about April and the champagne. It was having a bigger effect on him than he'd thought. As they walked, April tripped, then stumbled against Austin. His friend's arm slid around her, stopping her from falling.

She giggled. "You're right. The champagne did go to my head."

Quinn was very conscious of the fact that Austin's arm stayed around her as they continued walking. He wasn't jealous as much as *he* wanted to be the one taking care of her. April seemed so comfortable with Austin. So willing to let him do things to help her, but with Quinn, she insisted on paying him back.

Which confused him because if she really were a gold digger, why wouldn't she just take the money? He'd thought it was pride, or more likely she'd make a lot of noise about paying him back while they both knew it would never happen because she didn't have the means.

Back in college when they'd been dating, he never would have believed that she'd be the type to go after a man's money. Not until she'd broken up with him and within weeks was hanging on Maurice's arm.

He stopped walking. A moment later, Austin and April stopped, too, and stared at him inquiringly.

"April, why did you break up with me in college?" Quinn asked.

She frowned and drew away from Austin. "I told you, it just wasn't working between us."

It had been a shock to him when she'd ended it, simply saying that the relationship wasn't working. He'd thought it was more because she thought he was frustrated about them not having sex. He'd even brought it up, assuring her that he was okay with her reasons for waiting, but she'd denied that was the problem.

"Was it because you'd already met your next boyfriend?" The accusation flashed through his mind and out of his mouth before he could stop it.

Her eyes widened, and the pain in those depths told him he'd hurt her. His heart compressed at his callousness.

"April, tell him the truth," Austin said.

She gazed at Austin, then bit her lip as she turned back to Quinn.

"The truth?" Quinn glanced from Austin to April. "What's going on, April?"

Then she shook her head and stared down at her hands.

"Then I'll tell him," Austin said. "April broke up with you because she was afraid of being hurt. You didn't understand it back then, and she was just trying to deal with her issues, but you were throwing yourself into your work, as usual, and she felt abandoned. She didn't want to make you choose between her and your work, so she chose for you."

"That's not fair. If I had known—"

"There are a lot of ifs, buddy. But April was struggling with new feelings. Of belonging. Of being cared for. Being with you prompted needs in her that she didn't know how to deal with. When you seemed to be pulling away, she was afraid. So she decided to end it before she fell in love with you. But in my opinion, it was too late."

Quinn remembered that during their conversation this morning, she'd commented on how hard he'd worked in college. He'd taken it as an accusation that he had neglected her, but she'd denied that was why she'd left. Austin's words gave him more insight. Of course she wouldn't admit that was the reason, because she wouldn't even consider laying blame on him for the relationship ending.

"I don't understand. I wasn't gone that much."

Then he remembered canceling their date on the night she'd wanted to make a special dinner for him. He'd finally figured out a bug in his software program, and he'd wanted to fix it right away. He'd wound up working through the night. Then he'd canceled the concert a week later.

But he hadn't been neglecting her. He'd loved being with her.

He also knew, however, that when he was really caught up in a project, he was so focused he tended to lose track of time.

"Was I really gone that much?" he asked, more of himself.

April didn't answer, still staring downward.

He stepped toward her and took her hands. "Why didn't you tell me?"

Slowly, she raised her face. Her blue eyes were haunted with sorrow.

"Because I would never ask you to change who you are for me."

"Ah, fuck." He pulled her into his arms. "I was such an idiot back then." He hugged her tightly against him, pain searing through his chest. "If I had known . . ." He nuzzled her hair. "You were the most important thing in the world to me. I would have given anything to keep you in my life."

"I know," she whispered.

And she'd already said she wouldn't ask him to.

"Fuck, it was my fault." He held her tighter, never wanting to let her go.

Several long moments passed while he clung to her. Finally, Austin cleared his throat and rested his hand on Quinn's shoulder.

"Let's get back to the hotel," Austin said.

Quinn drew back, but then slid her to his side and kept his arm around her as they walked.

Why hadn't he been able to see what was happening back then? He had lost so much. *She* had lost so much.

He had to question everything. He'd labeled her a gold digger because . . . well, fuck, it had been easier to believe that than anything else. His whole world had tumbled off-kilter when she'd left him, and that was the only explanation that had made any sense to him.

Maurice might be a total asshole, but he'd lavished April with attention back then, and that had been exactly what she'd needed. He could see how she would convince herself she was in love with the guy.

Fuck, Quinn now realized it had been his fault she'd wound up with Maurice. That meant everything that happened after was his fault, too. Like the predicament she was in now.

Hell, she wasn't in *his* debt. *He* was in hers.

Sure, he'd paid off the bill the asshole had left her with, but she'd lost so much more than that. This arrangement they had . . . it wasn't fair to expect her to honor that.

But how could he give it up? He thought he'd die if he didn't satisfy his primal need to be with her.

She leaned her head against his shoulder with a sigh, warming his heart.

The hotel was two blocks away. He felt his pulse accelerate as they walked, knowing they were getting closer to that moment.

When he finally had her in his bed, he'd show her how much she meant to him.

A couple ahead of them turned and entered a neon-lit wedding chapel. Before they reached the door, another couple burst into the night, laughing, the woman clinging to a small bouquet of flowers wrapped with lace and ribbon.

April slowed to a stop as she watched the couple hurry away, holding hands and laughing. Quinn gazed at her wistful eyes.

"What's wrong, April?" Austin asked.

But then understanding flared in Austin's eyes as he saw where she was looking. At the same time Quinn figured it out.

She chewed her lip. "Nothing. It's just . . . today was supposed to be my wedding day."

Fuck, he knew she'd lost a lot, but all he'd thought about were material things. And the loss of a guy she was better off without.

But there was so much more. She'd lost the promise of a future with a man who loved her. Someone who would be there for her and support her when she needed it.

"That's true." Quinn squeezed her hand. "And you know what? You deserve to have that special day." He led her toward the chapel.

13

"What are you talking about?"

Confusion swirled through April as Quinn clung tightly to her hand and hurried her toward the neon sign.

"You and I," Quinn said. "We're getting married."

She stopped dead in her tracks, pulling Quinn to a stop.

"You can't be serious. You've been very clear that's not what you want."

"I am serious. And don't worry. We can have it annulled later. I just want you to be a bride today. I don't want you to lose that, too."

"Hey, that's a great idea," Austin said. "I want to marry her, too. Then her wedding day will be twice as good."

Quinn chuckled. He leaned in and whispered, "I haven't seen Austin drunk very often, but when he is, he makes terrible decisions, and he's very exuberant about them. Clearly, tonight is no different."

"And your decision isn't bad?" she asked.

He grasped her shoulders and stared at her intently. "No, baby. Marrying you could never be a bad idea."

She gazed into his decisive blue eyes. The warmth and caring there left her speechless.

Oh, God, she knew she should protest as he tugged her into the building, but her head was so foggy, and deep down, she didn't want to stop this.

What happened next became hazy, but she remembered saying, "I do," and Quinn slipping a ring on her finger. Then she was walking outside again, and it was Austin holding her hand. They went a block or so, and there was another building and another "I do."

Austin kissed her, and they walked into the night again, April clinging to a bouquet of lovely pink roses. When did she get those? The first wedding, she was pretty sure. She remembered clinging to them as they walked to the second place. She held them to her nose and breathed in the delicate scent as they walked.

Finally, they reached the hotel. When they stepped inside, the lights and noise from the slot machines, paired with the thrum of voices and frenetic energy around them, revived her.

Quinn hurried her into the nearest elevator, and the doors whooshed closed behind them.

Quinn held on tightly to April's hand as if afraid that somehow she would slip away. Austin pressed the button for their floor, and the elevator started to move.

Quinn couldn't believe she was his wife now. Legally married. His ring on her finger.

And now they were headed to their suite. On their honeymoon.

His body ached at the thought of finally being able to make

love to her. To hold her close. To touch her. Feel her soft, naked skin. To caress her breasts and stroke her intimate places.

His groin tightened. He couldn't wait to pull off her clothes and see her completely naked. Then to explore every part of her. His cock swelled at the thought of sliding inside her.

His urgent need for her pulsed through his body. And knowing she was his wife made the anticipation more intense. She leaned her head against his shoulder, and his cock pulsed with need. He slid his arm around her and drew her soft body close to his.

Fuck, he could take her right here in the elevator.

She gazed up at him and smiled. He couldn't help himself. He cupped her cheek with one hand and captured her lips, thrusting his tongue inside. He pulled her against him as he stroked her tongue, then suckled it into his mouth.

Her arms slid around his neck. The bouquet still clutched in her fingers brushed the back of his head. He arched, pressing the bulge of his straining erection into her belly. It was heaven having her in his arms like this.

Austin chuckled. "I'd tell you two to get a room, but we already have one."

A ding signaled that the elevator had arrived, then the doors slid open. Austin was out first, and Quinn grabbed April's hand again and hastened her down the hall. He needed to get her behind closed doors.

Austin slid the key card into the slot, and as soon as the green light flashed, Quinn dragged her frantically into the suite. Once Austin was inside, Quinn grabbed the bouquet from April's hand and tossed it to his friend, then surged forward, trapping her between his body and the heavy wooden door.

He felt like a wild man, desperate to be inside her. Now.

He kissed her deeply, then arched his hips, pressing his hard cock against her. She whimpered.

"This dress is in the fucking way." He reached around and unzipped it, then slid it down until it fell to the floor.

His gaze fell to her naked pussy, and his cock lurched. He reached around behind her and unhooked her bra, then stripped it away.

Oh, God, her breasts were full and round, with beautiful dusky rose nipples blossoming to tight buds as he watched. He cupped her soft mounds, heat jolting through him at the exquisite feel of them. His thumbs glided over her hard nubs, teasing them lightly.

Austin stood a few feet away, leaning against the wall, watching them. He was clearly mesmerized by the sight of April's glorious breasts, too.

Quinn found her mouth again, pulling her tightly to his body, loving the feel of her bead-hard nipples pressing into his chest. He loved how soft and surrendering she was in his arms. Against his mouth.

He eased back and stared at her breasts as he pulled off his tie, then stripped away his jacket and shirt and tossed them aside. He stroked her breasts again, then leaned down and licked one delicious tip. The feel of it against his tongue drove his need up several notches.

"Fuck, you're so beautiful, baby."

He pulled her against him again, his mouth merging with hers, and almost died when he felt her nakedness against his skin. His cock pulsed with need, and he was desperate to be inside her. His cock ached so badly he could barely think straight.

He slid his hand down her belly, then between her legs. She

murmured against his lips. He stroked her soft folds, delighting at the warm slickness he found there. He unzipped his pants and pulled out his hard, aching cock. When he glided his tip over her wetness, he groaned.

Fuck, he could barely hold back.

She clung to his shoulders and whimpered softly.

Without thinking, he drove into her. Oh . . . God . . .

His head started to spin at the incredible feeling of being inside her tight, hot body.

Then his chest constricted. What the hell had he been thinking?

But when he gazed down at her, he saw the same desperate longing in her eyes, not anxiety at his clumsy penetration.

His need overrode all else. He pulled back and drove in again. Her softness surrounding his aching cock drove him wild. He thrust into her again and again, spiraling toward heaven with each one. His body was ablaze, the heat in his groin coiling tighter and tighter until it burned through him.

Then it released, to his guttural groan. Her moans of pleasure echoed in his ears as fireworks exploded in his head, the lights glittering behind his eyelids as he crushed her against the door, her softness a sweet comfort he'd never realized he'd needed so badly. Not just the sweetness of her warm passage around his cock or her soft breasts snug against his body, but more. The sweetness of who she was. Of how she made him feel.

She slumped, and her breathing was labored. He eased back, realizing that with his weight on her she probably couldn't catch her breath.

Her cheeks were flushed and her hair disheveled. The long,

cascading waves fell around her breasts in a golden shimmering mass.

He knew he'd taken her to orgasm, but he was ashamed to think that in his own desperation, he might not have waited for her.

Fuck, why was he always such an idiot around her? He'd waited all this time for her, desperately wanted to be with her, and had wanted this first time to be special. But he'd ruined it by taking her against the door in a twenty-second fuck session.

He was a fucking asshole.

As he stepped back, he reached for her hand.

"Oh, no," Austin said with a smile and took hold of it himself. "Now I'm going to take my wife to bed."

Quinn frowned, pushing back his hair as Austin led her toward the bedroom. Fuck, he deserved to be shut out. Austin would make sure April would be treated right.

Austin glanced over his shoulder. "Are you coming?"

April drew in a deep breath as she followed Austin into the bedroom. Her body was still quivering from the intense orgasm Quinn had given her. It was exhilarating that he'd wanted her so badly he'd taken her against the door in a primal explosion of passion.

Now it was Austin's turn to make love to her. As he led her across the bedroom, she became self-conscious that she was naked and he was fully clothed. Then she saw a powder-pink box on the bed, bound with a white satin ribbon and a beautiful tied bow.

"Open it," Austin said.

She walked to the bed and pulled the ribbon to untie the bow, then lifted the top off the box. She pulled back the pink tissue paper to reveal a sexy, white lace baby doll nightie.

"Put it on," Austin urged.

"Really?" She turned to him and grinned. "I'm naked and you want me to put clothes on?"

Austin placed the bridal bouquet on the bed, then lifted the small garment from the delicate paper and held it up. It was fastened together at the front with a tied ribbon between the breasts.

"It's not like it's going to cover much," he said as he ran his hand under the sheer lace.

He untied the bow on the front, then held the nightie by the shoulder straps as if holding a coat for her to put on.

She laughed. "Okay."

She slid her arms through the straps, then adjusted it over her breasts and tied the ribbon into a bow again. It was open down the front, the soft lace fabric curving down to her hips in cascading waves. The fabric over her breasts wasn't lace but a completely sheer white fabric showing her nipples clearly. She pulled on the tiny thong, which had scalloped lace around the waist, but the crotch was also completely sheer.

"How did this get here?" she asked.

"I made a quick call to the concierge right after our wedding," Quinn answered. "You didn't have a white bridal gown, so I wanted you to have something to make you feel more like a bride."

Her heart fluttered. "That was very considerate, Quinn. Thank you."

"There's more." Austin pulled at the tissue and lifted out a white robe.

He slipped it on her arms. It flowed to the floor in an elegant waterfall of Chantilly lace. She tied the white satin sash at her waist, and as she moved to the mirror to take a look,

Quinn stepped behind her and placed a headpiece of white silk flowers and pearls on her head with a spray of tulle forming a double layer veil that brushed her shoulders. Then Austin handed her the bouquet of pink roses.

Her jaw dropped. "I . . ." Her throat tightened. "I look like a bride."

Quinn wrapped his big hands around her shoulders and leaned close.

"Yes, you do. And you're the most beautiful bride I've ever seen."

Their gazes locked in the mirror, and the warmth in his eyes stole her breath away.

She turned to face him. His warmth, his intense masculinity, and the fact he clearly wanted her again filled her with need. She tipped up her face, and her lips parted, ready for him to kiss her.

He stared at her, a battle waging in his midnight eyes. Then he took her hand and turned.

"Austin, your bride is waiting." Quinn placed her hand in Austin's, then walked across the room and settled on the love seat near the bed.

Austin smiled and drew her close. "You *are* a beautiful bride."

The warmth of his words made her feel special. Almost as special as the look Quinn had given her.

Austin pulled her into his arms, and their lips met. His kiss was sweet and gentle. She slid her arms around his neck as his tongue glided inside her mouth and curled over hers, coaxing it into a seductive dance.

When their lips parted, he smiled, his eyes crinkling at the sides. He stepped back, unbuttoning his shirt, then tugged it off and dropped it to the floor. Her gaze followed his hands to his belt, and she watched in anticipation as he unbuckled, then pulled the belt from the loops and tossed it aside. His chest was broad, and his abs were tight ridges.

He pulled down the zipper on his pants, watching her the whole time. She licked her lips as he dropped the pants to the floor. Then he pushed down his black boxers and stood up. His erection also stood up, tall and proud. She wanted to wrap her hand around it and feel it pulsing.

He walked backward to the bed and sat down. She set the bouquet on the dresser and stepped forward until she was in front of him, and also facing Quinn in the love seat on the other side of the bed, then she untied the sash. Slowly, she drew the delicate lace robe from her shoulders and let it fall. Both men's gazes jerked to her breasts, clearly visible through the sheer fabric. She stepped closer to Austin, then into his arms. His lips brushed along her collarbone, sending goose bumps flashing across her skin.

He drew back and smiled at her, then turned his head to look over his shoulder.

"Do you want to take charge, Quinn?" Austin asked.

"No. You've got this."

Austin laughed. "Any requests, at least?"

"Yes. Make her happy."

April's heart compressed at his words.

Austin's teal eyes darkened. "Oh, I promise I'll do my best."

He tightened his arms around her waist and pulled her with him as he turned and leaned against the cushions, stretching his legs out on the bed. She knelt over his thighs, facing him. Excitement quivered through her as she leaned forward and brushed her lips against his, then across his cheek. The stubble on his face was coarse against her skin, and she loved it. She dragged her teeth over the short whiskers.

He laughed and rolled her over, then dove in for a deeper kiss, thrusting his tongue inside briefly, then leaning back and staring down at her.

"Now, let me have a good look at these gorgeous breasts of yours." He stroked over the thin fabric covering one of them, then teased the nipple until it thrust straight up, straining at the cloth.

He dipped down and took the nipple into his mouth, then suckled. His other hand stroked her other breast, his thumb toying with the nub. At the exquisite pleasure, she arched against him and moaned.

He rolled onto his side facing Quinn and drew back one side of her nightie, exposing her stomach. He glided his fingertips down to her belly button and stroked around it in circles.

"Quinn, you going to come join us?" Austin asked.

"I'm good here for now," Quinn answered.

"Yeah?" Austin's fingers continued their journey down her stomach and under the thin elastic of her thong.

She knew Quinn would see every movement of Austin's fingers clearly through the transparent fabric.

Austin dipped into her folds and stroked her slickness. Heat rippled through her.

"Mmm. You left her nice and wet," Austin said.

His finger pushed inside her, and she arched against his hand.

Austin chuckled. "And eager for more." He gazed down at her. "You do want more, don't you, sweetheart?"

"Oh, yes. I want you inside me."

"You mean another finger?" he asked, sliding in a second one.

She squeezed around the two thick fingers as he stroked, excitement swirling through her.

"Ah, yes, that's good," she said, "but I mean your cock."

He laughed again. "You hear that, Quinn? My pretty little bride wants me to fuck her."

"Good," Quinn said. "Because I want to see that."

Austin wiggled his fingers inside her, sending heat rippling through her body.

"Well, you know, I think she deserves the very best experience . . ." Austin's eyes glittered. "So I think I could use some help."

14

April groaned in disappointment as Austin withdrew his fingers from her body, then stood up and scooped her into his arms. He carried her to the love seat and set her on Quinn's lap. Quinn had shed his pants and now wore only his boxers, which barely contained his erection. The thick shaft now pressed against her back.

"Cup her breasts and keep those nipples nice and hard for me," Austin instructed.

Quinn's arms came around her, and his large hands covered her breasts. Gently, he stroked her nipples.

"Yeah, that's good," Austin said with a smile. "Now open her legs."

Quinn widened his thighs, and his knees drew her legs open.

Austin stroked a fingertip over her crotch, then hooked his finger under the fabric and pulled it sideways, exposing her slick flesh.

"Man, look at that beautiful pink pussy," he said to Quinn.

Quinn's fingers were circling over her hard nubs, igniting a deep need inside her.

"Fuck, buddy, I want to watch you shove your cock deep inside it," Quinn practically groaned. "What the hell are you waiting for?"

"Ha ha. What about you, April?" Austin asked.

"Yes, please. I want you inside me now, Austin."

His gaze locked with hers, and the depth of desire shocked her.

He glided his fingers along her cheek and through her hair, then curled them around the back of her head and leaned closer.

"Whatever you want, sweetheart."

He captured her lips and drove his tongue deep, then thrust several times, leaving her breathless. He eased back, a wicked smile on his lips, and she felt his hard, hot flesh brush over her soft petals. Then he pressed forward, sliding into her.

At the feel of his hard member stretching her wide, she leaned back against Quinn and moaned, delightful sensations dancing through her.

"Do you like that, baby?" Quinn murmured against her ear. "Feeling Austin's big cock sliding into you?"

She opened her eyes and found herself staring into Quinn's midnight-blue ones.

"Oh, God, yes," she whispered hoarsely.

Austin's pelvis bumped against her, his cock all the way inside. "Is it deep inside you?" Quinn asked. "Is it hard and thick?"

"Yes. Oh, yes," she moaned, squeezing Austin's cock with intimate muscles.

She was still so aroused from Quinn's lovemaking that the combination of Quinn's fingers circling her aching nipples and Austin's rigid shaft inside her had pleasure quivering through her entire body.

Austin stroked her hair, his face inches from hers. His eyes were full of need.

"Damn, it feels so good being inside you." Austin's cock twitched, sending thrilling ripples of heat through her.

She grasped his shoulders and pulled him tighter.

"Please, Austin. I need you to fuck me now. I'm so close."

Austin's eyes widened, and he smiled. "Are you going to come for me?"

He drew back and glided deep again, igniting rippling waves of pleasure inside her.

"Yes," she breathed.

He glided back and forward again, his cockhead dragging along her sensitive passage. His thumb stroked her cheek, and he pulled her into another kiss, not missing a stroke with his cock.

In and out. She squeezed tighter around him. She gripped his shoulders as the pleasure skyrocketed.

"Ohhh, it feels so good," she moaned.

He sped up, driving deeper and faster.

"Oh. God." Her heart pounded, and then pleasure exploded through her, blazing into a thousand sparks inside her head as she rode the wave of pure bliss.

"Are you coming, baby?" Quinn asked, his lips brushing her ear.

"Yes. Oh, God, yes. Austin's making me come," she said through labored breaths.

"Ah, fuck, baby," Austin groaned, then drove deep and held her to him. His cock exploded inside her, driving her orgasm higher still.

She clung to him as he continued to pump inside her, keeping her on the edge of ecstasy.

Then he laughed and rolled backward onto the floor, his arm firmly around her waist. She was on top of him now, her ass in the air. She squeezed his cock, the fading embers of the orgasm still smoldering through her.

"This is really where I need your help, buddy," Austin said. "You see, I'm done, and she's still raring to go."

He cupped her ass and spread her for Quinn to see. Then his cock slipped away. April was still quivering in his arms.

"Fuck," Quinn uttered, then stood up.

She saw his boxers fall to the floor beside her, then felt him prowl over her. His hard cock stroked her wet opening, sending tingles through her again. When he drove deep into her, pleasure jolted through her again. She rested her head on Austin's chest with a sigh. He stroked her hair to the side and cupped her head, gazing at her with a smile.

Quinn drew back and thrust deep. At the same time, he found her clit with his fingers and stroked.

She gasped at the joyful sensations surging through her.

He pumped into her steadily now, still teasing her sensitive bud. Austin kept stroking her hair while Quinn fucked her from behind. The whole thing was so wildly outrageous and exhilarating, her body vibrated with the intensity of her arousal.

Quinn's cock drove deep again, and she moaned.

"Oh, yes, Quinn. I'm going to come again."

"Fuck, yeah, baby. Come for me."

At his command, her body exploded into bliss. She was swept into staggering ecstasy, and the world shattered around her.

As she moaned, Quinn surged deep again, then groaned his own release.

Although he stopped thrusting, he kept stroking her clit, keeping her orgasm going on and on.

Finally, she slowed, the pleasure fading to a warm glow. Quinn rested his head on her back, and they all drew in slow, deep breaths.

It was so warm and cozy between these two men. And she felt so well loved.

She closed her eyes and drifted off to sleep.

April woke up with blinding sunlight flashing across her eyelids. Her head throbbed, and she just wanted to fall back asleep so she didn't have to deal with it. She shielded her eyes with her hand and kept them closed against the onslaught.

Her head was foggy, but she knew she had to get up. For the past several months, with planning her wedding, her to-do list was always jam-packed. And the big day was . . .

Yesterday!

Her eyelids snapped open as a slew of memories fluttered through her brain. Of packing for the trip to Las Vegas. Of meeting Maurice at the hotel.

Oh, God, then the rehearsal dinner . . .

Her head ached even more as she remembered that disaster. She rubbed her temples.

As her bleary eyes focused, shock surged through her. There was a naked, masculine back facing her. Big and muscular with a small red birthmark on the right shoulder blade that looked like an eagle with its wings spread.

She sucked in a breath and realized there was an arm around her waist, too. Strong and thick. On the wrist, there was a gold watch with the iconic Rolex crown on the black face. On the back of his hand was a small scar.

Her breath caught when she saw a wedding band on the ring finger of the hand. Oh, God, she'd gone to bed with a married man? She'd never do such a thing.

The other man's hand was draped over the covers, and she was shocked to see a wedding ring there, too.

She drew in a deep calming breath. No, she couldn't have.

Then she glanced at her own hand and . . .

Red spots flickered in front of her eyes, and if she hadn't been lying down, she probably would have fainted.

She was wearing a wedding ring, too.

She had to think, but her mind swirled in confusion.

All she knew for sure was that yesterday had been her wedding day.

And neither of these men were her fiancé, Maurice.

The arm around her waist tightened, and lips brushed the back of her neck.

"Good morning, Mrs. Taylor."

That voice.

"Quinn?" she gasped.

She glanced over her shoulder. His lips were turned up in a lazy smile.

Then it all came tumbling back. Maurice ditching her at the hotel, leaving her with an exorbitant bill. Quinn bailing her out. Then . . .

Oh, God, the arrangement.

Her cheeks flushed at the memory of giving Austin a blow job in the gaming suite while Quinn watched, followed by Austin bringing her to orgasm with his talented mouth. Then when they'd walked back to the hotel . . .

Her chest clenched. "So you and I are actually married?"

"You're definitely married." Austin rolled over and leaned on his elbow, gazing at her. "But I think calling you Mrs. Wright would be more appropriate."

She rolled onto her back, slumped between them, her head spinning.

"I don't know," Quinn responded. "I married her first, so that gives me dibs."

First? Oh, God, she was married to both of them.

Her chest tightened. This couldn't be happening.

"You know, we're doing a lot of chatting," Austin said as his hand settled on her chest, then scooped her breast into his hand.

He kneaded it softly, and her nipple blossomed to a tight bud. Awareness rippled through her, and her body heated with a deep yearning to feel him continue to touch her. To run his hands all over her body.

"But we're in bed naked." His grin broadened. "And we're newlyweds. So I think . . ."

He leaned down and nuzzled her neck, his lips brushing along that one supersensitive spot that sent shivers dancing along her spine and caused her inner passage to clench tightly in need.

He kissed her ear, his breath sending wisps of hair fluttering around her face, and both nipples swelled.

"We should do something about it," Austin finally continued.

A single pink rose sat on the bedside table in a bud vase, and vague memories of last night fluttered through her brain.

"Wait," she said. "I want to understand. How did we wind up like this?"

"You really don't remember, sweetheart?" Quinn asked softly.

Tingles danced down her spine. He usually called her *baby*. Not *sweetheart*. Austin did that. But hearing it from Quinn warmed her.

She shook her head. "I remember being in the gaming suite. Then going outside to walk back here." She ran her hand over her forehead and back through her hair. "I guess I had a lot to drink."

Austin chuckled. "We all did."

He continued to stroke her breast, keeping her nipple tight and aching. She wanted to arch against him, then invite him to touch more of her.

"You got sad when you saw a couple coming out of a wedding chapel," Quinn said.

She glanced at the white lace robe draped over a nearby chair, scraps of lace on the floor that a flash memory told her was the sexy wedding-night lingerie he'd given her, then the wedding bouquet sitting on the dresser.

"You didn't want me to miss out on my wedding day. You . . ." Tears prickled at her eyes. "You wanted me to feel like a bride."

Quinn smiled warmly, and a tear escaped April's eye.

"That is so sweet." She rested her fingers on his raspy cheek. "Thank you." Her words came out a mere whisper.

She glided her hand around his neck, and he dipped down and captured her lips. The kiss was sweet and tender, unlike the demanding kisses that had been his style yesterday.

"Don't forget Austin," Quinn said. "He wanted in on it."

She shifted her gaze to Austin. "Thank you, Austin. But isn't a second marriage illegal?"

"We didn't worry much about that," Austin said, "since we're getting it annulled. Not that we were really thinking all that much." He caressed her breast gently, his finger brushing over her nub. "And I don't much feel like thinking now, either."

He nuzzled her neck, and she giggled. Then she felt lips brush her other nipple, and a warm mouth close around it as she gasped. Her fingers glided through Quinn's dark, wavy hair as he suckled on her, pleasure catapulting through her.

Austin stroked one nipple, and Quinn teased the other with his tongue. Then Austin leaned down and captured her nipple, too. She arched upward, pushing farther into both warm mouths.

"Oh, God, that feels so good." She sucked in air as heat washed through her in waves.

Austin was on his hands and knees beside her as he drew her nipple deeper into his mouth. She stroked down his taut stomach and found his growing cock. She wrapped her hand around it and squeezed, then stroked his length.

"I love it when your cock is big and hard," she said with a smile.

"That's good, because it's going to be that way anytime you're near me." Austin licked her nub as his glittering teal eyes shifted to her face. "Or even in the same room."

She filled with delight at the fact he was so turned on by her.

Quinn chuckled. "Then maybe we'll have to keep her in the suite so we don't have some embarrassing incidents." He sat up and wrapped his hand around his pulsing erection. "Because I'm going to be in the same state."

Just the sight of April naked had his cock in a raging hard-on. Seeing Austin sucking her breasts and her hand wrapped around his friend's cock drove Quinn's need off the charts.

"Oh," she said, "it might get boring being stuck in the same place, even a suite as luxurious as this."

She reached for Quinn's cock and grasped it, too, then began stroking. "But maybe I can find a way to satisfy these big, hungry monsters even when we're out."

"Really?" Quinn asked, his eyebrows arching. "What do you have in mind?"

"Well, the hotel has various outdoor courtyards with large plants for privacy." She squeezed the two hard shafts in her hands as she stroked, eliciting groans from Austin and Quinn. "There are elevators with emergency stop buttons. You might be able to persuade the security staff to delay rescuing us if we're stuck inside. And . . ."

She paused while Austin stopped her hand and slowed it down. Ah, he obviously liked the elevator idea.

"And what, baby?" Quinn asked, a little breathless from the hormones spiraling through him at her attention.

"And there are a couple of nice restaurants with tablecloths."

"Tablecloths?" Austin arched into her hand as she stroked down his cock.

"Yes. If I dropped a napkin and crouched under the table to get it, no one would see me under there. Right?"

"Goddamn, Quinn. If she's suggesting what I think she is, let's go out for some fucking breakfast right now."

Quinn laughed. "Maybe we'll save that for dinner. Right now, I'm quite comfortable where we are."

He drew his cock from her hand and swooped down to capture her breast again, pulling the soft flesh into his mouth. Her nipple immediately hardened, and he dragged his teeth over it lightly.

"Ohhh." She arched against him.

Then he released her bud and kissed down her stomach. He dabbed his tongue deep into her navel, then continued downward. Austin was still lapping at her other nipple, and his hand covered the breast Quinn had abandoned.

When Quinn reached her beautiful pussy, he stroked over it with his fingertips, satisfied by her answering murmur. The feel of her slick flesh make his cock throb. He drew the petals apart and licked her. Her long, soft moan was like silk gliding over him. Stimulating his senses. Making him harder and eagerer to be inside her.

He dipped his tongue into her again, this time stroking deep. Caressing her passage. Her fingers glided through his hair, and she clung to his head. Urging him to pleasure her.

Satisfaction swelled through him. She was his wife, and she wanted him. As much as he wanted her.

He licked up to the nest of folds surrounding her clit, then opened the petals to find the sensitive nub. He smiled at the sight of it, then covered it with his mouth and teased with his tongue.

Her moans echoed alongside Austin's. He glanced up to see that she was stroking his friend rapidly now. Clearly, the more excited she got, the faster her hand moved on Austin's cock.

Quinn began to suckle her delightful bud.

"Ohhh . . . yes . . ." she moaned.

Austin groaned and grasped her wrist, stilling her hand. Quinn continued to tease and suck her. She moaned again, arching against his mouth. He stroked her slit with his finger and glided into her wetness. His cock twitched, wanting to be inside her warmth.

He lifted his face and gazed up at her. "Are you close, baby?"

"Yes, sir, I . . ."

He suckled again, and she mumbled incoherently.

"What was that, baby?"

"Yes, I'm so close."

"Do you want me to make you come right now?"

"No," she murmured, to his surprise. Then she reached her hand to him. "Please fuck me, Quinn."

Heat blazed through him, and he found himself prowling over her body, then pressing his cockhead to her wetness. Her hands stroked over his shoulder, and she pulled him closer.

"Oh, yes. Now. Drive into me."

15

April gasped when Quinn thrust forward, his thick, hard cock filling her all the way.

"Are you all right?" Quinn murmured against her ear, his voice filled with concern.

She giggled softly. "I'll be better when you start moving."

She tightened her arms around him, luxuriating in the feel of his hard body against her and the glow of blissful pleasure shimmering through her.

She nipped his earlobe. "I'm so close," she whispered seductively into his ear.

He groaned, then moved back, his shaft caressing her passage. Then he thrust forward again, stealing her breath.

Austin's head was on the pillow beside them as he watched, his hand firmly around his cock, stroking its generous length.

Quinn drew back again, then thrust deep.

"Ohhh, yes." Her insides melted into a quivering mass.

Quinn kept thrusting. When she squeezed around his massive shaft, her pleasure skyrocketed, and she felt dizzy.

He pumped deeper. And faster.

"Oh, God." She felt tears welling in her eyes.

Having Quinn making love to her . . . Being married to him . . .

Her heart swelled as bliss surged through her. She arched against him, taking his cock deeper still.

"Are you close, baby?" Quinn whispered in her ear, his voice raspy.

She nodded, unable to utter words. She wrapped her legs around his thighs and pulled him tighter, arching up again to take him as deep as she could. His cock twitched, and then he groaned and erupted inside her.

The heat of his liquid seed filling her threw her over the edge. She clutched his shoulders and moaned, flying to ecstasy. He continued rocking his hips, keeping her orgasm going on and on.

Finally, he collapsed against her. She slid her arms around him, holding him in a tight embrace. Her breasts were crushed against his chest, and their hearts pounded in unison.

After several long moments, Quinn drew back. He smiled warmly, then kissed her, a long, lingering kiss. Then he rolled to his side beside her. His hand covered her breast, then glided down her stomach and over her mound. She sucked in a breath as he stroked her clit.

"Austin, she's still primed."

Austin still stroked his cock, and she watched the purple head bob up and down from his fist.

She smiled. "I don't want to neglect my second husband." She opened her arms to him.

Immediately, he prowled on top of her, his cock still in his fist. He pressed it to her slick flesh and glided the top along her length several times,

"It was fucking hot watching the two of you go at it," Austin said, his teal eyes sparking with need.

"And now you want to fuck me really badly, right?"

He eased into her wetness just a little. Her insides ached, wanting him deeper.

"You fucking know it." His voice was coarse with desire.

"So fuck me, Austin. I'm all yours."

He groaned and impaled her.

She gasped. "Oh, yes."

He gathered her close and thrust into her again. Her head started to spin, her last orgasm still vibrating through her.

"I'm going to make you come, sweetheart. Just like Quinn just did." His voice was deep and urgent.

"Yesss," she hissed, tightening her arms around him.

He pumped into her, sweeping her right back into bliss. Her body quivered, and pleasure pummeled through her with each thrust of his cock.

"Ohhhh, Austin."

"Yes, sweetheart." He drove deep again. "Tell me."

"I'm . . . coming," she murmured in a bare whisper.

Then she moaned as exquisite delight rippled through her. He began pounding into her, then jerked forward and groaned. More hot male essence filled her as he found his release.

She moaned as the orgasm continued to wash over her in waves. Quinn covered her breast with his warm hand and stroked while Austin found her clit with his fingers as he kept moving inside her. Her pleasure crested, then slowly faded back to a soft glow of delight.

Finally, Austin rolled onto his back and sucked in air.

"You are the most fucking amazing woman I've ever met," Austin said.

"That's the truth," Quinn agreed.

She gazed up at Quinn. His face was perched on his hand, his elbow digging into the pillow, as he watched her. His eyes glowed with warmth, filling her with a delightful quivering feeling.

"Well, I think my two husbands are pretty amazing, too."

Her time with these two men might be short, but she was thankful for every second she had with them. And would cling to these memories for the rest of her life.

April stepped out of the shower and grabbed a fluffy towel to dry off. Both her enthusiastic husbands had joined her, and while their big soapy hands stroked over every part of her body, she'd never felt so thoroughly clean . . . and so deliciously dirty.

She walked into the bedroom and glanced around for her dress but couldn't see it anywhere. Quinn, who was right behind her, a towel draped casually around his waist, walked to the dresser and pulled out some new boxers, then dropped his towel. Her gaze fell to his hard, muscular butt. She felt the urge to walk right over and cup that firm ass and squeeze.

Austin stepped behind her and rested his hands on her shoulders, then nuzzled her neck.

"Looking for something?" he asked.

Austin hadn't bothered with a towel, and his naked cock nestled against her ass. Then his hand stroked lightly over her breast, and she knew it wouldn't take much for her to suggest they hop right back into bed.

"I'm . . . uh . . . looking for my dress, but I don't see it."

"Ah, yes. Well, that would be because you and Quinn were a little anxious to get started on the honeymoon last night, and you shed it at the front door."

A memory flashed through her of Quinn holding her pinned

against the door, then driving into her with a savage thrust. Then he'd pounded her fast and hard against the wooden surface until they'd both shuddered in release.

It had been primal and exhilarating. A powerful wave of arousal swept through her, and she nearly spun around to grab Austin's cock and start pumping it.

Instead she drew in a deep breath.

"You really don't remember what happened last night?" Quinn asked, now wearing a pair of jeans and pulling on a shirt.

"I remember everything until we left the other hotel where we played poker, but after that . . . just fragments."

"Do you want to talk about it?" Quinn asked. "I don't want anything hidden from you. Like the fact the three of us had sex last night."

Austin pulled her tightly to him, his lips brushing her ear. "I sure hope you haven't completely forgotten the first time I made love to you." His lips trailed down her neck. "And then when I held you while Quinn—"

"Austin. Give her a minute to breathe," Quinn said.

She remembered now. Being on the floor on top of Austin, then Quinn prowling over her and making love to her from behind. Her intimate muscles clenched at the memory, wanting him inside her again.

"All right. If you insist." Austin turned her around and kissed her, then let her go. "But if you need a reminder of what it was like, sweetheart, just let me know."

His wide grin and the twinkle in his teal eyes made her laugh.

"I promise. Right now, I'm going to get dressed. I assume my undies are with the dress?"

"Well, your bra is," Quinn responded. "You gave your panties to Austin as a gift."

"Oh, right."

She walked out of the bedroom and crossed the living room to the front door.

She picked up her discarded bra and slid the towel down around her waist while she pulled the lacy garment on. She dropped the towel to the ground and slipped her dress on, then zipped it up.

She bit her lip. "Uh . . . my only other panties are the black ones I wore in the pool yesterday. I hung them to dry in the bathroom, but I didn't see them there when we showered."

"I sent those out with the other clothes to be cleaned." Austin grinned. "Sorry, they're not back yet."

Both men now stood in the living room, fully dressed. And both were staring at her skirt, knowing there were no panties underneath. She turned back to the door, not quite ready for another onslaught of male hormones, so she picked up the other clothes lying there. She draped Quinn's shirt over her arm. She remembered him peeling it away last night. Then the suit jackets scattered across the entrance floor. She picked them up and hung them in the closet. She noticed a pink rose in the breast pocket of each, and she pulled them out.

"Are these supposed to be boutonnieres?" she asked, heading to the bathroom to put them into a glass of water. "They look pretty sad."

There was no foliage or baby's breath to adorn them. They'd gotten a lovely wedding bouquet for her from the chapel or a florist. She was surprised they hadn't gotten proper boutonnieres, too.

Austin laughed, and Quinn joined in.

"What's so funny?" she asked as she followed them into the living room. She sat on the couch and gazed from one to the other. Quinn sat beside her, Austin on the armchair.

"When we went to the second chapel to get married—"

"The second chapel?" she asked.

"Yeah, I didn't think that the guy would agree to marry you and me," Austin explained, "right after performing the ceremony for you and Quinn. So we went somewhere else."

"Good thinking," she said wryly.

"And when we got there," Quinn said, "we realized they might suspect something if we walked in with a bouquet."

Her eyebrow popped up. "Wouldn't they just think we came prepared?"

"Well, yeah, that makes sense now, but last night . . ." Austin shrugged.

"Okay. So why did you laugh when I asked about the roses?"

"We had to ditch the flowers," Quinn continued, "but you wouldn't let us throw away your wedding bouquet. You were quite insistent, even getting a little weepy, saying it was special."

"It was a small bouquet," Austin said, "made up of three pink roses, so we pulled out the three flowers and broke off the stems on two of them and tucked one in each of our pockets as makeshift boutonnieres. When we walked in, the guy thought we were nuts."

Quinn laughed harder. "But not because of that." He grinned at April. "You insisted on clinging to the third rose. When the guy saw the three of us, he raised his eyebrows uncertainly and said, 'I see you already have flowers.' Then Austin said, 'Yes, but I'd like something more substantial for the bride.'"

Austin chuckled. "He really did think we were crazy."

April vaguely remembered her hand wrapped tightly around the short stem, the lovely blossom a symbol of love and marriage. Of everything she'd lost.

In the end, the flower would always remind her of how

Quinn, in his infinite kindness, had tried to give her back that dream, even if only for one night. Of course she wouldn't let them throw it away.

She smiled tremulously, trying not to let them see the moisture in her eyes.

"So how did you get the rose away from me?"

Quinn stroked her arm. "I promised you I'd keep it safe. You let me take it from you then, and I slid it behind your ear."

She gazed into his midnight eyes, so filled with warmth, and smiled.

"That's nice. Thank you for that."

"I get some credit, too," Austin said. "Quinn didn't even notice that it fell out of your hair while you and he were . . . enjoying yourselves in the entryway. After we all went to bed, I was the one who came back out to get it and put it in water."

Quinn stood up and slapped him on the back, laughing. "As husband number two, you really are trying harder."

Quinn offered his hand to April, and she took it and stood up.

"Now let's get this woman some breakfast," Quinn said.

"Good thinking," Austin said. "That way she'll have lots of energy, so when we get back, we can remind her exactly what else happened last night."

He winked at her. Her heart fluttered, and she was already looking forward to returning to the suite.

April stood beside Austin as Quinn told the hostess that they'd like a table for three for the Sunday buffet, preferably in a quiet corner. The woman led them to a nice booth, already set with silverware and crystal glasses.

"Would you like mimosas, Mr. Taylor?"

Austin groaned. Quinn glanced at April, and she shook her head. Champagne was the last thing any of them wanted this morning.

"Just coffee and some orange juice, please," Quinn said.

A waitress showed up promptly with a silver carafe of coffee and filled their cups.

"We have an extensive Sunday buffet," she said and listed several items, including lobster tails, shrimp, prime rib, omelets made to order, and eggs benedict. "I'll be right back with your orange juice."

"I'm going to get some eggs benedict and a lobster tail," April said.

As she started to rise, Quinn held up his hand. "Hold on."

The waitress had already poured three juice glasses and was heading back toward them. She set them on the table.

"Can I get you anything else?" she asked.

"Actually," Quinn said, "would you save us a trip and bring us our entrées? One eggs benedict for the lady, a plate with four lobster tails for the table, prime rib for me, and . . . Austin?"

"Uh, yeah, I'll go for the prime rib, too."

"Of course." She smiled and hurried away.

"But it's a buffet," April said. "Don't you want to see all the goodies?"

Quinn laughed. "We can go up for dessert. Right now, I'd rather spend time with you and talk."

"Talk?" Her smile faded. "Oh, of course. Quinn, it's okay. I know we're getting an annulment. You both did this to give me a wonderful wedding day to remember, and I think that's really sweet. None of us have to feel awkward about it. I assume you'd like to go right after breakfast."

"Hold on," Austin said. "There's no rush. I'm enjoying this marriage thing."

She turned to Austin. "You know, to quote Julia Roberts in *Pretty Woman*, 'I'm a sure thing.' At least for the next month." She turned her lips up in an amused smile, even though she felt sick at the thought of walking away from Quinn and Austin at the end of the month. "We have an arrangement, remember? You don't have to have a wedding ring on my finger."

"Can we forget about the annulment for now?" Quinn asked. "I had something else—"

"Actually, that's exactly what I'd like to do," Austin said. "Forget about the annulment."

April was stunned. "What do you mean?"

Austin took her hand and squeezed it gently while he gazed into her eyes. The feel of her hand nestled in his and the loving glow in his eyes made her feel wanted. And cared for.

"April, I want to settle down with a good woman, and you and I have a strong attraction to each other. I'm a good judge of people, and I believe that the two of us could make a go of it. Since we're already married, I'd like to give it a trial run, at least for the next month."

"What the hell, Austin?" Quinn demanded.

"I'm sorry, buddy. I've watched you resist your feelings for her, and I think you're crazy. The bottom line is, if you want to stay married to her, and she wants the same thing, of course I'll step aside. But if not, I don't want to miss my chance at happiness."

"Well, I'm fucking not going to get it annulled now. If I did, you would be legally married to her."

"I don't want the two of you to fight about this," April said. "It's not worth hurting your friendship over. Austin, we've only known each other for a day. Staying married doesn't make any sense. I think you're just caught up in your desire to settle down, and you've convinced yourself that I'll make a good wife for you. But really, I'm just convenient right now."

"No way. I—"

She raised her hand to stop him. "And, Quinn, you don't have to worry about me running off with Austin's wealth. Though I know I won't be able to convince you of that."

She frowned as pain tugged at her heart. She'd been so happy only moments ago, blown away by the generosity of spirit both men had shown her, but it had all soured when she remembered that Quinn would never trust her.

She crumpled up her cloth napkin and tossed it on the table.

"You know, suddenly I'm not hungry." She stood up and strode from the restaurant.

16

Quinn glared at Austin. "What the hell were you doing?"

"I was trying to jar you into realizing that you really want that woman. You'd be an idiot not to, and"—Austin stared at him squarely—"one thing you're not is an idiot."

The waitress arrived with a tray and placed the plates around the table.

"Would you like me to take the eggs benedict back until the lady returns?" she asked.

"No, thank you. It'll be fine," Quinn said.

The waitress smiled and hurried away.

"So you're not angling to stay married to April?" Quinn demanded.

"Hey, don't get me wrong. I would absolutely love to stay married to her. But as I said, if you love her . . ."

"Fuck, I don't know what to think anymore. I thought I knew what she was all about. But everything's changed since I've spent this time with her. Now that I understand her background and why she really broke up with me."

"So you admit you're in love with her?"

"I don't know. But either way, I've royally screwed up."

"What are you talking about?"

"Fuck, the first time I made love to her . . . on our wedding night . . . I was like a madman. You saw how I behaved. It wasn't exactly a special moment."

Austin's lips turned up in a half grin. "She seemed to enjoy it."

Quinn scowled. "Maybe, but if she did, it wasn't because of any consideration from me. I just took from her. And you don't know about what happened before. When we made the arrangement. I demanded she give me a blow job, and when she was done, I did nothing for her. In fact, I practically rushed her out the door. Not like you. You treated her properly."

"Look, none of that matters. You're struggling with the past, and she knows that. In case you haven't noticed, she's a sweet and loving person, and I'm sure she's in love with you. I suggest you get her into bed alone and show her how you feel in your heart. You won't have to say a thing. After that, just see where things go."

"Yeah, if she'll even talk to me." He shook his head.

"We'll deal with that when the time comes. Right now, why don't we have the food sent up to the suite? I'm sure she'll appreciate that once her stomach starts to rumble."

Austin signaled for the waitress.

Quinn glanced at his watch, his foot tapping as nervous energy thrummed through him. Where was April?

He and Austin had been back in the suite for over an hour, finished their meals, and now sat in the living room. Austin was happily reading a book in the armchair, but Quinn couldn't settle.

"Relax, buddy. She'll be back," Austin said.

"Maybe I should go look for her," Quinn said, glancing at his watch again.

Austin closed the book and set it on the coffee table, then leaned forward.

"It's not like she has bus fare or anywhere to go," he pointed out. "And she promised a month. From everything I've seen, she's a woman of her word. Do you really think she's going to skip out on us, especially when she's so concerned about paying off the debt?"

Quinn needed to sort out his feelings for her. He hated struggling with his emotions like this. And not having her here was driving him crazy.

His chest tightened another notch. "I just want to know she's okay."

A light knock sounded at the door. Quinn strode to the entrance and swung it open.

April stood on the other side, her expression subdued.

His heart swelled at the sight of her.

"Quinn, I'm sorry I ran out on breakfast."

He gently grasped her elbow and drew her inside, letting the door close behind her.

"It's okay, baby." Quinn guided her into the living room.

"Austin, I'm sorry," she said as she sat down on the couch across from him.

Quinn sat down beside her, his arm sliding around her waist and drawing her close.

"It's okay," Austin said. "Things did get a bit emotional."

She pursed her lips. "You and Quinn have been so good to me. I should have let it go."

Quinn tightened his hold. "Never mind about that. I'm just glad you're back."

Austin grinned. "You'll be happy to know we brought your breakfast up to the suite. I can nuke it for you. Coffee, too. Or I can order a fresh breakfast from room service."

She smiled. "No, that's okay. I'm fine with reheated, and I'm starving."

Austin strolled into the small kitchen. Quinn walked with April to the table and sat down. A few minutes later, Austin returned with a tray containing a covered plate, a thermos of coffee, and three mugs. He filled her cup as she started to eat.

Quinn sipped his coffee, watching her the whole time. Things had changed over the past day. Everything he'd thought he'd known about her and why they'd broken up had changed. He'd never realized how alone she'd felt her whole life. How that had affected her feelings of self-worth.

He had thought she'd left him for someone who had more money, but she had left him for other reasons. He'd been too much of a fool to see he was losing her because she was insecure about his feelings for her and thought he was pulling away. She'd been afraid of losing him, so she'd ended it first.

The fact she'd fallen for Maurice . . . even she had admitted that money might have been a factor, but not for reasons of greed as he'd surmised . . . but because what she'd needed most was security. And love.

Fuck, he could have given her both back then. He hadn't had wealth, but he'd had a brain and could make a good living. She could, too. Together they could have built a sound foundation. But more, he'd been in love with her, and if he'd been able to see what was happening and assure her, his love would have helped heal her wounds.

She cut another bite of egg, Canadian bacon, and English muffin, pushed the forkful through the béarnaise sauce, then put it in her mouth. When she noticed he was watching her, she smiled timidly, then swallowed. She was down to her last few bites.

He'd wasted so much time. He couldn't let this opportunity slip away. To reestablish what they'd had.

Austin sipped his coffee, watching both of them. When April finished her last bite, Austin tipped back his cup and drained it, then picked up her plate and placed it on the tray, along with his empty cup.

He stood up. "Well, I'm going out for a walk. I'll probably be gone for a couple of hours."

In response to Austin's pointed gaze, Quinn nodded. Austin headed out the door.

"What was that about?" April asked.

"That was my friend being not so subtle about letting me know he's giving us some time alone."

"Oh." She sipped her coffee, then set it down and stared at the cup, avoiding looking his way.

It was clear she wasn't sure what he expected. He might want to talk. Or he might order her down on her knees in front of him again.

He took her hand and cradled it in his. "Baby, I just want to tell you that I'm sorry about the things I've accused you of and the way I've treated you."

Her gaze jerked to his. "You've treated me very well." She shook her head. "You didn't think twice about paying my bill yesterday. You let me stay here—"

"And I agreed to a sexual arrangement with you. Then when I had a chance to finally be with you—something I'd wanted for so long—I had you suck me off, then right afterward dragged

you down to the casino without even a thank-you, let alone sat-
isfying your needs, too."

"It's all right," she said hesitantly. "Austin was waiting."

"Fuck Austin," he said sharply.

She glanced up at him. Her hand tightened around his, and
he noticed amusement shimmer in her eyes.

"I did, thank you." Her lips turned up in a grin. "I quite
enjoyed it, too."

He couldn't help it. He chuckled, tension releasing
from him. At least she was okay with the whole threesome
thing.

He smiled. "I'm glad about that. I'd hate to think I trauma-
tized you by including that in the arrangement."

"It's really okay, Quinn. You have nothing to be sorry about.
All you've done is help me. And the arrangement was my suggestion, so you didn't take advantage."

"I did blow it, though." He stroked her cheek, gazing into
her eyes with regret. "The first time I made love to you was a
twenty-second bang against the door." He shook his head.

She leaned closer, her eyes bright and a smile on her lips.
"Yes, I remember." Her voice was sultry. "I loved that you wanted
me that much."

A surge of need rose in him. "Damn straight I want you."

She smiled. "So what are you going to do about it?"

His fingers curled tighter around hers, and he stood up,
drawing her to her feet and pulling her toward the bedroom.
Once inside, he closed the door, then drew her close.

He gazed into her eyes, his arms around her.

"This time, I'm going to do things right." He gently stroked
her cheek, loving the feel of her silken skin beneath his fingertips.

He pressed his lips to her neck right at the jawline, below her ear. He nuzzled, and her soft sigh and the way she melted against his body sent heat rushing through him. He fluttered light kisses along her jaw, then tipped her face up until her luminous blue eyes gazed into his.

"God, you're beautiful."

Hesitation flickered in her eyes. "You know you don't have to flatter me. I'm yours no matter what."

He knew she wanted this. She'd practically suggested it. But now that he was opening up to her, he could tell that she was fearful. Trying to keep a distance. He couldn't blame her with the way he'd made it clear what he thought about her. She didn't want to be hurt.

Fuck, the last thing in the world he wanted to do was hurt her. She'd been hurt so much by her bastard of a fiancé. And by life.

Whatever he'd thought of her and her motives in the past, right now, all he saw was a vulnerable woman who needed love.

And that's just what he was going to give her.

"Baby, I know we have an arrangement. But right now, I want you to be with me because you want to be, not because you feel obligated. Is that possible, or have I ruined any chance of that between us?"

Her eyes softened, and the haunting pain that had shadowed them ever since he remembered, even though he hadn't recognized what it was, faded ever so slightly.

She stroked her hand over his whisker-roughened cheek. "Quinn, I do want to be with you."

His heart pounded at her words.

She eased closer, her full lips parting slightly, and he dipped down and captured them. The sweetness of her kiss filled him with desire. He glided his tongue forward, nudging her lips. She opened, welcoming him inside.

He slid into her mouth, finding her tongue. He stroked it, then suckled. Her soft, delighted murmurs sent his heart into a staccato beat, and his cock surged to life.

His hands glided down her back, and he pulled her tighter to him. The hard ridge of his cock pressed against her, and the feel of her warmth made his groin ache.

"Oh, God, baby. I want you so bad."

"I know. I can feel it." Her hand stroked down his stomach, then over his bulge. Then she squeezed lightly, driving him insane with need. "What would you like me to do now, sir?" she asked as she started to crouch down.

But he grasped her arms and drew her back up.

"No. No *sir* or *Mr. Taylor* right now. Call me *Quinn*."

She pressed her lips to his jawbone, then fluttered light kisses to his ear.

"Yes, Quinn," she whispered. Her soft breath in his ear sent tingles dancing down his neck and along his spine. "Whatever you want."

His cock twitched against her.

"You don't get it, April. I want this to be us. A husband and wife making love for the first time. I want to forget what happened when we got back to the suite last night. The way I took you against the door. I want this to be special."

She tipped her head, and a soft smile played on her lips. "That *was* special, Quinn. I've never felt more wanted."

"I acted like an ass. Taking what I wanted without worrying about your needs."

She laughed softly. "Well, then you really are a talented man because you met my needs with spectacular success."

She stroked her fingers through his hair, then pressed her lips to his temple and nuzzled.

"And if you really want to meet my needs now"—she nibbled his earlobe, then murmured softly—"then make love to me."

April felt Quinn's big hands cup her butt, and he pulled her tightly to him again. His thick, hard shaft pressed against her.

Oh, God, she longed to have it inside her again. When he'd taken her against the door as if he couldn't wait a moment longer, it had been primal and exciting. Now he would take it slow and easy, gliding his incredible cock inside her in long, deep strokes.

Her insides melted, and she felt her knees growing weak.

She stepped back and unzipped her dress, then let it fall to the floor. Now she stood before him in only her bra. His gaze glided down her body, the heat of it igniting a blaze of desire inside her. She reached around and unhooked her bra, then slowly eased it from her breasts.

When she dropped it to the floor, too, he rested his hands on her shoulders, then glided them down her arms, his gaze falling to her breasts. His eyes glittered with desire.

She unfastened the buttons of his shirt as quickly as she could, then pushed it from his shoulders. He shrugged out of it, then wrapped his arms around her and hugged her close. The feel of his hot, smooth skin against her sensitive nipples caused them to harden and spike forward.

"Oh, fuck, baby."

His hand cupped one breast gently. As his thumb brushed over her hard nub, she sucked in air.

"Mmm, that's so nice." She rested her head against this shoulder, enjoying his caresses.

He nuzzled her neck, then kissed down her chest until he found one hard bud. He took it in his mouth and suckled softly.

She arched her head back. "Oh, yes."

He drew away, a big smile on his face, then he scooped her up and carried her to the bed. After he laid her down, he stared at her naked body so long she almost wanted to cover herself, sure he'd find flaws.

"I've dreamed of seeing you like this so many times. I can't believe it's finally happening."

17

The look of awe in Quinn's eyes moved April. She opened her arms to him in invitation. He shed his pants, then his boxers. Her attention focused on his impressive cock, standing straight up, ready for her. He lowered himself onto her, and it pressed tightly against her belly. Hot and hard.

She reached down and wrapped her hand around it, then pressed the tip to her slickness.

But he stilled her hand and drew it away.

"Not yet, baby," he murmured in her ear. "I'm going to take my time. To explore your body. To find out what you like."

She giggled and wrapped her hand around his cock again. "I like *this*."

He chuckled. "That's good."

He rolled them over. Now she was on top of him.

"What do you like about it?"

His grin warmed her, making it easier to relax.

"I like how thick it is." She stroked its length. "And how long." She squeezed it. "And I *love* how hard it is." She smiled. "I think it'll fit perfectly inside me."

"Really? Where inside?"

She laughed. "Well . . . In my mouth."

She kissed the tip of his cock, then opened her lips around it and eased downward until she took the whole cockhead inside. She suckled, to his moan.

She drew her mouth from him, her hand still firmly around the shaft, and pushed herself up on her knees. She brushed his cockhead against her intimate flesh again.

"And right in here." She teased him by gliding his tip back and forth through her slickness.

"Right where, baby? I'm not sure I know what you mean."

His teasing grin delighted her. But he wanted an answer. He wanted to hear her talk dirty.

And why not? She wanted to talk dirty to him.

To be dirty for him.

"Inside my pussy." She glided it along her length again, longing to feel it push inside her aching passage. "I'm getting desperate to feel your cock there. It's so thick it'll stretch me wide. And when you drive it in, I'll moan at the sinful pleasure it'll give me."

"Really? You're saying you want me to drive it inside you?" His voice was thick with need.

He drew her hand from his cock and wrapped his own around it. She glided her hands over his taut, ridged stomach to his chest, then teased his bead-hard nipples.

"That's right. I want you to fuck me hard," she murmured. "To drive that long cock of yours into me so far, I'll feel it in my throat."

His midnight-blue eyes glittered, and he laughed. "You are a vixen. You're determined to hurry me up, but . . ." He rolled her over again and trapped her under him, holding her wrists over her head. "I insist on having my way with you."

He captured one nipple in his mouth and suckled, to her soft moan. Her bud ached as he pulled it deeper into his mouth. His tongue played over it, rolling it, then spiraling around it. Then he suckled again.

"Oh, God, that feels so good," she moaned.

He chuckled, then moved to her other nipple and toyed with it in the same way.

She arched against him, pushing her bud deeper into his warmth. His tongue played over it, lapping hard, then delicately teasing. She moaned softly, and he suckled. His cock was rock-hard against her belly, and she rocked her hips upward, pressing his shaft tightly between their bodies.

He chuckled against her soft flesh. Then he glided downward, releasing her wrists. He nuzzled her stomach, then licked her navel. His tongue dipped inside and swirled. He kissed sideways next, his lips brushing over her hipbone, then back toward her stomach again.

Her breathing was increasing as she longed for him to find her slick flesh. His mouth grazed her outer folds and she murmured, opening her legs for him. His lips brushed her sensitive inner thighs, and delightful shimmers of pleasure quivered through her. She arched her hips, hoping to draw him back to her needy place, but he moved down her thigh to the inside of her knee, then shifted to the other leg. She held her breath as he kissed upward again.

Finally, his lips brushed her outer folds again. She licked her lips, aching inside at the feel of his mouth so close to where she wanted it.

He gazed up at her with a smile. "What is it you want me to do now, baby?"

"I want you to . . . uh . . . lick my pussy. And to slide your fingers inside."

His eyebrow arched. He pressed his tongue to her pussy and gave it a quick lick. Her whole body quivered with need.

He gazed at her again. "Is that what you want?"

She nodded vigorously.

His deep chuckle rumbled through her. Then his lips found her intimate folds and glided her length, drawing her delicate petals into his mouth as he moved. Her fingers tangled in his wavy hair. His tongue dipped inside her opening and swirled around. She ached, wanting him so badly.

He eased back and stared at her wet flesh. He glided his fingers over it, an expression of wonder on his face. Then his fingers slid inside her, and her eyelids fluttered closed. He pressed in deep, then began to move in and out gently. His tongue found her again and he licked upward to her clit.

"Oh, God, yes," she said as pleasure rippled through her.

He lapped at her sensitive bud, his tongue curling over and around it. When he covered her and began to suckle, she tightened her hands around his head, holding him close, as blissful sensations blossomed inside her.

His fingers continued to glide into her. His thumb found her clit as his mouth moved away, but she could still feel his breath on her. She opened her eyes to see him gazing at her.

"Baby, I love tasting you like this."

He continued watching her with his warm, midnight-blue eyes as the pleasure stormed through her. Then he captured her clit with his mouth again, still watching her.

She arched again, needing him desperately.

"That feels so good, Quinn. I'm getting close."

His eyes glittered, and he suckled her nub as his fingers slid deeper inside her, then began to thrust. Her whole body tightened as electricity danced over her nerve endings, lighting a fire inside her.

"Ohhh," she murmured softly, tossing her head back on the pillow. The pleasure kept rising as his fingers thrust into her and his mouth suckled her nub.

She rocked against his mouth.

"Yes, I'm going to come, I . . ."

He suckled her deeper, watching her with those dark eyes of his.

Then it happened. An explosion of pure ecstasy jolted through her, tossing her over the edge of eternity. She moaned, low at first, then growing louder until the sound filled the room.

"Fuck, baby. It's so beautiful when you come." After he uttered the words, his mouth was back on her immediately.

She arched and wailed, riding the wave of rapture. She wished he was in her arms, but at the same time didn't want him to move from where he was. Not now.

The orgasm rocked through her. Then slowly faded.

When he finally lifted his mouth, she was sucking in air, her body slumped on the bed. He prowled over her and nuzzled her neck, then lay down beside her. She glanced at his smiling face, then giggled at his expression of complete satisfaction.

"You're certainly pleased with yourself," she said, her own lips turning up.

"Shouldn't I be?" he asked.

Her eyebrows arched. "Actually, yes, you should be. That was spectacular."

He rolled on top of her, propping his elbows on either side of her face. "And now, my sweet bride, I'm going to make love to you." He nuzzled her ear. "For the first time."

She smiled, happy to live this fantasy with him.

"Well, my dearest husband, this is my first time ever." She hooked her arms around his neck. "But I'm not afraid, because I know you'll be gentle."

He gazed down at her, and the depth of feeling in his eyes tugged at her heart. If she hadn't broken up with him back in college, he would have been her first.

She bit her lip. She wished she could have given him that. It was clear it would have meant the world to him.

He stroked the hair from her face. "I will, my love," he murmured tenderly.

She felt his hand against her stomach as it wrapped around his rigid cock. His hips eased up, and she felt his hot tip brush against her slick flesh. He stroked her length several times, his gaze never leaving her face. The intensity in his eyes as he positioned himself at her center took her breath away.

"I'm going to fill you now, sweetheart."

She nodded, her body aching for him to be inside her.

Slowly, their gazes locked, and he pushed forward. His tip slid inside.

"Ohhh, Quinn." The feel of him filling her, his thick, hard shaft opening her as it glided in deep, stroking her canal, was exquisite.

Each breath she took was like a drop in a tranquil pool, ripples spreading outward. Filling her whole being with a quiet, yet deeply profound bliss. His eyes darkened to almost black as his cock became a part of her, so deeply imbedded in her body she could barely tell where he ended and she began.

His hips met hers, and she knew he was all the way inside her now. She squeezed him, wanting him deeper still. Wanting to become one with him.

His lips found hers, and the tender kiss opened her heart, drawing out her deepest feelings. The ones she kept hidden even from herself.

Oh, God, she loved this man.

But she couldn't allow herself that luxury.

She tightened her arms around him, not wanting this time with him to end. Ever.

Their lips parted, and he stared deep into her eyes, his own glowing.

Then he smiled and started to move. His cock dragged along her inner passage, triggering joyful waves of delight. Then it glided deep again. She squeezed around him, and he groaned.

He rocked his hips faster, filling her with his marble-hard cock again and again. She sucked in air, still enthralled by the mesmerizing spell of his eyes.

"You feel so good around me, baby." The ache in his voice echoed through her.

She tightened her arms around him. "I love you inside me, Quinn. I never want this to end."

He smiled, deepening the intensity of his eyes. "I'm afraid it's going to end soon because any minute now, I'm going to come inside you, my sweet. But I won't allow that to happen until I've fully satisfied you."

His cock filled her again, and he nuzzled her ear. Then he swirled his cock as he pulled back, then thrust hard into her. She moaned as sparks flickered through her.

He thrust again.

"Yes, Quinn," she murmured against his temple as she tightened around him, a sweltering need burning through her. "Please make me come."

His lips brushed her cheek, and his eyes glowed with determination. He thrust deep again and again. She arched against him, meeting him stroke for stroke. Her breathing increased as her insides coiled tighter.

"Oh, I'm so close."

"Tell me . . . baby. Are you . . . going to . . . come?" The words were punctuated by his thrusts.

She nodded, her whole body quivering with need. "Oh, yes. Quinn."

Bliss rose inside her, and she sucked in a breath.

"Oh, God." She catapulted over the edge, clinging to him as she fell into the void of rapture. "You're making me come."

The reedy words were a mere echo in her ears as her body shuddered with her release. Her world shattered as the rapture exploded through her, sending her into free fall.

Then he groaned, and his cock erupted inside her. She moaned again, flung back into euphoria.

Quinn continued pumping into her, keeping her at the height of ecstasy, until finally, the pleasure faded and she gasped for air. Then he rolled onto his side and held her against him, his arms wrapped tightly around her as if he'd never let go.

She rested her head against his muscular chest and nuzzled

his warm skin. At the comforting sound of his heartbeat pounding in her ear, she sighed contentedly and snuggled closer, feeling warm and protected in his arms.

Quinn woke up to the sound of his phone vibrating on the bedside table. He grabbed it and saw a text from Austin.

It's been 3 hours. Want to grab dinner or still getting busy?

Quinn pushed his hair back from his face as he sat up, then tapped in his reply.

Meet you at Casey's in 15.

He glanced at April and saw her eyes were open, if only halfway. He couldn't help smiling at the sight of her all sleepy and adorable.

"Is that from Austin?" she asked as she stretched her arms wide.

Her chest arched upward with the movement, her breasts pushing against the white sheet covering her. He'd love to pull back that sheet and reveal her lovely naked body, then ravish her all over again.

Fuck, it had been incredible being with her, making love to her the way he'd always dreamed of doing. A part of him had been afraid that the actual experience could never live up to what he'd imagined, but in fact, it had been even better.

"Hey, my eyes are up here."

At her words, Quinn's gaze shifted back to her face. Her lips were turned up in a teasing smile.

He chuckled. "Yes, and they're very lovely eyes." He reached for the sheet and tugged it down. "Almost as magnificent as your beautiful breasts."

He leaned down and kissed the soft flesh, close to but avoiding the budding nipple. If he took one of those in his mouth, then Austin would wind up waiting a lot longer than fifteen minutes.

He sat up and grinned at her. "But I'm not going to give in to your seductive persuasion right now." He stood up and walked toward the dresser, knowing she was watching his naked ass. "I promised Austin we'd meet him for dinner."

"What? I wasn't seducing you. It was you who pulled the covers down."

He chuckled. "Whatever you say, baby."

He grabbed a pair of clean boxers from the drawer and pulled them on.

"Quinn?"

He turned to see her sitting up in the bed, the covers around her waist. His cock immediately lurched.

Her expression was serious, and she opened her arms. Like a man in a spell, he moved to her, then sat beside her and took her in his arms. She squeezed him tightly. Her warm, soft breasts against him filled him with a deep yearning to be inside her again.

Then she gazed up at him, her blue eyes gleaming. "What we did earlier . . ." She shook her head, her golden-blond hair shimmering over her shoulders in sun-gilt waves. "It was amazing."

She tipped up her face, and her irresistible pink lips called to him. He dipped down and captured them, kissing her with growing passion. His cock sprang up, ready for action, aching for her.

He stroked her hair back and gazed into her eyes. "I think Austin can wait a few more minutes."

She smiled and nuzzled his neck, sending tingles dancing across his skin. Then her head popped up, and her smile turned to an impish grin.

"Oh, I don't think that would be fair to Austin."

To his shock, she slipped from his arms and hopped from the bed. Totally naked, she strolled across the room toward her dress, which was lying in a heap on the floor. As he watched her delightfully round ass sway, she glanced over her shoulder.

"You see? If I were going to seduce you, that's how I'd do it."

18

Quinn laughed. Damn, but she was a delight.

April picked up her dress and then glanced around the floor. He noticed her bra lying near his feet and leaned over to hook his finger through the strap and then held it out to her.

"Looking for this?" he asked, stepping toward her.

She took it and slipped it on. He leaned against the dresser and watched as she straightened her breasts in the cups, wishing he was the one handling those soft, round mounds. Then she pulled her dress on and smoothed it down.

"Aren't you going to put on panties?" he asked.

"Austin has them. Remember?"

"Right. And the black ones you wore in the pool still aren't back?"

"Apparently, they got damaged in the wash. But you don't really want me to wear panties anyway, do you?"

He grinned. "Well, that's true." He stepped close and slid his arms around her waist, drawing her close to his body. "But you really should get some new ones. And some clothes, too. I love this dress, but you need something else to wear."

She drew away from him, a little stiff.

"That would be nice, but I don't have any money."

He could feel her withdrawing from him, and he hated it. She tried to step away, but he caught her hand.

"You know, I'm happy to pay for some new clothes for you."

She drew her hand free and put a little distance between them.

"I'm not borrowing more money from you."

"Sweetheart, be reasonable. You can't go an entire month with just one dress and no underwear."

She drew in a breath and shook her head, but he caught her quick glance in the mirror and the doubt flickering across her eyes. He wanted to insist, but now was not the time.

"When did you say we're meeting Austin?" she asked.

He glanced at his watch. "In about three minutes."

She arched her eyebrow. "You should get cracking then."

Quinn walked to the closet and retrieved a fresh shirt, then donned a charcoal-gray suit and a silk tie in a gray and violet pattern. He offered her his elbow. She curled her fingers around it and accompanied him to the door.

They'd have a nice evening, then in the morning, he'd ensure that one way or another, she had some nice things to wear.

Austin saw Quinn and April walk toward the table, accompanied by the hostess. April had a subtle glow, and Quinn seemed more relaxed than Austin had seen him in . . . forever.

"I'm sorry we kept you waiting," April said as she sat down.

"It was my fault," Quinn said. "I was a little slow getting dressed after our nap."

Austin smiled. "If I had been napping with April, I would resist getting back into my clothes, too."

The waitress appeared and set two drinks on the table.

"I went ahead and ordered drinks for you," Austin said.

"Would you like a refill now, Mr. Wright?" the waitress asked.

"No, I'm good, thanks." Austin's glass was still half-full.

"This doesn't have the same liquor I was drinking last night, does it?" April asked, eyeing the cocktail.

"No, I didn't think you'd want something that strong tonight. I ordered you today's special, which has mango, pineapple, and vodka. If you'd rather have something else, we can change it."

"No, it sounds delicious. Thank you." She sipped it, and the look of delight on her face made him smile.

"I thought we might catch a show after dinner," he suggested. "I hear they have a great new magician."

"No gambling tonight?" April asked.

"No, that's what I've been doing for the past couple of hours. I wanted to reserve the rest of the evening to spend with the two of you."

April lifted the spear of fruit from the top of her drink and pulled off a chunk of pineapple. As she chewed, the spear fell from her fingers and landed on her skirt. She glanced down and swept the fruit from her lap into a napkin.

"Oh, no. The maraschino cherry juice will stain." She stood up. "Excuse me."

They watched as she hurried in the direction of the ladies' room.

Austin turned to Quinn. "I take it things went well."

Quinn nodded, his gaze lingering in the direction April had disappeared.

"They went spectacularly well."

"That's great. Unless that means I'm spending the rest of our trip in the guest room."

"I'm glad you mentioned that, because I didn't want to ask."

Austin's jaw dropped. "Really?"

Quinn chuckled. "No. I'm kidding. But you should see your face. Do you really think I'd shut you out like that?"

"Well, if I was in love with the woman—which you are— and especially if I was married to her—which you are—then, yeah, I'd probably shut you out."

"First, you're married to her, too. Second, we don't need to start bandying about the *love* word. We have a month together."

"Are you still denying you love the woman?"

"I'm just saying we need to take it slow."

"Despite the fact you married her within twenty-four hours of meeting again?"

"*Especially* because of that," Quinn insisted. "She just got out of a really bad relationship, and we've just connected again. She can't really trust my feelings for her. She knows what I believed about her before. If I jump in now with talk of love, she's not going to believe it and she might bolt. Or more likely, in the position she's in, she'll stay, but feel trapped. I want to make this as easy on her as possible."

"So we proceed as if nothing's changed?"

"That's right."

Austin was happy for Quinn, who seemed to have finally come to terms with his feelings for the lovely April. It also made Austin a little sad. He'd have the next month with her, and probably fall deeper under her spell, only to have to give her up at the end.

April stood at the door of the suite, her fingers curled around Austin's bent elbow as Quinn unlocked the door. The magician had been talented and funny, amazing them with spectacular illusions.

Quinn opened the door, and they followed him inside. Then Austin turned and drew her into his arms and stole a kiss. Then he deepened it. She reacted to his masculine heat and melted against him, gliding her tongue along his, but when he drew back, guilt surged through her. Her gaze darted to Quinn. After this afternoon's tender lovemaking, would Quinn assume the threesome was off?

But he smiled, then stepped behind her and nuzzled her neck. Austin kissed her again, and her body ached being between these two powerful men.

Quinn took her hand and led her across the living room toward the bedroom, Austin right behind them.

April sat up in bed and glanced from Quinn to Austin in the morning light. Quinn was turned away from her, and Austin was stretched out on his back on the other side of her. She tried to slip out from under the covers without waking them, but as soon as she freed her legs, Austin's arm slid around her and pulled her close.

God, she'd never get used to waking up between these two hot, hard men.

"Morning," Austin rumbled from his chest. "Where you going?"

His eyelids were barely open, so she could only catch a glimpse of his teal-blue eyes.

"Bathroom," she whispered. "Trying not to wake you and Quinn."

"Okay." But he pulled her closer. "Don't be gone long."

Then he rolled her over his body and set her on the edge of the bed. The feel of his hard muscles and warm skin pressed against her as he'd spun her over left her breathless. She scooted to her feet and headed to the bathroom, her heart pounding. When she returned to the bedroom, she didn't feel like going back to sleep, so she glanced around for her clothes. She couldn't see her dress or bra anywhere. Nor could she find one of the men's discarded shirts to put on, and she didn't want to walk around naked.

She looked in the closet and found a white velour robe supplied by the hotel. She pulled it on. It was miles too big for her, but it would have to do. She tied the sash around her waist and wandered into the living room, hoping to find the clothes in a heap out there somewhere.

No luck.

"I thought you were coming back to bed."

She glanced up to see Austin standing a few yards away, naked and sleepy-looking. And oh, so sexy.

"I didn't want to go back to sleep, and now I can't find my dress." She peered behind the couch.

"Well, there are other things we can do in bed besides sleep," he suggested.

She glanced at him with a grin. "Are you saying I didn't do enough to satisfy you last night?"

His lips turned up as he walked toward her.

"Oh, sweetheart, you did more than satisfy me." He pulled her into a kiss. When he drew back, he gazed down at her. "I just can't get enough of you."

"What are you two doing up?" Quinn asked from the bedroom doorway.

"It seems I've woken the whole household," April said. "Sorry, Quinn."

"Not a problem." He walked to the couch and sat down. "I'll order some breakfast."

Austin took her hand and led her to the couch as Quinn dialed the phone. She sat down between Quinn and Austin. Quinn ordered a breakfast platter for three and coffee.

"She's looking for her dress," Austin mentioned as Quinn hung up the phone.

"Yeah, I sent it out with the other clothes to be cleaned."

"But that's the only dress I have to wear," April protested.

"That's why I did it. Now you'll have something clean to put on, even if it is the same dress." Quinn grinned. "You're welcome."

"What she really needs is to buy some new clothes," Austin said. "April, I know you don't have any money, but we can arrange for you to charge them to the room."

"I already told her that, but she refused."

Austin turned to her. "Sweetheart, we're happy to give you the money. But if you won't accept it, we can consider it a loan. You can pay us back whenever you can."

She glanced from Austin to Quinn. She didn't want to be in any more debt to Quinn, but she knew she was being stubborn. What Quinn had said yesterday was true. It didn't make sense to keep wearing the same dress for a month. And she missed wearing panties.

"When will the clothes be back?" she asked. "I don't relish wearing this oversize robe for long."

Quinn smiled. "I think you look adorable in it. But they'll probably bring up your dress with breakfast. I told them to rush it."

"Good. Thank you."

"And then after breakfast, you'll go out shopping?" Austin persisted.

She hesitated.

"We could always refuse your dress when it arrives," Quinn

said. "Then you'll be stuck wearing this robe." His lips crept up into a grin. "Or nothing at all."

"No fair. The two of you are ganging up on me."

Austin laughed and slid his arm around her. Quinn did, too, and they moved in closer, their bodies pressing tightly against her.

"But, baby, we love ganging up on you," Quinn said. "Especially in bed."

"You're both terribly wicked, you know."

"And you love it," Austin teased.

Quinn took her hand, then turned her to him. "Seriously, April, we've come so far. Let me do this for you."

She gazed into his solemn blue eyes and bit her lip. Finally, she nodded.

"Okay, I . . . uh . . . thank you."

Once she was finished breakfast, April donned her clean dress and headed to the shops in the hotel. Austin and Quinn wanted to come with her, but she refused. Although it could be fun, she didn't need them helping her pick out bras and panties or trying to talk her into more expensive clothing than she was comfortable buying. She intended to pay this back, and the fact she had to shop in the hotel meant it would already be a hefty bill.

By the time she walked out of the third store, she wore new lingerie and a simple, fitted, royal-blue dress that could be worn during the day or dressed up for evening. It was comfortable and flattering. She wore new shoes, also royal blue. She knew it was more practical to stick with her one pair of black, but she'd indulged, mainly because she loved the iridescent panel along the front that shimmered like a fairy's wings.

"Ms. Smith. Wait."

She turned to see the salesperson who'd been helping her standing in the store entrance.

April walked back to her. "Is there a problem?"

"Could you come back inside for a moment, please?"

"Why?" But she followed the woman into the store again.

"I don't know why. I got a call from the manager."

April's stomach clenched. Were they going to confiscate her packages? Tell her she couldn't put them on Quinn's bill?

But that didn't make sense.

Unless Quinn had changed his mind.

Her head started spinning, but she knew Quinn wouldn't do that. She was just gun-shy from the way the manager had treated her on Saturday.

The woman led her to a pair of comfy chairs, and April sat down, her stomach fluttering. She set her bags down on the floor beside her.

"Ms. Smith, I'm glad I caught up with you."

She turned to see Mr. Gunter, the hotel manager walking toward her. She cringed inside.

She felt conspicuous with the many shopping bags around her, sure he believed she was a gold digger taking advantage of yet another wealthy man.

"I needed some clothes," she babbled as he stopped in front of her, knowing she shouldn't be trying to justify her actions.

"Of course, Ms. Smith. I hope enjoy your purchases."

"I'm sure I will."

He sat down in the chair beside her. "The reason I wanted to find you is that Mr. Dubois called me. He asked if I knew where you were, and I told him you're still in the hotel."

Her heart stammered, her chest was so tight. "What does

he want now? Does he think I'm still holding something back from him? Because your staff already went through my luggage—"

"No, nothing like that, Ms. Smith."

Now that he was sitting beside her, she realized he seemed a little nervous, and she saw the look of deference in his expression.

He reached into his pocket and pulled out a folded sheet of paper. "He asked me to give you this message."

She frowned. "Why didn't he just email me? Or call?"

"He told me he didn't think you'd take his call after all that happened. And he very much wants you to read this."

Anger surged through her, and she stood up. She snatched the paper from his hand and tore it in two, then handed it back to him.

"Well, Mr. Dubois doesn't always get what he wants."

Then she stormed from the store.

When April entered the suite, Quinn glanced up from his book. Her heart raced as his heated gaze glided over her. It was very clear he liked her new dress.

And she was sure he was wondering what she wore under it.

"That dress looks lovely on you," he said.

"I second that," Austin said with an appreciative smile.

"Thank you," she said. But she couldn't muster a smile. She was still unnerved by Maurice's attempt to contact her.

She took off her new shoes and put them in the closet, then walked into the sitting area and sank into an armchair.

"Did your shopping trip go well?" Quinn asked.

"Uh . . . yes. I bought three dresses, a pair of shoes, and a nice assortment of lingerie. They're sending the packages up."

After she'd hurried from the store, she'd realized she'd left them behind. Not wanting to go back, she'd called the store on a hotel phone, and they assured her they'd handle getting the packages safely to her suite. Then she'd taken a long walk outside to clear her head.

"They already arrived," Austin said. "I put them in the bedroom."

"Thank you." She felt stiff and distracted. Not quite sure what to do with herself.

The fact that Maurice had tried to contact her had shaken her more than she would have thought. She was over him, but the pain of his betrayal still left her devastated.

"April, is there something wrong?" Austin asked.

"No, nothing. I'm just . . . tired."

Her phone chimed, and she opened her purse and pulled it out. She felt the blood drain from her face when she saw that it was Maurice calling her. She ended the call with a jab of her finger and shoved the phone back in her purse.

"Who was that?" Austin asked.

Nervously, she glanced at Austin's concerned expression. She did not want to tell them about Maurice trying to contact her. They'd want to talk about it, and she just wanted to put it behind her.

"No one. Just one of those spam calls."

Quinn leaned forward, his midnight-blue gaze locking on her.

"You're sure there's nothing wrong? Did something happen while you were out?"

"I'm fine. Really." She stood up. "As I said, just tired. I think I'll take a nap before dinner."

April sipped her drink, waiting for Quinn and Austin. They'd been out playing golf this afternoon and had arranged to meet her in the lounge overlooking the garden. She wore one of her new dresses, a slinky red strapless that made her feel sexy.

Over the past several days, she'd immersed herself in enjoying her time with them. They were both very attentive, and Quinn had a glow in his eyes whenever he looked at her. She could almost convince herself that he was falling for her all over again, but she knew that was just wishful thinking. He was just relaxed and enjoying the free and easy sexual relationship the three of them were sharing.

Her stomach tightened. A relationship that would be over all too soon. Then she'd be on her own again and have to figure out what she was going to do next. How she would start over again with nothing.

A waitress walked toward her table with a smile. "Ms. Smith, I have a message for you."

Panic raced through her. "I'm sorry, if it's from Mr. Dubois, I don't—"

"No, ma'am. It's from Mr. Wright. He said you left your cell phone in the suite. He said to tell you the game went late and asked that you meet them in the casino in about ten minutes. He said you'd know which one."

"Oh, thank you." Her racing heart slowed.

"Would you like me to let him know you'll be there?"

"Yes, that would be great. Thanks," April said.

The waitress placed the bill on the table before she left.

Damn it, just because Maurice had tried to have a message delivered to her, then attempted to contact her a couple of times, was she going to jump every time hotel staff approached her?

She added a tip to the total on the bill and signed, then grabbed her purse and headed to the casino.

•   •   •

Quinn walked into the living room as he finished knotting his tie. He'd just showered and shaved and was looking forward to the evening.

"That was a great game." Austin was sitting on the couch tying up his glossy black shoes.

"Better for you than me since you won." Quinn grinned. "Now we're going to that poker game tonight where you'll be the biggest winner at the table, I'm sure."

Austin chuckled. "You do all right. And you love the rush as much as I do."

"To tell the truth, what I'm really looking forward to is getting my arms around my wife and enjoying another kind of game. One where I'm sure I'll be a winner."

"Hey, she's my wife, too."

"I didn't say you weren't going to win, too. I think it's safe to say all three of us have been winners in this particular arrangement."

Instead of laughing, Austin's expression grew serious. "I'm not so sure about April."

Quinn's eyes narrowed. "What do you mean by that?"

"Don't get me wrong. I know she's enjoying the sex. It's just that . . . haven't you noticed that she's been distracted the past few days? Withdrawn. Something's definitely bothering her."

Quinn had noticed. He'd felt a growing distance between them and wondered if she was pulling away so she didn't get too attached.

Although he needed time to get used to these new feelings for her and for her to see that his attitude about her had changed, he wished he could tell her how much he cared about her. He would have loved to buy her flowers or other gifts to show her, but he knew that would make her uncomfortable, so he'd focused on showing her as best he could in bed.

"She's been through a rough time," Quinn said, "and I'm sure she's worried about what's going to happen at the end of the month."

"I wish there were some way we could reduce her anxiety," Austin said.

Quinn glanced at his watch. "One way is not to keep her waiting in the casino."

Austin stood up. "Don't forget to grab her phone."

Quinn strolled to the counter and picked up April's cell phone. As he walked across the room, following Austin to the door, the phone beeped. He glanced down to see a text message display on the screen.

I really am sorry. We need to talk. Call me.

Quinn's gut clenched. "Fuck."

"What is it?"

"It's a text from her ex. He's trying to get her back."

19

After sitting through a few games of roulette with Quinn and Austin, April walked with them to the suite where the exclusive poker game was to take place. As soon as she stepped into the room, she saw Sarah and Jon. Austin and Quinn followed her gaze and spotted them, too.

"We can leave if you want," Austin murmured in her ear.

She straightened her back and held her head high. "No. I made you miss one of these games because of them. Not tonight. I'm not going to run every time I see a friend of Maurice's."

Austin and Quinn sat down at the table, and April sat in a chair behind them since she wasn't playing. Sarah glanced her way, and their gazes locked briefly. Instead of the look of scorn April expected to see, Sarah's expression was subdued.

Sarah and her husband sat farther down the table, so April chose to ignore them. Everyone anted up, and the game began. After about forty minutes, Austin's stack of chips had doubled. Quinn had lost several rounds but was still ahead.

A waitress took April's empty glass and asked if she'd like

another. April shook her head, and as soon as the current hand was over, she leaned in to Quinn.

"I'm going to the ladies' room. I'll be back in a minute."

He glanced her way and smiled, then took her hand and pressed it to his mouth. The gentle contact paired with the complete and focused attention he gave her left her knees weak.

"Don't be too long. I'll miss you," he said.

Her heart pounded as she stood up. His attitude toward her had changed radically since that first day. Gone was the distrusting, angry man. He was so relaxed around her now. And wonderfully attentive.

She didn't allow herself to read anything more into it other than he was enjoying their sexy arrangement.

She stood up and made her way to the door. There were washrooms just off the atrium outside the suite. She walked into the sumptuous room with potted plants, large mirrors, and black sinks embedded in granite countertops, then stepped into one of the stalls with solid wood doors. After she was done, she walked to one of the sinks and washed her hands, then opened her purse to retrieve her lipstick.

As she gazed in the mirror to put it on, Sarah entered and stepped behind her.

"New dress? It looks very nice," Sarah said.

April frowned as she turned to face the other woman, not in the mood for any nasty games.

"What do you want, Sarah?"

"I want to help, actually."

"Help? I don't understand."

Sarah's disapproval had been wholly evident, and it made no sense she'd suddenly change her mind about April.

But Sarah's expression was genuine.

"You've been through a terrible experience with the wedding, and . . . well, Maurice contacted me and told me what really happened."

April's eyebrow quirked up. "He did?"

"He said that it wasn't you who'd cheated on him. It was the other way around. That when you walked away, he panicked and his ego got in the way. He knows what he did was wrong and that blaming you was unforgivable." Sarah stepped forward and took April's hand. "But, dear, he does want you to forgive him. He wants you to give him a chance to make it up to you. He says you won't take his calls, so he contacted me and asked if I'd talk to you."

April shook her head. This was crazy.

"I know he doesn't deserve it," Sarah continued, "but he really does love you. And from everything I've seen over the past two years, I believe you love him, too. I totally understand why you want to walk away, but I urge you to at least listen to what he has to say."

Quinn smiled at the huge stack of chips in front of him. Both he and Austin had done exceptionally well tonight.

He turned to April and took her hand. "You are a great lucky charm."

Austin settled their winnings as Quinn drew her to her feet and hugged her tightly. Her body stiffened, and he drew back.

"What's wrong?"

She shook her head. "Nothing."

"I don't believe you." He smiled encouragingly and tipped up her chin. "Does it have anything to do with the fact those friends of your ex's were here? Because they left over an hour ago, so you can relax and enjoy your husband's attention."

Austin stepped beside her and leaned in with a grin. "If we go back to the suite, you can enjoy both your husbands' attention."

Quinn loosened his hold on her, and the three of them strolled to the door.

They walked through the atrium and took the elevator down. Soon they were in the hustle and bustle of the main level, with shops and restaurants around them and a steady flow of people, even at midnight.

"I would love to buy my beautiful wife a diamond necklace or at least a big bouquet of roses to celebrate our winnings." Austin glanced at her with a smile. "What do you say?"

Her lips turned up in a wistful smile that tugged at Quinn's heart. He wanted to give her the world but couldn't even suggest it.

"No jewelry," she said. "But maybe I'll accept one of those."

She pointed to a woman carrying a basket of roses, and Austin grinned and waved her over.

"But just one," April said firmly.

Austin purchased the rose and handed it to her. A soft blush set her face aglow as she pressed her lips to Austin's cheek in a light kiss. Jealousy washed through Quinn—not directed at Austin but because he wished he'd been the one to give her that small joy.

They reached the elevators that would take them to their floor, and soon they were inside the suite. Austin pulled her into his arms and kissed her. Quinn watched her fingers stroke through Austin's sandy-brown hair, and his heart ached. Then he heard the sound of her zipper unfastening. Austin's hands stroked up her sides, and he leaned back to gaze at her lovely body, then eased her strapless gown downward until it tumbled to her feet, leaving her in a stunningly sexy red-and-black lace bra and panty set.

She turned to Quinn and stepped close, then glided her hands over his chest, and around his neck. He wrapped his arms around her and captured her lips. The sight of her exquisite body had caused his groin to tighten, and now with the warmth of her curves against him, his cock swelled.

Once he got her in the bedroom, he could barely control himself. He stripped off her lingerie and stood admiring her naked body. She unfastened his zipper and reached in to find his cock, but when she crouched down to take it in her mouth, he drew her back to her feet.

"No. I want to be inside you. I want to make you come."

He shed his clothes and backed her up to the bed. Austin was there, too, naked. But all Quinn could think about was being with April. Giving her pleasure.

Their lovemaking was sweet and tender. And absolutely breathtaking. Quinn made her come. Then Austin did, too. The three of them collapsed under the covers in a tangle of limbs, and Quinn watched her in the moonlight as she fell asleep.

"Maurice?"

April stared at her ex-fiancé, her stomach coiling into knots at the sight of his handsome face, his lips turned up in that charismatic smile of his.

"I want to win you back. I want to start over. I want you to be mine."

She stepped back. She was a challenge to him. That's all. He wanted to own her. To control her. She shook her head, continuing to back away from him. Then she bumped into something. She turned to see Quinn standing there, his eyes glowing with love.

"Come to me, baby," Quinn said. "I'll take care of you."

He opened his arms, and she surged into them. They closed around her, and she felt safe in his warm embrace. Protected.

He kissed the top of her head. "I'll love you."

She smiled and gazed up at him. "Yes."

"For a month," he continued. "Then it's over."

Her chest compressed. She stared at him, shaking her head.

"But I love you." Tears streamed down her face as she stared into the depths of his midnight eyes.

He continued smiling, his eyes still glowing with warmth.

How could he look at her like that, his face filled with love, oblivious to her pain? How could he love her and yet exile her from his life?

Her heart sank as she realized it was because he didn't really love her.

Quinn's chest ached as he stared at April's face awash in the moonlight. He'd fallen asleep with a smile on his face, watching her. Feeling close to her.

Then he'd awakened to her murmurs. She'd become restless, then she'd shocked him by uttering her ex's name clearly. She'd shifted and turned in her sleep, then cried out, "But I love you."

Fuck, could it be that she still had feelings for that jerk, despite all he'd done to her?

His stomach knotted. She had been with the man for two years. The guy might have treated her like crap, but if she had genuine feelings for him, if she actually loved him . . .

Quinn knew that Maurice was actively trying to get her back. If she loved him, he might be able to convince her that he would change. That he'd be faithful to her. Because sometimes love is blind.

April shifted again, then rolled toward him. Her hands glided over his naked chest, sending tremors of need through him, then she snuggled in close and sighed. He closed his arms around her, unable to resist.

But when her lips trailed across his skin in soft kisses, he stiffened.

"Is something wrong?" she murmured.

"Do you even know whose arms you're in right now?" He rolled away from her. "Do you even care?"

Fuck, she'd just told another man that she loved him. Sure, it was in her dream, but that didn't make Quinn feel any less rejected. In real life, she had chosen Maurice over him once, and it looked like she was going to do it all over again. She was going to break his heart all over again.

She stared at him, confusion in her eyes. "I don't understand."

He just shook his head and pushed himself from the bed, needing to get away from her.

20

April watched Quinn go, wondering if she should go after him. She glanced at Austin uncertainly. The moonlight washed across his face, and strands of his sandy-brown hair curled over his forehead. But his eyes were closed.

Hesitantly, she shifted on the bed, but his hand grasped hers.

"I don't know what started all of that," he said, his voice raspy from sleep, "but I suggest you let him stew for a bit. He probably had a bad dream that put him in a mood. Better to see how he is in the morning."

She lay down facing him. "I'm worried that maybe he's jealous. He seems to like the three of us being together, but . . . I don't know. Maybe he doesn't like that I like it so much." She bit her lip. "Maybe his suggestion that you two share me was supposed to be a punishment of sorts."

"Do you think it's a punishment being with me?" His tone was serious, but there was a teasing glitter in his teal eyes.

"No, of course not. I'm really enjoying what we're all sharing together. But I was nervous at first."

He slid his arm around her waist and leaned forward to kiss

her lightly. "I think the two of us sharing you is a huge turn-on for him, so I wouldn't fret about it. If it'll make you feel better, though, I'll talk to him."

"I don't want to do anything to hurt your friendship."

He pulled her close to his hard body and stroked her hair. "Don't worry. Everything's going to work out fine."

She relaxed against him, listening to his steady heartbeat. Letting it relax her. But she couldn't help gazing back at the door, hoping Quinn would return soon.

"Hey, sleepyhead. Time to get up."

April opened her eyes and stared bleary-eyed at Quinn's cheerful face as he stared down at her. Sunlight filled the room, and she blinked a few times.

"It's a beautiful day, and I think we should go for a swim," he said.

He wore his swim trunks, leaving his sculpted chest and arms naked to her appreciative view.

He pulled the covers off her. Sometime during the night, she'd pulled on one of the guys' T-shirts. Quinn scooped her up and carried her into the living room, then outside to the pool.

"There she is." Austin sat on the side of the pool, his legs dangling in the water.

Was Quinn going to throw her in? She couldn't help smiling, happy that he'd gotten past whatever was bothering him last night, at least for now. Maybe Austin had talked with him.

Instead of tossing her into the water, Quinn walked down the steps with her still in his arms. She clung tighter to his neck.

Quinn laughed. "Don't worry. The water's warm."

She rested her head on his shoulder. "I'm not worried. Not when I'm with you."

His gaze washed over her face, his eyes looking troubled for an instant, then he smiled again.

She felt the water on her backside, then climbing up her body until she was immersed. Quinn lowered her legs in the water and took her hand, guiding her to follow him as he swam to the deep end, toward Austin. Once there, Quinn rested his elbow on the side of the pool. She tread water beside him.

Quinn wrapped his arm around her waist and pulled her tightly to his body, then captured her lips. His tongue glided into her mouth and stroked. Her heart stammered at the delightfully possessive kiss, and when he finally drew back, she was breathless.

"Hey, I'd like one of those, too," Austin said.

He held out his hand, and she grasped it, then he pulled her from the water and onto his lap. The T-shirt clung to her body, showing every curve, including her hard, puckered nipples, the tips jutting out from the cloth like arrows.

Austin claimed her lips, thoroughly exploring the inside of her mouth. Their tongues tangled together as his hand glided up her back, pulling her tightly to his chest. The warmth of his sun-drenched skin was delightful against her hard, cold nipples.

Then he leaned back and admired her body with a grin. "You might as well be naked."

He ran his hand down her side, his gaze focused on her breasts. He slid back on the deck and set her between his legs facing the pool.

"Yes, a glorious sight," Quinn agreed.

But Quinn's view wasn't blocked by cloth. He could see her naked pussy.

She squirmed a little in Austin's arms, feeling an ache inside, growing the longer Quinn watched her with those darkening midnight-blue eyes. She liked him looking at her like that, and she opened her legs wider to give him a better view.

Austin's hands slid down her hips, then along her inner thighs. Heat rushed through her having his fingers so close to her melting folds. He drew her legs wider still.

"I want to see you touch that pretty pussy, Austin," Quinn said.

"Really? What about you, April?" Austin asked. "Would you like that, too?"

Need spiked through her. "Yes, please."

Austin's fingers slid up her inner thigh. Painfully slowly. Sending tingles racing along the sensitive flesh. Finally, he reached the outer folds, and she groaned at the first brush of his fingertip. He teased along the outside. She arched forward, wanting him to touch her slick flesh. When his fingers found the smaller petals and glided over them, she moaned softly.

"Do you like Austin touching you, baby?" Quinn asked.

She froze, not sure what to say. Not after last night.

Austin stroked over her again, and pleasure rippled through her body.

"Tell me," Quinn insisted. "I want to know."

"Yes," she breathed. "I love him touching me."

Quinn smiled. "Good."

Quinn grasped her calves and drew her forward until her ass was balanced on the very edge of the pool. Austin wrapped his hands around her waist and lowered her a little more.

With a devilish gleam in his eyes, Quinn leaned forward and pressed his mouth to her soft flesh. At the feel of his tongue stroking her, she whimpered. Then he suckled her clit. Very lightly. Teasing her. She arched against him, depending on Austin to hold her steady.

Quinn's tongue pushed inside her and swirled around, then he glided forward until he was over her clit again. His fingers found her opening and slid inside at the same time as he began to suckle again. She gasped at the exquisite sensations flooding her.

"Oh, yes, Quinn. That feels so good."

His fingers pulsed inside her as he sucked deeply on her bud. Pleasure swelled quickly, at the same time filling her with a desperate, throbbing need.

"Oh, God, make me come, Quinn. I'm so close."

He drove deeper into her, pumping faster. His tongue swept over her clit, then he sucked harder. She coiled her fingers in his dark, wavy hair, pulling him tightly to her, then wailed her release.

He kept her in the throes of orgasm, letting it ease off, then intensifying it again with his talented mouth and fingers. Finally, she collapsed against Austin, gasping for breath.

"Well, someone enjoyed her morning wake-up call."

She stared up at Austin's smiling face and giggled. "Definitely a great way to start the day."

Quinn pushed himself from the pool and stood beside her, dripping on the wooden deck.

"Since you recommend it so highly," Quinn said, "why not give Austin the same treatment?"

Quinn offered his hand, then drew her to her feet. Austin followed as Quinn guided her to the rattan love seat, and she sat down on the thick cushions. Quinn sat down beside her and slid his arm around her, pulling her against him, while Austin dropped his trunks and stood in front of her. Austin's cock was rigid and pointing to the sky.

She wrapped her hand around it and stroked. His hard flesh was thick and hot. She watched the rising desire in his eyes with satisfaction. She leaned forward and licked his tip, then covered it with affectionate butterfly kisses. Next she softly nibbled the ridge.

"Oh, yeah, sweetheart," Austin murmured. His breathing was accelerating.

She smiled, then dipped down to his root and licked the length of him. His teal eyes were dark and filled with need as she opened and took him inside. His cockhead filled her mouth. She ran her tongue all over his hard flesh, then glided deeper.

Quinn's hand slid over her hip, then between her legs. The brush of his finger over her slick flesh sent heat thrumming through her.

"God, I love how wet you are." Quinn stroked back and forth, setting her on fire.

She took Austin deeper still, loving the feel of his thick, hard shaft filling her mouth. Quinn pushed a finger inside her. She squeezed around him while she drew back on Austin's cock, then surged forward to take him deep again. He moaned softly.

Quinn's fingers slipped away, to her disappointment, then she felt him rolling the wet cloth of her T-shirt up her body. He freed her breasts to the warm sunshine. She let go of Austin's cock long enough to tug the garment over her head and toss it aside, leaving her completely naked, then grabbed Austin again and swallowed him inside.

She bobbed up and down on the thick column, savoring the feel of the hard flesh moving across her lips and caressing the inside of her mouth. Quinn cupped her breast in his warm hand. Her nipple was so hard it hurt as it burrowed into his palm. He stroked, then squeezed her aching bud between his fingertips. Burning desire spiked through her. She wanted it in his mouth. She wanted him to suck on it. Hard.

She kept bobbing on the big cock in her mouth, taking it deep into her throat. Squeezing it as it moved between her lips.

Quinn found her pussy again. He slid in a finger and stroked softly, starting a slow burn inside her.

"I love watching you make Austin come." Quinn's voice was hoarse with need as he whispered close to her ear. "I want you to pull him out just before so I can see it."

Pleasure kept building inside her as Quinn continued to stroke her sensitive passage. She glanced up at Austin's face, trying desperately to keep her focus. His eyes were half-closed and his cheeks flushed. He smiled and nodded, then glided his hands around her head and urged her to move faster.

She could feel Austin's body tensing. He would come any moment.

And so would she if Quinn kept it up.

"Now," Austin blurted, then pulled from her mouth.

White liquid pulsed from his cock. Some splattered on April's breasts, but most landed on Quinn's torso. She stared at the glistening white foam on Quinn's bronzed, gleaming flesh, and need drove her to lurch toward him and lap at the wetness. She ran her tongue over his hard muscles, tasting the saltiness of his skin and Austin's semen. She lapped downward, over his taut, sculpted abs, licking all of Austin's essence from Quinn's body.

"Fuck, baby." Quinn grasped her hips and flipped her onto her back, then feasted on her breasts, licking away the white residue on her skin.

Then he captured her lips, driving his tongue into her. Sharing the taste with her.

"Oh, God, Quinn. Please fuck me," she pleaded, practically panting.

Something hot and hard brushed against her pussy, and she moaned. She glanced down to see his hard cock jutting from his trunks, firmly in his hand as he guided it over her wet flesh. He moved the tip up and down, caressing her. Driving her wild.

His hard cockhead settled at her opening, and excitement burned through her as he pushed forward. Just a little.

"Is this what you want?" he asked.

She nodded vigorously, unable to catch her breath.

Her flesh opened to him as he pushed the tip a little deeper.

"You want me to thrust inside? To fuck you hard and fast 'til you come?"

"Yes." The word, uttered on a short exhalation, was filled with need.

He grinned, then pulled back. She whimpered softly.

"I'd love to, baby, but not right now. I want to watch Austin fuck you."

"Austin's not ready yet." But when her gaze flicked to the other man, she saw his hand wrapped around his fully erect cock.

"Sweetheart, you underestimate how intensely sexy it is seeing you turned on," Austin said.

"Kneel in front of me," Quinn instructed as he settled back on the love seat. "And keep your lovely ass high."

She got down on her hands and knees. Austin stepped behind her, then knelt. His fingers found her slickness and he stroked, then she felt his hot tip brush against her. She stared at Quinn's cock standing tall in front of her and wrapped her hand around it, ready to take it in her mouth. But Quinn stopped her.

"No, baby. I want to keep my full attention on you. I want

to watch your face as Austin makes you come." He moved her hand from his cock and rested it on his thigh. "No distractions."

Austin glided forward, pushing inside.

"Ohhhh," she moaned.

He kept moving, filling her with his long, thick member. Then he stopped, his groin tightly against her ass, his cock twitching inside her.

Quinn's midnight eyes burned with desire. "How does it feel?"

"He's really hard and thick," she murmured, squeezing Austin with intimate muscles, setting her head spinning. "I'm squeezing him inside and—"

Austin twitched again, and she moaned.

Quinn chuckled, his face beaming. "I love the fact that Austin's hard cock inside you is turning you on so much." He glanced behind her. "Austin, why don't you start fucking her?"

She felt Austin's cock drag along her passage as he drew back. Then he thrust forward again. Quinn watched her intently as Austin moved in and out, his cock filling her in long, deep strokes.

Her eyelids drooped as the pleasure built inside her.

Quinn cupped her chin and lifted. "Baby, look at me. I want to see your face when you come."

His eyes locked on hers, and she stared into the midnight depths as Austin filled her over and over again.

"Who's fucking you, baby?" Quinn asked. "Who's giving you this pleasure?"

21

April began to tremble in delight. Austin pumped faster. Every stroke of his pulsing column drove her pleasure higher.

"Austin," she answered, still staring deep into Quinn's eyes.

"Are you close?" he asked.

She nodded, barely able to catch her breath. The intensity of Quinn's focus on her amplified every sensation.

"Tell me when you come," he insisted, "and who's making you come."

Austin's hand glided over her hip to her pelvis. He found her clit and stroked it. Pleasure skyrocketed through her.

"Ohhh, yes. I'm going to come. I'm . . ."

He drove deep inside her, and she felt his spasms as hot liquid filled her.

Immediately, she plummeted over the edge. Sparks quivered across every nerve ending, and she found herself drawn into the depths of Quinn's eyes.

"I'm . . . coming. Austin is . . ." she moaned.

Quinn covered her mouth in a quick kiss.

She sucked in a breath as Austin kept rocking his hips. Driving her higher.

She rode the wave of bliss, intensifying with every stroke of his cock. Lost in Quinn's eyes, she plunged into sheer ecstasy.

Quinn's hand cupped her cheek. "You are so beautiful when you come."

The pleasure shimmering through her slowly ebbed. Finally, Austin drew back, his cock dragging from her depths and falling free.

Quinn immediately pulled her into a tight embrace.

"Fuck, I need to be inside you."

He rolled her back until she was lying on the wooden deck. As he prowled over her, her gaze locked on his gigantic cock, swollen and pulsing. She ached inside, anticipating his first thrust.

He pressed his hot cockhead to her opening, then eased in.

"Ohhh, yes," she cried.

He filled her in one long stroke. With her pinned to the deck, their groins tightly together, he leaned forward and kissed her. Deeply. With a tenderness she found almost disturbing.

Then he began to pump, and her thoughts scattered.

His big cock filled her again and again.

"Oh, yes. Make me come again."

"I will, baby. Just tell me. Who's making you come?"

She opened her eyes and stared at his handsome, loving face. "You are, Quinn."

He pumped faster, filling her deeper. The pleasure ignited, catapulting her into a mind-numbing orgasm. She clung to his shoulders, their gazes locked. The depth of tenderness in his eyes made her heart swell.

Then he groaned and erupted inside her, driving her pleasure higher still.

Finally, they collapsed together on the deck, panting. He rolled to his side, smiled, and stroked back her hair. Their gazes locked, and she was sure he was going to say something, but then he kissed her. A sweet brush of lips.

"I don't know about you two, but I'm going for a swim," Austin said, grinning down at them.

She and Quinn sat up as Austin walked to the pool and dove in. Quinn stood up and helped her to her feet, which was good because her knees were a little weak after that.

As she followed Quinn to the pool, her mind wandered back to last night.

He seemed totally all right with sharing her with Austin. In fact, as Austin had pointed out, Quinn seemed to find it a real turn-on.

So what had set him off last night? And why this morning had he looked at her as if . . . Her heart swelled. Well, as if he were actually in love with her?

After a nice lunch delivered to the suite, April curled up on the couch and read a book while Austin and Quinn played chess. After the game, Austin stood up and stretched, then glanced at his watch.

"I've got that tennis court booked for 3 p.m.," he said. "That gives me an hour to hit the casino first. Want to join me?" he asked Quinn.

"No, you go ahead. I'll meet you at the court."

"What about you, April?" Austin asked. "You can hang out at the tables with me, maybe bring me a little luck, then we can play a round-robin of tennis."

"No, thanks. But I think I'll go out and explore a bit. I'll walk down with you. I'll just take a minute to change first."

After their swim, she'd just thrown on a robe.

She hurried into the bedroom and donned her royal-blue bra and panty set, then pulled on the royal-blue dress she'd bought on her shopping trip. She couldn't believe almost a week had passed since then. In fact, it was her one-week anniversary as Mrs. Quinn Taylor. And Mrs. Austin Wright. She couldn't help grinning as she reached behind her to pull up the zipper.

"Let me help you with that," Austin said.

She turned around to see him standing in the doorway, his large frame filling the space, a smile on his face. He walked toward her, and she turned around so he could slide the zipper up. When he reached the top, his hands glided to her shoulders and he squeezed, then his lips played lightly along her neck. Heat simmered through her.

"I don't have to go to the casino now," he murmured.

She turned to face him with a smile. "But you will. Because you know I'll be here when you get back." She curled her arms around his neck and kissed him lightly. "And we can continue this then."

She stroked his cheek affectionately, then kissed him again.

His dark teal eyes gleamed, and he glided his fingers through her hair and drew her in for a deeper kiss. His tongue nudged at her lips until she opened, then he slid inside. Their hearts pounded together as the passion of his kiss seduced her. She was ready to drop her dress on the floor right now.

Then their lips parted, and he grinned. "Okay, so at least give me something to bring me luck at the tables."

"Like what?" she asked, still trying to catch her breath.

His grin broadened, and he dropped his gaze until it rested a few inches below her waist.

"You want my panties?"

He stroked over her hip. "Yes."

"I could give you a pair from my drawer," she suggested, but his glittering eyes told her that just wouldn't do.

He laughed. "That's nowhere near as much fun."

She smiled. "Okay, but just because I like you so much."

His eyes turned serious, and he cupped her face, then tipped it up until their gazes locked.

"You like me?"

She felt her cheeks heat. From the look in his eyes, he wanted her feelings to be more than that.

"I . . . it's more than that. But—"

"So what's going on here?"

Quinn's voice startled her, and her gaze jerked to the doorway to see him standing there with a grin.

"Am I missing out on something?" he asked as he strolled into the room.

Austin's expression lightened as he turned to Quinn, a smile spreading across his face.

"Not much. She's just going to strip off her panties for me. I need a good-luck charm."

Quinn chuckled. "Not likely, but if you're going to have one, that's a brilliant choice."

The two men turned to her expectantly.

The skirt on the dress didn't have a lot of extra room, so she shimmied it up, revealing a lot of leg. She tucked her thumbs under the fabric and slid the panties down her hips, then dropped

them to the floor. She smoothed the skirt back down and retrieved the panties from around her ankles.

"Here you go," she said, pressing them into Austin's large
hand.

He grinned as he stroked them over his cheek. "Ah, still
warm." He slid them into his jacket pocket. "Even if they don't
bring me luck, they'll remind me of the big win I'm looking
forward to later on."

Quinn glided his hand over her hip, then across her
behind.

"And all afternoon," he said, "I'll be thinking of you
wandering around in public with nothing on under that sexy
dress."

He pulled her in close, his hands cupping her ass firmly,
and kissed her. She was intensely aware of her breasts crushed
tightly against his broad chest. Delighting in the feel of his
hands squeezing her round flesh. Her insides ached, and she
could feel a melting heat build between her legs.

"Break it up, you two," Austin said. "If I don't get down
there soon, I'll run out of time."

Quinn eased back, then pressed his hand to the small of her
back and guided her toward the door.

"Have fun," he said as April and Austin walked across the
living room toward the door.

Moments later, they were riding the elevator down to the
lobby.

"I take it you talked to Quinn this morning about his strange
mood last night?"

"I told him you were worried that he was jealous of you being with me, and he definitely wanted to straighten you out on
that."

"Yes, he made it abundantly clear that he loves watching us together."

"And I'm sure if we wanted to be together when he's not around, he'd have no problem with it. As long as we told him about it. In detail." Austin grinned. "Thought I'd mention that in case you're craving some kinky elevator sex."

Austin was such a wonderful, caring man, and he was such fun to be around. She could fall for him. Hard. And he seemed to be developing feelings for her.

"Austin, I just want to be sure . . ." She drew in a breath, not sure exactly what to say.

"Sure of what?" he prompted at her hesitation.

She turned her gaze to his. "Quinn may enjoy the sharing we're doing, but he would not be okay with anything continuing between us. He made that clear. I just want to be sure you understand that once the month is done, this is over."

Austin's expression grew serious, and he took her hands. "Well, maybe things will change."

She shook her head. "No. I want to be really clear because I don't want to lead you on."

He squeezed her hands and released them, his gaze flicking to the floor number lit up above the door. They were almost at the lobby.

"You're not leading me on. I just prefer to keep a positive attitude."

The doors whooshed open, and he guided her out of the elevator before she had a chance to respond.

"Have a nice walk," he said. "I'll see you later in the suite."

He strolled away, and she sighed as she walked to the doors leading outside. She was sure Austin wouldn't do anything to hurt Quinn or their friendship. She just hoped Austin wouldn't get hurt along the way.

April sat in the hotel garden listening to the birds twittering in the trees. She'd walked around outside the hotel for about a half hour, then returned to the hotel and the lovely garden where she could sit quietly and enjoy the sunshine and beautiful flowers and greenery.

Her phone chimed. She pulled it from her purse.

"Hi, April," Austin said on the other end when she answered. "I'm leaving the casino now, and I wanted to let you know that I cleaned up."

She smiled. "That's great."

"It is. And to thank you, I've made an appointment for you at the spa in twenty minutes."

"But, Austin—"

"I know, you're going to say you're uncomfortable with me spending the money. But it's money I wouldn't have without the delightful lucky charm you gave me. *And* . . . if you don't go, the money will go to waste. So don't even think about fighting me on this."

"Austin, you are—"

"A sweetheart? The man of your dreams?"

"Exasperating," she interjected. Then she laughed. "But yes, also a sweetheart and exactly the type of man any woman would dream of."

"Good. And if that argument hadn't worked, I would have pointed out that it's our one-week anniversary, and as your husband, I should be able to treat my wife to something special."

The wistfulness in his voice when he called her his wife melted her heart.

"I'd better get a move on if I'm going to find the place in time," she said.

April stepped from the spa feeling more relaxed than she had in months. In her hand was a small, fancy gift bag the receptionist had handed her when she'd arrived, saying that her husband had left if for her.

She'd opened it when she was in the changing room getting ready for her massage, and inside was a lovely bra and panty set with a note from Austin. He'd decided to keep her lucky charm, so this was a replacement.

She smiled broadly as she walked through the hotel, looking forward to getting back to the suite so she could thank him. Maybe even model it for her two husbands.

"April, you look good."

Her back stiffened, and ice ran through her veins as she turned around to come face-to-face with Maurice.

Her relaxation and happiness disintegrated.

22

"What are you doing here?" April kept her expression calm and indifferent, despite the roiling emotions inside her.

"Looking for you. When you didn't respond to my messages, I decided to come and talk to you in person. I asked the manager to help me track you down, and he found that you had an appointment at the spa." His expression turned contrite. "April, I know I'm the last person you want to see. What I did to you was totally inexcusable. I was an idiot."

"I won't argue with you there."

"I know what I did hurt you, but I'm hoping you'll give me a chance to make amends."

Anger spiked through her.

"Maurice, there is nothing you can do to make amends. You left me with a huge hotel bill, which I have no means to pay. I'm lucky I'm not in jail. Then you took away my job, my town house. Everything."

She wouldn't even bring up the fact he'd had sex with another woman.

"I know. And I regret all of it."

He stepped closer, and she stiffened but forced herself not to back away.

"At least have a drink with me so we can talk." He gazed at her with big brown eyes that at one time had held her enthralled and made her heart thump loudly . . . but now left her cold.

She frowned, but considered. Every time he contacted her . . . every time she saw another message from him . . . she went into a tailspin. She didn't want him to have that much control over her life.

And seeing him now, the man she'd spent the past two years with, brought back a lot of memories. And aside from what happened last weekend, which had caught her totally off guard, they had all been good memories. Times when she'd felt safe and secure. A part of her wanted to believe that the whole fiasco had been a big misunderstanding.

Except that the memory of him humping that woman against the wall was still too fresh in her mind.

She sucked in a deep breath, driving the image from her mind.

No matter how they'd arrived at this point, it was time to listen to what he had to say. Only then could she put this chapter of her life behind her.

"One drink," she said firmly.

Before April sat down, she subtly slipped off her wedding ring and slid it into her purse. She didn't want Maurice asking any questions about it.

As she sat back in the chair watching him order their drinks, dazzling the waitress with his boyish charm, she wondered what he was up to. She knew better than to think Maurice actually cared about her.

So what did he want from her? She didn't believe for a minute that he was actually in love with her and wanted her back.

Once the waitress was gone, he turned to her, his expression serious.

"April, I know it's not enough, but let me start by saying I'll pay the hotel bill and tell them it was all a misunderstanding and that I take full blame. That way, everyone will know it wasn't your fault."

Appearances were important to Maurice, so of course he'd think she cared about that, too. And unfortunately, she did worry about what people thought of her.

One thing she'd learned in the system as a child was that it was important that people like her. She'd had no control over who took care of her or how well. But if she acted the way people wanted her to, and did what people told her to, things went better than if she didn't.

But she was grown up now and knew she shouldn't care what the hotel manager and staff believed about her. Nor should she care that Maurice's friends thought she had cheated on him. It only mattered what the people close to her thought. Unfortunately, although Quinn protected her and was extremely generous with her, she was sure he still had doubts about her.

"What about my town house?"

He nodded. "I'll give it back for you. With the mortgage paid off so you'll own it outright." He took her hand, and she tried not to cringe. "But if we get married, you won't need it."

"I don't want the town house anymore," she said, ignoring his comment about getting married. "All I want is that you give me the equity I'd built up."

"Of course. And if you come back to me, I'll give you a generous allowance once we're married. I know you said you wanted to keep on working, and you can if you want to, but this way you won't have to ask me for money if you want something. I know how you hate that."

She drew her hand back, needing to be free of his touch. "How can I trust you to follow through on any of this?"

He pulled out his phone and tapped a few times, then showed her the screen. It was his bank app.

"I'll transfer the money for your town house to your bank account right now. Then I'll send an email to the hotel manager to move the bill payment to my credit card. I understand an old friend lent you the money, so your friend should get notification tomorrow morning."

"So you're telling me you regret sleeping with that woman? And that it won't happen again?"

"That's right. I'll be totally devoted to you."

"And why do you think I won't just take the money and walk away?"

"Because I'm also offering you a big fat signing bonus. The minute you become Mrs. Maurice Dubois, a half a million dollars will be put into your account."

She kept her expression even, but inside she was reeling. Just like Quinn, Maurice obviously thought she only cared about money.

And why was he willing to throw so much money her way to convince her to come back?

He leaned toward her and gave her the smile that had once charmed her but now turned her blood cold.

"You see, darling, I do care about you," he said.

Then he pulled something from his pocket, which she immediately recognized as the box for the engagement ring he'd given her. He opened the small black velvet box, displaying the dazzling diamond ring inside.

"Just put this on again, and I'll start everything in motion."

Austin watched in horror as the man who'd been having a drink with April presented her with an engagement ring.

Austin had been sitting in the lounge having a drink while he caught up on his email. He'd noticed April come into the bar with a strange man. She hadn't seen Austin sitting there, so he left them to it. He assumed this was a friend who'd come to Vegas for the wedding. Austin kept an eye on them, though, in case the guy said anything to upset April. If that happened, he was ready to step in.

Never in a million years did he think the guy would propose.

And never in a million years did he expect that she would allow him to slip the ring on her finger.

As she gazed at her hand, Austin realized two things. She was no longer wearing the wedding ring. And the engagement ring she now wore was the same as the one she'd worn last Saturday when he'd met her.

Goddamn! This guy was her sleazy ex-fiancé, Maurice.

He lifted his phone and snapped a picture of them, then texted it to Quinn.

Quinn enjoyed the sun warming his skin as he relaxed on the outside deck by the pool. His phone vibrated on the table next to him. He picked it up and opened the text Austin had sent him. He clicked on the image, and a photo of April sitting at a table with Maurice filled the small screen.

His heart pounded, and he jabbed the quick dial.

"Are you fucking kidding me?" Quinn demanded as soon as Austin picked up.

"No, I'm looking straight at them."

Quinn stood up and paced, his blood racing through his veins.

"I'm coming down there right now."

"Not a good idea," Austin said. "You don't want to cause a scene. And it looks like they're leaving anyway."

"Well, fucking catch up to her. I don't want her going back to the guy's room."

"Not a problem. I heard her say she has to go but she'll talk to him tomorrow. Just in case she's heading back to the suite, I'll try to beat her up there. If I don't make it, please don't say anything to her until I get there."

"I make no promises," Quinn said through gritted teeth.

April slowed as she approached the suite door. How was she going to tell Quinn and Austin why she was wearing Maurice's engagement ring?

She could just stroll in and say, "Hey, guess what? I ran into Maurice, and we're now officially engaged again."

She sucked in a deep breath, then slid the key card into the slot and opened the door. When she stepped into the entrance, she saw that both Quinn and Austin were sitting in the living room staring her way.

"Oh, hi. It's really nice outside. Sunny and warm." She took off her shoes and dropped her purse beside them. "I had a nice walk and then sat in the garden for a while. Then I went to the spa. Did Austin mention about the spa?"

She realized she was babbling, which she did when she was nervous.

She walked into the living room, sensing a tension she hadn't noticed before because of her own anxiety.

Austin's expression was guarded, but Quinn's rippled with displeasure. She sat down in the armchair between the couch where Quinn sat and Austin's chair.

"Is something wrong?" she asked.

Quinn scowled, then picked up his phone and tapped it. "I hear you ran into an old friend." His voice was tight and hard. He held the phone up facing her, revealing a photo of her and Maurice talking in the bar.

Her back stiffened. "Yes, as a matter of fact. I ran into Maurice while I was leaving the spa."

"And you went out on a date with him," Quinn accused.

"It was a drink, not a date. And yes, I accepted his invitation. He wanted to talk about what happened."

She wanted to say more. Like he had no right to interrogate her like this. She could talk to whomever she wanted. But she didn't want to inflame the already tense situation.

"So are you going back to him?" Quinn's midnight eyes were somber.

Shock and anger surged through her at his question. She could feel her cheeks burning with it.

"No, of course not. Do you think I'm an idiot?"

He grasped her hand and jerked it up, glaring at the diamond on her finger. "Then why are you wearing his ring?"

She glared back at his angry face, but said nothing.

"And last night, you murmured his name in your sleep. Then you said you loved him."

She felt the blood drain from her face. That's why he'd been upset. She'd babbled out loud. God, she couldn't tell him that her proclamation of love in her sleep had been to him. Not when he didn't return those feelings.

"I see you just ditched our wedding ring without a thought."

"It was for a fake wedding."

"The wedding was real," Quinn countered. "You are my wife."

"But the feelings are fake."

She turned and stalked off toward the bedroom. Once she reached the door, she turned.

"By the way, tomorrow my debt to you will be paid off in full."

Then she slammed the door behind her.

Quinn stared at the door to the bedroom, his heart hammering in his chest.

"I really screwed that up, didn't I?" he said.

"Yeah, I'd say so." Austin stood up and poured them both a drink, then handed one to Quinn.

Quinn tossed back a swallow. "Do you think I should go in there?"

Austin settled back in the chair. "I think you should give her some time alone. She's got a lot to sort out."

Quinn sighed and raked his hand through his hair. "That dream she had last night . . . Fuck, it really messed with my head."

"Look, whatever you heard her mumble in her sleep, I wouldn't let it get to you. It could mean anything."

Quinn swirled the liquid around his glass. "She said she's not going back to him, but she didn't explain why she's wearing the ring."

"I'm sure she has a good reason. Probably related to the fact that it seems he's paying her back some—or hopefully *all*—the money she lost because of him. It'll take some time to get it to her, so maybe she's playing a bluff until she has the money in hand."

Quinn's hand tightened around his glass. "Fuck, do you think this means she'll walk away from us, too? Since her debt is paid off, she has no reason to continue with the arrangement."

Austin stared at the bedroom door wistfully as he sipped his drink.

"I don't know, man," he said.

From the moment Austin had told him April was talking to Maurice, fear had surged through Quinn. His gut had knotted at the thought of losing her again. He was glad she wasn't going back to that bastard who had treated her so badly. But it seemed far too likely she would walk out of Quinn's life again, just as suddenly as she'd stumbled back into it.

Unless he did something about it.

23

Once April was inside the room, she crumpled on the couch. She should be happy. Maurice would be reimbursing her every cent she'd lost because of his abhorrent treatment of her. That meant she could pay back Quinn. And she was getting enough money from her town house to get started somewhere new.

But seeing Maurice had forced her to relive the pain of losing the dream of happily-ever-after all over again.

She couldn't believe she'd been so thoroughly fooled by him. But when she thought about it, she realized he was like the magician from last night's show. Keeping her attention focused on things like flashy gifts and talk of love while making things disappear. Like her self-esteem. Her independence. Her happiness.

With Maurice, she'd thought she was in love because she'd wanted the security his love and wealth would give her. But in fact, she would never be secure with Maurice because he could rip it all away from her so easily. In fact, anyone she came to depend on could do the same.

Her sense of security had to come from within herself. She had to believe she could keep herself secure and happy. Even when she'd been with Maurice, she'd held down her own job and paid her own bills, but everything she'd built had toppled because of Maurice.

She straightened her shoulders. But she'd learned from that. She wouldn't let herself be in that position again.

Getting the money to pay back the hotel debt from Maurice meant she no longer owed Quinn, except for the clothes she'd bought, and she'd pay for those from the equity she was getting back from her town house. She'd use the rest of that money to get set up in an apartment somewhere and get back on her feet.

Her heart ached as she thought about living in that apartment alone. Without Quinn. Or Austin.

She'd never doubted that she loved Quinn. She'd never stopped loving him. And now she'd been falling in love with Austin, too.

She sighed and stared at the door wistfully. When Quinn had demanded answers from her, jealousy coloring every word, she'd become annoyed and rebellious, but she realized that he'd acted that way because he cared about her. He was worried that she'd go back to Maurice. And given her current situation and her past actions, she couldn't really blame him for that.

If she hadn't had Quinn and Austin's help during ths desperate time, it would be all too easy to jump at a lifeline. To convince herself that Maurice was telling the truth and really did regret what he'd done. Because fear could do that to a person. She'd seen other women return to worse situations out of fear of the alternative.

It all came down to wanting to be loved and cared for.

Maurice was doing everything he could to convince her he still cared. By giving her money.

Quinn had given her money, too. But he'd also given her so

much more. And all of it with no strings. He'd only agreed to the arrangement to satisfy her need to pay him back.

She sighed and stood up, then walked toward the door.

Austin watched Quinn with a somber eye. His friend had come a long way dealing with his feelings for April. Austin had hoped over the next few weeks that Quinn would finally realize he wanted to keep her in his life.

Austin sure as hell did, and he had no idea how that was going to work.

But now April could just move on, and as happy as Austin was about April having her independence again, selfishly he wished the turnaround could have come a little later.

Quinn sipped his drink, and Austin saw the resolve in his eyes. That was good. It meant Quinn was going to fight for her.

The sound of the bedroom door opening snagged his attention, and his focus jerked to it, along with Quinn's.

April stepped into the living room. The anger was gone from her eyes, and she looked almost sheepish.

She sat down. "Quinn, I'm sorry I got mad." Her fingers twisted together on her lap. "It was hard seeing Maurice again, and when you got angry and started questioning me . . ." She bit her lip. "I just reacted."

Quinn stood up and moved to her chair, then knelt in front of her and took her hand.

"It's okay, baby. I didn't mean to badger you."

She wiped an errant tear from her eye. "I know you were just looking out for me, and that means a lot to me."

Quinn drew her forward and slid his arms around her. She rested her head on his chest, and her gaze now fell to Austin. He smiled and nodded. He was rewarded by a small smile turning up her lips.

She drew back from Quinn's embrace.

"And that dream didn't mean anything. I don't have any lingering feelings for him, except what you'd expect for someone who hurt me."

The glitter in Quinn's deep, blue eyes told Austin that he'd love to get his hands on Maurice and make him answer for that pain.

"Now I'll answer your question about why I'm wearing the engagement ring," April said.

Quinn drew her to her feet and guided her to the couch with him, then, when they sat down, slid his arm around her protectively.

"When he told me he wanted to talk to me, I was going to turn him down," she said, "but I wanted to know what he was up to. And I needed to find closure. When we sat down for a drink, he apologized for his actions and promised never to cheat on me again. He started offering me money by paying back the hotel debt and returning the equity in my town house. He even offered a huge bonus payment that I would receive if I married him."

Why the hell would the guy be throwing around all that cash to win April back? He didn't love her. That was clear from his affair and his subsequent treatment of her. Yet he was spending a lot of money to try to get her to marry him.

An idea prickled through Austin's brain. "How huge? If you don't mind me asking."

"Half a million dollars. But I don't want his money. I just want the debt cleared and the equity in my house that I worked so hard to build." She turned to Quinn. "He insisted I wear his ring again and that we talk tomorrow once the money shows up in my back account."

"April, did Maurice ask you to sign any papers leading up to the wedding day?" Austin asked.

"Yes, a prenup."

"Anything else?"

A prenup. An image flashed through April's brain. Quinn sliding a small piece of notepaper toward her. There'd been a sentence or two scrawled on it . . . she couldn't remember . . . but at the top was written PRENUP in Quinn's distinct block printing.

Her stomach twisted. Even drunk and spontaneously marrying her in an essentially fake wedding, he had protected himself with a prenup. Not that she could blame him. It just . . . hurt.

"April? Is something wrong?" Austin asked.

"No, I just . . ." She shook her head. "A memory from Saturday night."

"When we all got married?" Quinn asked.

She nodded.

"Anything you want to share?" Quinn coaxed with a smile.

"No," she said a bit too quickly, still reeling from the mélange of feelings swirling through her. "It was just a flash. Nothing substantial." She turned to Austin. "I'm sorry. What were you saying?"

"I asked if you signed anything besides the prenup."

"Yes, there were other papers. He signed over some properties and one of his companies to me. He said it would help with taxes." Her eyes widened. "That wasn't illegal, was it?"

"No, not illegal, but that's what he's worried about. You still own those things. And with the amount of money he's offered to get you back, I take it they're worth a hell of a lot."

She shook her head. "But I assumed since we didn't get married that they'd revert to him. The date of ownership was set at the day after the wedding."

"It sounds like he was depending on the prenup alone to get the holdings back if you wound up getting divorced, never imagining the wedding itself wouldn't happen."

"So it sounds like you just became a multimillionaire," Quinn said.

"I don't want his properties," April said. "I'll tell him so tomorrow. I just want to be rid of him."

"You should wait a little longer and make him sweat," Quinn suggested.

"Whatever you decide to do, if he asks you to sign any papers, will you let my lawyer look them over?" Austin asked.

"Yes, thank you." She smiled. "Now why don't we forget about all this right now and just enjoy the rest of our day together. What would you like to do?"

After a long but wonderful day April would never forget, they stepped into the suite, and she slumped on the couch. They'd gone on a helicopter tour of the Grand Canyon, had a sumptuous dinner at a very exclusive French restaurant with a twenty-third-floor view, and finally enjoyed a hilarious comedy show.

She pulled off her shoes and tossed them under the coffee table. "You two spoiled me. I had such a good time."

"You deserve to be spoiled," Quinn said as he sat down beside her.

"Talking about having a good time," Austin said as he settled at her other side, "the whole time we were out, all I could think about was coming back here and having a good time with you."

She grinned at him. "Is that a proposition?"

"If it is, will I get a yes?" he asked, his eyes glittering.

"I don't know. I'm pretty tired." She stretched her legs out in front of her.

"Maybe we can find a way to revive you," Quinn suggested, then ran his hand down her thigh and over her calf.

Austin turned her and tugged her onto his lap as Quinn drew her legs onto the couch. Then Quinn wrapped his hands around her foot and started to massage. She sighed as she rested against Austin's chest, his strong arm holding her close. The pressure of Quinn's fingertips moving over her foot sent waves of delight through her.

"Mmm, that feels wonderful."

Austin's lips brushed her ear. "Did I tell you how beautiful you look in this dress?" he asked as he slid the zipper down her back.

"At least three times tonight." She'd worn the red strapless again because she knew it was their favorite. "But if you like it so much, why are you trying to take it off?"

"Because I love looking at your stunning body even more." Austin nuzzled her neck. "And I'm curious about your underwear."

He slipped her dress from her shoulders and glided it down to her waist, revealing her black satin bra embroidered with gold thread and edged with delicate black lace. It was part of the set he'd left in a gift bag for her at the spa.

Quinn, who was still rubbing her foot, watched her dress slide away with a fiery glint in his eyes. Then he focused on the swell of her breasts.

Austin wrapped his hands around her waist and lifted while Quinn slid the dress down her hips then off. He dropped it on the floor, his gaze falling to her matching panties that were so skimpy they were mostly black lace edging with a small triangle of embroidered black satin front and back.

As Quinn started on her other foot, Austin captured her lips. The light pressure of his mouth on hers, paired with the sensual feel of Quinn kneading her foot, caused sparks of pure sensation to flicker through her. Austin's tongue dipped into her mouth, and she suckled on it, drawing it deeper. His large hand glided over her breast, and she arched against him as he caressed, her nipple blossoming into a hard bud.

Quinn massaged up her calves, squeezing and gliding over her skin.

Austin stripped off her bra and let it drop to the floor as he covered her breast again. She arched into the warmth of his hand. Quinn passed her knees and continued up her thighs. Her intimate muscles clenched as a deep yearning to feel him stroke her soft folds blazed to life.

Austin lifted her enough to slide out from under her, then knelt on the floor beside her and smiled. She was now stretched out on the couch, a cushion under her head.

"I think you're enjoying all this attention," he said.

She curled her hands around his neck. "Oh, yes. Definitely."

His lips found hers, and his tongue glided into her mouth again, then swirled deep. She tightened her grip on his neck, holding him close as her tongue stroked his. He tasted of aged scotch and wintergreen.

Then his lips veered sideways, kissing along her cheek, then down her neck. Her skin erupted in goose bumps, flashing along the path of Austin's light kisses and trembling up from Quinn's massaging fingers as he moved up her thighs, ever closer to her aching flesh.

Austin's warm breath washed across her breast as his lips

moved up the swell. His mouth covered her swollen nipple just as Quinn's fingers reached the satin of her panties. Austin teased her hard nub with his tongue. She sucked in a breath, pushing herself deeper into his mouth, then exhaled in a soft moan.

Quinn's fingertips stroked along the side of her panties, toying with her. She clung to Austin's head, pulling him tighter as his teasing mouth sent thrilling sensations sparking through her.

Then Quinn stroked over her satin crotch. She arched against his warm hand, moaning in need. He chuckled and cupped her, massaging with a gentle pressure. Heat thrummed through her. She widened her legs and arched again, offering him greater access.

When his hand slid away, she murmured a protest. He stripped off her new panties and crumpled them into a ball, then slid them into his pocket with a smile.

As she watched them disappear, she pursed her lips in a mock frown. "And I was just getting used to wearing panties again."

Austin released her nipple to the cool air and chuckled loudly. "It's a good thing Quinn's on that, then, because that's definitely not something we want you used to."

His fingers glided over her cold nub, then his mouth found her other nipple and he lapped at it. When Quinn's big, warm hand covered her again, his thick fingers pressing lightly, she rocked against them. They moved over her in the same massaging motion. Heat swelled through her, and slickness glazed her intimate flesh. He had to feel it.

Austin's hand slid down her stomach, then his fingers teased around her navel. He nipped her nub lightly, and she cried out in pleasure. Quinn's fingertips pressed into her petals, and he stroked her length. Austin flattened his hand on her belly, his fingertips so close to her aching clit.

Quinn's finger dipped deeper into her folds, continuing to stroke. She widened her legs, needing him inside her. Austin's hand moved, then his finger found her clit. An intense sensual blast jolted through her as he teased it lightly. Two of Quinn's fingers glided into her passage and stroked inside her.

"Ohh," she whimpered. "That feels so good."

Austin leaned forward, brushing his lips across her temple. "What does, sweetheart?" His finger never stopped stroking her sensitive nub.

"All of it," she nearly croaked. "Both of you touching me. Making me so wet."

They both laughed in deep male rumbles.

"We love it when you're wet, baby." Quinn dipped farther into her, then curled his finger and drew it out. He licked it, then smiled broadly. "Especially when we can taste you."

Austin leaned down and licked her clit. She arched and moaned at the feel of his tongue flicking over her. When he straightened again, Quinn dipped down and licked her length. Her fingers twisted in his hair as she held him close to her.

He nuzzled in deep, his tongue curling into her, and lapped enthusiastically. He gazed up at her, his midnight eyes dark and glittering with desire. Then he glided to her clit and suckled.

"Oh, yes," she cried, pulling him tightly to her.

Beside her, Austin had released his cock from his pants. It sprang out, rock-hard and ready. She grabbed it, loving its hefty weight in her hand. She squeezed and stroked as Quinn continued to suckle softly.

She tugged on Austin's member, drawing him closer.

"Quinn," she said in a trembling voice. "I'm going to suck your friend's cock now."

Quinn watched her brush Austin's cock against her lips.

"Do you want me to do that?" she asked, her body trembling from the rising pleasure he was giving her.

"You know I do, baby," he murmured against her wet flesh.

She opened her mouth and took Austin's cockhead inside, to his groan.

Quinn's mouth lifted, and she rocked her hips, wanting him back on her.

"But I doubt you'll have time to finish the job," Quinn said with a grin. Then he dove down on her again.

She squeezed Austin in her mouth and drew him deeper, the pleasure thrumming through her from Quinn's suckling leaving her light-headed. Austin helped by gliding in and out of her mouth in short, slow strokes. She glided her tongue over his crown, lapping at it as Quinn lapped at her.

Pleasure pummeled her now, and she squeezed around Austin's hard shaft.

"Oh, fuck, sweetheart," Austin groaned. "That's so good."

She arched against Quinn's mouth as pleasure spiraled higher. Then he glided two fingers deep inside her and began to pump.

She moaned around Austin's cock, then began to suck. Quinn's fingers thrust over and over as his tongue quivered over her clit.

Blissful sensations surged through her with a blinding intensity. She squeezed Austin in her hand and sucked harder, then stiffened as her body exploded in ecstasy. Quinn kept his fingers thrusting into her and suckling her nub. As she shuddered her release, Austin groaned. Hot liquid flooded her mouth and trickled out the side of her lips.

She fell back on the couch, letting the afterglow wash over her. Austin drew his deflating cock from her mouth, then leaned in and kissed her. Then he turned and slumped to the floor, sitting on the carpet with his legs outstretched.

Quinn took a last lick, then kissed up her belly to her breasts. He licked one nipple and suckled for a moment, the bud hardening in his mouth. Then he nuzzled her neck and finally found her lips.

The kiss he gave her was deep and poignant, filling her with an intense need to join with him.

"Make love to me, Quinn. I want to feel you inside me."

His midnight eyes grew darker, and he stood up, then scooped her into his arms.

"Come on, Austin," he said as he carried her into the bedroom.

24

When Quinn laid April on the bed, her naked body still carrying the soft blush of the orgasm he and Austin had given her, his heart ached.

She was his wife. She was in his bed, her blue eyes begging him to fuck her. And his friend was by his side. Life couldn't get any better than this.

He stripped off his jacket, then his shirt and tie, his focus on her the whole time. Her hungry gaze as she watched him strip sent heat blazing through him. His cock, already swollen with need, pushed against the constraining fabric painfully. He unzipped and dropped his suit pants to the floor, then shed his boxers. She reached out her hand as he stepped forward. When her fingertips brushed his tip, he felt he might explode on the spot. He wanted her so badly.

She wrapped her fingers around him and stroked as he knelt on the bed and arched his leg over her. He stared down at her as she pumped up and down his straining erection.

"Oh, fuck, baby," he said, his words strained as he kept a

tight leash on his need to drive into her. "I love it when you touch my cock."

She smiled. "I think you love it when I do this, too."

With one hand still firmly around his shaft, she glided the other over her lovely rose-tipped breast and toyed with it. Stroking lightly at first, then flicking her fingertips over the hard bud.

"Oh, yeah," Austin said as he lay down beside her, watching intently. "I love that, too."

When she started pinching the peaked nipple with her fingertips, Quinn groaned. He grabbed his cock and glided the tip over her wet flesh. His eyelids flickered closed at the exquisite feel of her melting heat on his aching member, then he opened them again and focused on her lovely, glowing face as he eased forward.

"I'm pushing into you now, baby. Do you like that?"

"Ohhh, yes," she whimpered, sending goose bumps dancing down his spine.

He sank into her slowly, her slick flesh swallowing him into her heat.

"Ah, fuck, your pussy feels so good around me."

He kept pushing in. Deeper. Her softness stretching around him in a sweet embrace. God, it was like going home. This was truly where he belonged.

"Ohhh, Quinn. Yes." Her fingers curled around his shoulders, her head tossed back on the pillow.

The knowledge that he was giving her pleasure made his heart soar. Damn, he fucking loved this woman so much.

He glided deeper still until there was no distance between their bodies. They were joined together as one.

Austin drew her long hair to the side, then stroked the golden strands shimmering across the pillow as he gazed at her.

Quinn's cock twitched inside her, urging him to move. He leaned forward and brushed her mouth lightly with his. Her lips parted, and he ran the tip of his tongue over them, then surged inside. At the same time, he drew back and glided into her in a slow and steady stroke.

"Ohhh, yes." She opened wider and wrapped her legs around his thighs.

He drew back and glided in again. Her quivering moan ramped up his excitement. He pulsed into her.

Her breathing quickened, and she tightened her legs around him, arching her hips to take him deeper still.

His groin grew taut, the pleasure coiling tighter and tighter as he pumped into her in rhythmic strokes.

She sucked in a breath. "Quinn, I'm . . . going . . . to . . ." She rocked against him, her eyelids fluttering. "Come."

The word, barely audible, trailed off on a breath, but it was enough to send him skyrocketing to orgasm. He drove into her in deep, hard thrusts as she moaned loudly, clinging to his shoulders.

As his own burning need seared away with his release, he marveled at the ethereal beauty of her face as she cried out in ecstasy. He kept pumping into her, wanting to keep her there as long as possible.

When it started to fade, he pressed his hand between their bodies and found her clit. His touch sent her rocketing off again, breathing his name in a loud moan.

Finally, he eased off, letting her orgasm fade away slowly. When she was finally lying gasping beneath him, he kissed her cheek, then found her lips in a gentle kiss. She gazed into his eyes, then cupped his face and deepened the kiss. His heart ached at the love shining in her sapphire eyes.

All he could think about was how much he needed her by his side. And in his bed. She completed him. He wanted her in his life forever.

When their lips parted, she gazed up at him and smiled. "That was fantastic."

He smiled and kissed her again, then rolled off her soft body. He wanted to say something. To tell her he loved her. But her gaze flicked to Austin, and she opened her arms.

Quinn watched as his friend prowled over her and pressed his cockhead to the warm, welcoming passage Quinn had just left.

Austin glided deep in one stroke. Seeing Austin's thick cock impale his woman sent another wave of arousal through Quinn.

Austin kissed her, then began to thrust in deep, even strokes. At her moans, he sped up until he was pounding into her body. Driving that hard cock deep again and again.

"Ohh, yes," she cried, her voice stretched taut with urgency.

Austin's face tensed as he fucked her, ready to come any minute.

"Oh, God," April wailed as Austin flung her into orgasm again.

Quinn watched her beautiful face, her cheeks flushing a dark rose, her eyes glowing with delight, as Austin kept filling her. Then his friend groaned and pinned her to the bed, his cock deep inside her, and shuddered.

A moment later, he rolled back, taking her with him. April giggled, and Austin chuckled along with her.

"What's so funny?" Quinn asked with a smile, his hand gliding along the graceful curve of her hip, then over her round ass.

"I just can't believe how lucky I am winding up in bed with both of you," she said.

She snuggled against Austin, who was holding her tightly.

Quinn moved closer, needing to feel her body against him

again. He slid his arm around her stomach and kissed the back of her head.

"Running into you again was definitely a stroke of luck for all of us," he murmured.

April's eyes opened, and she blinked. Moonlight streamed across the bed, and she felt warm and snug. After she'd fallen asleep, she'd rolled away from Austin's solid chest, but both men were pressed to her sides in a cozy arrangement.

She turned her head to face Quinn and was startled to see that his eyes were open and he was watching her.

"Oh, hi," she whispered, not wanting to wake Austin.

Quinn smiled. "Hi."

"Are you having trouble sleeping?"

"Not really. I just couldn't help watching your beautiful face as you sleep."

He stroked a tendril of hair from her face. The gentle touch sent shimmers of heat through her.

"I'm really glad I ran into you last weekend," he said. "This time together has made me realize something."

Her heart clenched, and she grasped his hand and moved it from her cheek. After the flash of memory she'd had this morning, she did not want to hear any more.

"Quinn, I don't know where you're going with this, but I don't want to discuss what our relationship is or where it's going. We both know this is a temporary thing. Let's leave it at that."

"But that's just it. I don't want it to be temporary. I know things have gotten all twisted up and backward with us being married already, but I want to turn that around."

She didn't like where this was going.

"When I thought you might go back to Maurice," he continued, "I had to face the fact that I'd be losing you. Again. I knew I couldn't let that happen."

He leaned in and kissed her, and the tenderness of that kiss took her breath away. Then when he drew back, and she saw the depth of emotion in his midnight eyes, her heart ached with the desire to have something she knew she couldn't.

"Sweetheart, I love you." He took her left hand and pressed it to his lips. "And I want our marriage to be real."

Her breath locked in her lungs as she fought back the swell of tears that threatened. Tears that should be happy ones, since she'd dreamed of having this chance with him for so long. But these tears came from a desolation that was rooted deep inside her soul.

"I'll do whatever I can to make it special," he said. "Of course we can have a big, fairy-tale wedding. And if you want, we can even annul our current marriage and date for a while leading up to a romantic proposal. Anything you want, I'll do it."

She shook her head, desperately pushing back the bitter pain swelling through her.

"It won't work."

She pushed herself up and wiggled out from under the covers, then dodged off the end of the bed. As soon as her feet hit the floor, she hurried to the nearest shirt sprawled on the carpet and snatched it up as she strode from the room.

25

Quinn stared at the door April had just closed behind her. He wasn't sure what had just happened. He'd anticipated she might want some time to think about it. It had been a whirlwind ride these past couple of days. But a flat-out rejection left him in shock.

"Go after her."

Quinn's gaze jerked to Austin, whose sleepy face was still resting on the pillow. Austin sat up and pushed his hair back.

"You need to talk her into it, because if you don't, I will," Austin said. "I don't want us to lose her. And yes, I mean *us*, because whether you're married to her or I am, we both know we're going to share her, and I'm in love with her, too."

Quinn nodded and got up, then pulled on his boxers and walked out the door. He glanced around the moonlit room and saw April standing at the window staring into the night.

He walked to her side and rested his hands on her shoulders. She stiffened a little but didn't move away.

"April, I know I've been a jerk, but tell me what to do to make it up to you. I love you, and I want you to be a part of my life."

She shook her head. "It just won't work." Her words were spoken so softly he could barely hear them, but the depth of sadness in her voice filled him with dread.

"Why, sweetheart? You've got to tell me why."

She turned to him slowly, her eyes shimmering with unshed tears.

"Because . . ." She drew in a deep breath, clearly having trouble keeping her emotions in check. "A marriage won't work without trust. And you don't trust me. You never have."

He cupped her face. "No, baby, that's not true. I told you, that's all changed."

She jerked back and waved away his words.

"What about the prenup?" she asked, her expression taut.

"What prenup?"

"Things were pretty hazy when we got married, but when Austin asked me about the papers Maurice had me sign, I had a flashback. I remember a scrap of paper with *Prenup* hand printed on the top, and you insisting I sign it."

Quinn shook his head, confused. "I don't remember any of that. But I do know that I don't care about a prenup. We can find it and tear it up."

She sighed, then walked to the couch and sat down. He followed and settled beside her.

"The prenup itself doesn't bother me. It's not like I would ever take anything from you if we got divorced. But the fact that even when you were drunk, you thought about protecting yourself from me . . ." She shook her head. "That shows a deeply ingrained lack of trust."

"Sweetheart, whatever I did that night"—he took her hand and cradled it between his—"please don't let our relationship end because of it."

The haunting sadness in her eyes tore at his heart. But at her hesitation, he cupped her face and kissed her.

April's heart ached so intensely she thought she'd die. His tender kiss tore away her barriers.

She didn't want to walk away from Quinn. She wanted to spend a lifetime with him. But no matter what he said, deep in his heart, he didn't trust her.

He deepened the kiss, his firm lips lighting a fire inside her. Oh, God, she wanted to stay in his arms so badly.

She had to stay strong.

But that didn't mean she couldn't allow herself one more time with him. A memory to last a lifetime.

She melted against him, parting her lips to his coaxing tongue. It glided inside and stroked hers. She sighed, surrendering to him.

When she was totally breathless from his devastating kiss, his lips brushed across her cheek, then nuzzled her temple.

"I love you, baby. I never want to let you go."

He kissed down her neck, sending tingles dancing across her flesh. His fingers hastily released the few buttons of the shirt she'd fastened, and he slid it from her shoulders. He laid her back on the couch and smiled.

"You're so beautiful in the glow of the moonlight."

Her heart quivered as he gazed at her with devastating tenderness and awe.

He knelt and stroked her body from shoulders to hips, his thumbs brushing the sides of her breasts on the way down. Then he leaned down and captured one taut nipple in his mouth. His tongue swirled over it in circles, then he suckled softly.

She glided her fingertips down his chest, over the tight

muscles, then found his hardening cock under the thin fabric of his boxers. She stroked his thick, rock-hard cock, feeling it twitch under her touch.

He shoved down his boxers and prowled over her.

She was mesmerized by the glow of his midnight eyes, so filled with desire, as he lowered himself onto her. She wrapped her hand around his pulsing member and pressed it to her already wet flesh.

He rested on his elbows and cupped her face gently. His gaze stayed locked on hers as he eased his pelvis forward, pushing his hard member inside her. Her slick canal welcomed him, stretching as he glided deeper.

She began to tremble, needing him so badly she could barely think straight.

Staring into his dark blue eyes, focused firmly on hers, kept her grounded in one fact. And one fact only.

That she loved this man. So deeply she feared she'd lose herself.

His belly pressed tightly to hers, his cock deep inside her. She tightened around him, wanting him there forever.

He kissed her again, his fingers cradling her head and his lips moving on hers so tenderly it made her heart break. She felt so cared for, and she didn't want to walk away from that. But she couldn't let her blind need for love and security override her good judgment.

He drew back and glided deep again. She curled her fingers around his shoulders.

"God, baby. I love you so much," he murmured against her ear as he filled her again and again with long, smooth strokes.

She began to quiver, pleasure rising with each gentle

thrust. She wrapped her legs around him, wanting him as deep as he could go. Then she arched forward to meet each of his thrusts.

He groaned. "Oh, fuck, baby. I'm so close."

"Me, too. Quinn, make me come."

He smiled, his eyes glittering as he drove deeper. He pumped into her faster, and she felt a sweltering heat rise through her, setting every cell ablaze. Her breath caught, then a wave of bliss surged through her. She clung to him as the orgasm bombarded her with rapturous delight.

"Ohhh, yes," she moaned.

Quinn drove in hard, then jerked forward and groaned. She squeezed around him, the feel of his seed filling her sending her over the edge again. Her heart pounded as she soared into ecstasy, holding him tightly.

Finally, the pleasure eased, and she slumped on the couch. Quinn's lips trailed down her neck, then he rolled to his side and pulled her tightly to his body. He tugged on the plush throw, which was draped over the back of the couch, and covered them with it.

She snuggled against him, listening to his heartbeat, letting it soothe her. She didn't want to think. She only wanted to feel his solid body against her and his strong arms around her.

As the lulling sound stole away her worries, she found herself drifting off to sleep.

Quinn felt himself pulled back to consciousness by a sound in the room. Sunlight blazed against his eyelids, and he flung his arm over his face and rolled back. Or tried to. He was on the couch.

He opened his eyes, remembering he'd fallen asleep here

with April in his arms, but her soft, warm body wasn't next to his now. He sat up, his gaze scanning the room.

"She's not here." Austin walked into the room from the kitchen carrying two steaming cups. He set one down on the coffee table in front of Quinn.

Austin's eyebrow arched as he took in the sight of Quinn on the couch, the throw blanket draped around his waist.

"Funny. Usually when the husband sleeps on the couch, it's because the wife threw him out of bed. But as I recall, it was April who left the bed last night. Did you get tired and take a nap on your way to talk to her?"

Quinn raked his hand through his hair. "Damn it. I thought I'd convinced her. Are you sure she's gone and not just out for a walk or something?"

Austin shrugged. "Well, I suppose she might be out for a walk. Not sure why she'd take her suitcase, though. And a drawerful of lingerie, the new dresses she bought, and both pairs of shoes." He held up an envelope. "And a note with her lawyer's number so we can contact her about the annulments."

"Damn." Quinn's stomach seethed.

April was gone.

Austin sank into the chair across from him.

"So what was that all about last night?"

Quinn leaned back on the couch. "I basically proposed to April, telling her I wanted to stay married to her."

"Yeah, I heard that part. She said it wouldn't work, and you went to fix it. Why does she think it won't work?"

Quinn frowned. "She was upset about me insisting she sign a prenup."

Austin set his cup down, his jaw dropping. "You were trying to fix things with her and you suggested a prenup?"

"No. She had some memory flash, and . . ."

If there were a prenup, then he should be able to find it. He shot to his feet and grabbed his boxers, then pulled them on.

"Do you know where the wedding certificates are?" Quinn asked.

"Uh, yeah, they're in the desk. They were in my suit pocket, and I put them in the drawer the next day before we sent our clothes out to the cleaner's."

Quinn strode to the desk in the corner of the living room and tugged open the top drawer. He pulled out the paperwork and flipped through it but saw no sign of a prenup.

Quinn scowled. "You said the suits got sent out to the cleaner's. Where are they now?"

"In the bedroom closet."

Quinn marched to the bedroom, Austin trailing after him.

"If you tell me what we're looking for, I could help," Austin suggested.

Quinn opened the closet door, then flicked through the clothes until he found the two suits they'd worn that night. He ripped away the filmy plastic over his suit.

"April told me she remembered signing a prenup on the night of the wedding," Quinn explained as he rooted through the pockets. "After I insisted. That's why she's upset with me. She said that means that deep down I don't trust her. And a marriage without trust won't work."

He tore away the plastic on Austin's suit and searched the pockets.

"I remember that prenup," Austin said.

Quinn glanced at him in shock. "You knew? And you didn't think to remind me about it?"

"Well, I didn't know you'd forgotten. And I didn't really think about it until you just mentioned it." He shook his head. "But she can't be mad about that."

"The hell she can't."

Quinn finished going through the pockets, then noticed a clear sandwich-size bag taped to a trail of the torn plastic. Inside was a folded piece of white notepaper. He grabbed the bag and tugged out the paper. When he opened it, the word PRENUP was scrawled across the top in his block-letter printing.

"Damn it!"

26

April walked up the third flight of stairs and pushed the key in the lock of her small apartment. She dropped her purse and keys on the kitchen counter that was open to the living room, then sat on the couch she'd bought from the secondhand store down the street.

The place wasn't much, but it had been available to move into right away, was in a nice neighborhood, and the rent was modest. Even though she had money in the bank from her town house, she was going to live on a tight budget until she got established in a job. Once she had a steady, reasonably secure income, she'd think about moving into something nicer.

Not that getting a job was turning out to be an easy task. The only place she'd ever worked was Maurice's company, and that meant she had no glowing references to offer a potential employer. She may have sorted things out with Maurice, agreeing to sign documents to return his properties to his name, but he was still annoyed she wouldn't take him back.

Her phone chimed, and she grabbed it from her purse.

"Hello?" she said.

"Hi, April. This is Bev. I have good news. The annulment to Mr. Wright is done. He signed the papers today."

April's heart sank. "That's great news. What about the other one?"

"Well, there's a bit of a hitch there. Mr. Taylor insists on meeting with you."

Her hand clenched tightly around the phone. "But you said we could do this without me having to meet with either of them."

Seeing Austin again would be hard. Seeing Quinn again would be excruciating.

"I thought we could, but Mr. Taylor produced a prenuptial contract you signed."

Her lips pursed. "I don't see why that means I have to meet with him. I'm not asking him for any money, so . . ."

"It's not that simple. It seems from the terms of the contract, you actually owe him something."

April tugged on the bottom of her suit jacket as she stood outside the door of the hotel suite. Quinn had agreed to fly in to Sidney, OH. the small town April had decided to settle in, to save her having to travel back to Las Vegas, where he and Austin were still vacationing. Her lawyer, Bev, was meeting her here.

She knocked on the door. A moment later, it opened, and her heart stopped at the sight of Quinn in his tailored suit stretched taut over his broad shoulders and chest.

"April. Thank you for coming."

"I had little choice," she said as he stepped back to let her in.

She didn't know what she'd expected. That he'd pull her into his arms? Drag her into a kiss? Or be angry at her for leaving so suddenly?

But his unreadable expression, although preferable to those other choices, threw her off balance.

"My lawyer said that according to the prenup, I owe you something."

The prenup he'd said he didn't remember asking her to sign.

"We can talk about that when your lawyer gets here. Would you like some coffee?" He gestured to the table where he had a coffee service already set up.

She nodded as she walked to the table and sat down. Another knock sounded at the door, and Quinn went to answer it as she poured herself a cup.

What could he possibly want from her? She'd been racking her brain trying to figure it out. At the time she'd signed it, she'd already been in debt to him. Though the agreement they'd had was supposed to take care of that. Maybe he'd been worried that she'd walk out before the end of the month.

Which she had.

Maybe he'd wanted it as insurance that she'd stay. Or as punishment if she didn't. That would explain why he'd delayed the annulment.

So now would he take everything she had left?

Bev walked to the table, wearing a charcoal suit and red blouse.

"Hi, April. Sorry, I had hoped to be here first so it wouldn't be awkward." She sat down across from April.

"It's okay. I arrived early." She'd been so anxious she couldn't help herself.

Bev set her briefcase on the table and opened it as Quinn sat down. She pulled out a folder.

"Mr. Taylor, did you discuss the terms with Ms. Smith yet?"

"You mean Mrs. Taylor?" A hint of a grin curled his lips. Or was that her imagination. "No, I haven't."

"April, let me tell you first that this contract is unenforceable. That said, Mr. Taylor can refuse to go forward with the annulment, and in that case, you'd have to start divorce proceedings if you wish to end the marriage."

"I appreciate that you want to protect your client," Quinn said, "but before we get into the details of all of that, why don't you just explain the terms to April and we'll go from there."

"Very well."

Bev opened the folder, and April could see the sheet on top was a scan of a smaller piece of paper with some quickly scrawled words in Quinn's bold printing. At the bottom, she could see her signature.

"Basically, this document says you agree that if you end the marriage to Austin Wright—"

"You mean *Quinn Taylor*," April corrected.

"No, she's right," Quinn said. "This agreement is triggered if you annul your marriage to Austin, which you did."

Bev glanced from Quinn to April.

April pursed her lips in confusion. "Okay. Go on."

"If you end the marriage with Austin Wright—which, as Mr. Taylor pointed out, you have done—then you agree to stay married to Mr. Taylor."

"What?" April frowned. "But that makes no sense."

"We *were* pretty drunk," Quinn said. "The point is, I didn't insist you sign a prenup to protect myself from losing money. I had you sign it to protect myself from losing *you*."

Quinn's gut clenched. He couldn't read her expression, but the stunned, leaning-to-somber expression on her face wasn't a good sign.

"I had you sign that contract because I love you so desperately," he continued. "In that uninhibited state, the most important thing in the world to me was keeping you as my wife."

April glanced at her lawyer.

"Sweetheart, in case you're worried, I'm not going to force anything on you. I'll waive the prenup, and I'll sign the annulment papers if that's what you want. I just wanted this chance to prove to you that I do trust you."

April's teeth nipped at her lower lip. "I'd like a minute to talk to my lawyer," she said.

"Of course." Quinn's heart sank.

He stood up and walked to the window, giving them plenty of distance while April leaned forward and spoke to her lawyer in a low voice. A moment later, the other woman put the folder back in her briefcase and stood up.

"It was nice meeting you, Mr. Taylor. I'll be in touch." With that, she walked to the door and left.

He turned back to April, his heart pounding, as she stood up and walked toward him, her eyes filled with determination.

"There's one thing I have to say to you, Mr. Taylor," April said.

His chest constricted. Clearly, he hadn't convinced her, and now she was going to tell him to stay out of her life.

"What's that?" he asked.

She stood in front of him now, her gaze locked on his face.

She rested her hand on his cheek, and her beautiful blue eyes softened.

His heart skipped a beat.

When her lips turned up in a smile, his pulse raced.

"That I love you, too." She ran her fingertips along his jaw-line, her eyes gleaming. "And I would love to continue being your wife."

It was as if a cloud of butterflies fluttered through him. His spirit soared.

She stepped into his arms and tipped up her sweet face, her lips parting in invitation. He captured them, his arms encircling her, drawing her close. He ached at the feel of her so soft and warm against him. Exactly where he wanted her to be.

Their lips parted, and he laughed in joyous exuberance. Then he lifted her and spun her around.

"Oh, God, I love you so much, baby. It was hell on earth these past few weeks thinking I'd lost you for good."

"I've missed you, too, Quinn. Leaving you was the hardest thing I've ever done."

He stroked some hair back from her face. "I hope you'll never leave again. I want you in my life always."

Her beaming smile lit up her face, and she hugged him close, her cheek tightly against his chest, right over his heart. He cupped her head and stroked her silken hair.

After a moment, he slid his hands to her shoulders and eased her back. Then he knelt down on the floor in front of her and pulled out the small velvet box from his pocket.

"I never gave you a proper proposal." He snapped open the box, displaying the white gold engagement ring with a two-carat, pear-shaped diamond surrounded by a halo of smaller diamonds.

"April, I love you with all my heart. Will you be my wife?"

Her smile broadened until her whole face was beaming. "I will."

He took her hand and slipped the ring on her finger. She held up her hand, gazing at the dazzling diamonds glittering in the sunlight.

He stood up, and she hugged him tightly again.

"The offer still stands if you want to annul the marriage and start anew with a big wedding," he said.

"No. We can do a wedding for friends and family if you want, but I like the character of our inauspicious beginning. You helped me when you didn't have to, then you asked me to marry you because you are a profoundly caring man and wanted to turn my tragic wedding day into a dream come true." She smiled. "And you did. Especially when you brought in a second groom. That made it absolutely spectacular."

"Speaking of which, you know Austin is convinced we're going to continue sharing you."

She arched an eyebrow. "Really? And what are your thoughts on that?"

He ran his hand along the back of his neck. "To tell the truth, I like the idea. I think the two of you have a special connection and, well . . ." He shrugged. "I find it really hot watching you and Austin having sex."

She nibbled her lower lip. "And you won't be jealous if I tell you I've fallen in love with Austin, too?"

"If I thought you were going to pick him over me, then yeah. But it's me you're married to. And if the three of us agree to be together, then we have the best of all possible worlds."

Her eyes grew wide as she gazed into his.

"Is something wrong?"

She giggled. "No. Quite the opposite. I'm just amazed at how lucky I am. I've stumbled into the best situation ever. Having two doting husbands to fulfill my every desire."

He tugged her closer and wrapped his arms tightly around her. "I will absolutely fulfill every desire you have, baby." His lips captured hers in a deep, passionate kiss. "Starting right now."

He scooped her up and carried her into the bedroom. He set her on the bed and unfastened his tie, then pulled it free and tossed it aside.

"Aren't we going to phone Austin to let him know?" she asked.

"No need." He shed his jacket as he walked across the room, then dropped it on a chair and tapped on another door.

"Why are you knocking on the bathroom door?" she asked.

"It's not the bathroom. It's a second bedroom."

The door opened, and Austin stood in the doorway.

"Austin, my wife would like you to join us in bed. If you're not too busy."

27

Austin broke out in a big smile. "You two have finally figured out you're meant to be together. Thank God."

The happiness he felt for his friend and for April was heartfelt and joyous, but a part of him wished it could have been him she'd chosen.

"Not only that," April said. "We know that we're meant to be with you, too."

"Yeah, man," Quinn said. "It's official. We want you to be April's second husband. Even if it's not on paper."

Although Austin had made it clear to Quinn that he wanted them to keep on sharing April, he'd assumed that when they finally figured out they wanted to be husband and wife, Austin would be an occasional guest in their bedroom.

But he now filled with hope that maybe it would be more than that.

"It sounds like you two are proposing to me." He leaned against the doorjamb and crossed his arms, his grin broadening. "But I'm not sure. If it's really a proposal, it should be done right."

Quinn arched an eyebrow. "You want one of us to get down on bended knee and propose?"

April giggled. "Wait a minute, Quinn. I've got this."

She stood up, then with a slow, graceful fluidity walked toward them. It was the most seductive thing Austin had ever seen. He couldn't take his eyes off the sway of her hips.

Until she shed her suit jacket, then started unbuttoning the blouse. As her creamy breasts were revealed, his cock swelled. The blouse fluttered to the floor, and she unzipped her skirt. It slipped away, and she stepped out of it.

Austin's grin faded as he watched her step closer, desire surging through him.

When she stood in front of him, she smiled in a way designed to make a man's heart—and cock—leap. Then she reached around behind her back and unhooked her bra. When she revealed her firm, round breasts, the dusky rose nipples thrusting forward, his groin tightened.

"Austin," she said in a deep, sultry voice.

Then she took his hand and brought it to her mouth. The feel of her soft lips fluttering light kisses on his palm sent shivers through him. Then she turned her wide blue eyes to his, and he saw a sweet vulnerability in those depths.

"I'm married to Quinn, but I'm also in love with you," she said. "Ever since the first moment I met you, you've been kind and generous and truly caring. You tried to protect me, and you did everything you could to bring Quinn and me together again. You are a true friend, a very loving man, and I really want you to be a part of my life and our marriage."

At the sheen in her eyes, he felt his own eyes prickling. His heart swelled. She wasn't doing this just because having a threesome was a fun adventure. She actually loved him.

And he loved her.

To his surprise, she knelt down in front of him and kissed his hand again.

"Mr. Austin Wright, will you be my second husband and live with Quinn and me as husband and wife and husband, for the rest of our lives?"

"Oh, fuck." He dashed at a tear springing from his eye and dropped to his knees in front of her. He grasped her shoulders, staring deeply into her lovely eyes. "Of course I will. I love you, too."

He pulled her to him tightly, taking her lips with a depth of passion that soared from his soul. When he finally released her, she giggled, and he saw the pure joy in her eyes. He laughed, too.

His gaze shot to Quinn. "And you know that I love this guy, too." He grinned. "As a brother. But I don't mind getting down and dirty in the bedroom with him and the woman we both love."

He felt a tug on his shirt and realized that April was unfastening his buttons. She pulled his shirt open, then snuggled against his bare chest. The feel of her naked breasts against him made him groan happily.

"Talking about getting down and dirty . . ." He stroked her soft breast, his thumb brushing over her nipple.

She sighed contentedly. He drew her to her feet and cupped both breasts, lifting them in his palms. She turned in his arms so her back was to him and her delightful ass was tight against his erection. She wiggled it, causing his cock to grow and press tightly against his confining pants.

She took his hands and placed them over her breasts. Quinn, who was standing in front of Austin, watched with a smile.

Austin pinched her hard nipples between his fingertips, watching Quinn's dark blue eyes grow darker. In the mirror across the room, Austin could see April's hand slide down her taut stomach, then over the lace of her panties.

Then she dipped inside.

"Oh, my. I'm getting very wet." She smiled coquettishly. "I wish someone would help me out."

Quinn's hand was gliding over his thick bulge now. "Austin, I think it's your play."

Austin chuckled, then tugged the back of April's panties down. He unfastened his pants and let his cock spring free, then slid it between April's thighs, gliding over the hot, slick flesh.

"Damn, sweetheart, you *are* wet."

In the mirror, he could see his cockhead sprouting out from between her legs. Her fingers brushed his tip, sending sensual waves pulsing through him. He rocked his hips, his cock stroking over her.

She rested her head against his shoulder. "I want you inside me," she murmured, her voice full of need.

On the next stroke forward, he pushed his tip upward and pressed into her intimate folds. He moaned when he felt her welcoming flesh open around him. His cock slipped into her in a slow, even stroke. When he was all the way inside, he held her tightly against him, his arm snug around her waist.

Quinn stepped forward and cupped her breasts in his hands.

April moaned softly. Austin's thick cock was deep inside her, and Quinn's warm hands covered her breasts, his thumbs toying with her aching nipples.

Quinn leaned in and kissed her, his mouth gentle and loving on hers.

"Do you want Austin to fuck you now?" Quinn's lips nuzzled against her ear. "To make you come?"

"Yesss," she breathed.

Quinn smiled and slid her panties down her legs. Austin drew her backward a few steps, and then their bodies sank downward as he sat in a big, cozy armchair. He leaned back and wrapped his hands around her waist. The sight of them in the mirror, Austin fully clothed and her totally naked on top of him, his cock deep inside her, made her feel dirty. And exhilarated.

She leaned forward and rested her hands on his thighs, then lifted herself, his cock gliding inside her. Then she lowered herself again.

Quinn watched them, his midnight eyes simmering with desire. He was fully clothed, too, but he opened his shirt and cast it aside, then shoved down his pants and boxers. She watched Quinn wrap his hand around his thick erection and stroke it. She squeezed Austin's inside her as it plunged deep into her again.

She held out her hand to Quinn, and he stepped close. She wrapped her hand around his cock, then leaned down and took him in her mouth as Austin pumped into her from below. Her knees were shaking as pleasure quivered through her. She sucked on Quinn, moving her hand and mouth up and down on him to the same rhythm as Austin's moving cock.

Quinn knelt down in front of her, his cock escaping her hold.

"Baby, just enjoy Austin fucking you. I don't want to be distracted from watching your beautiful face as you come."

Then he stroked down her stomach and found her clit. Staggering delight rushed through her at the combination of a big, thick cock filling her vagina and swirling, intense sensations quivering through her bud.

"Oh, God, I'm going to come." Her voice was hoarse and deep with need.

"Fuck, sweetheart, me, too," Austin groaned.

He pumped faster, and her head swirled as a flood of pleasure surged through her.

"Ohhh," she moaned.

Quinn's finger kept moving on her, driving the pleasure higher. As she wailed at the top of her lungs, Austin spiked deep, and she felt him erupt inside her with a groan. He continued rocking his hips. Between that and Quinn's attention on her clit, she kept sailing on a wave of bliss.

After a long time, the orgasm finally waned, and she slumped forward into Quinn's arms. As he held her tightly, Austin sat up straight and kissed the back of her neck. Quinn drew her to her feet and led her to the bed, then perched her on the edge. He then pressed her knees wide apart, and his head swooped down.

When she felt his mouth on her, licking, then pulsing deep, her fingers curled in his hair and she moaned. Austin sat down beside her, watching Quinn's head between her legs.

Quinn found her clit and teased it mercilessly, and she arched against his mouth. Pleasure spiked through her again, and she fell back on the bed, moaning as another orgasm exploded inside her.

"Ah, fuck, you're so beautiful when you come, baby." Quinn surged onto the bed and pressed his hard cockhead to her opening, then drove inside. His thick shaft, so stiff and hard, pushed in deep.

"Oh, yes, Quinn," she wailed, flying high with the pleasure.

He wrapped his arms around her and pulled her to him as he kept driving into her.

As she soared to heaven, he groaned, and she felt a flood of hot liquid inside her. After a few more deep thrusts, he slowed, and she drifted back to earth. She sighed and snuggled in his arms. She could see Austin watching her from his perch on the bed beside her, and she smiled at him.

"You two are amazing," she murmured against Quinn's skin.

Quinn kissed the top of her head. "And you are an amazing woman."

He rolled to his side.

She smiled. "Mmm. You know, I'm feeling really greedy tonight. I want both of you inside me at once. But sadly, you're both spent."

Austin chuckled, then stood up. "That won't take long to fix."

He walked to the audio system in the armoire and turned on some sultry music, then he held out his hand to her.

"Would you like to dance?"

She smiled as she and Quinn stood up. "Really?"

Austin took her hand and drew her close to him, his arms curling around her. A second later, Quinn was pressed close to her back, and the three of them were moving in time to the slow music.

It wasn't long before she felt their cocks nudging into her. Austin slowed down their dance even more, then reached down and glided his cock between her thighs. With every movement, his shaft massaged her sensitive, slick flesh.

Quinn laughed, then she felt his cock slide in above Austin's, until both their cocks were between her legs, snug against each other's. She couldn't believe they didn't mind their cocks touching like that, but she was glad. It opened so many more variations for them.

Quinn's hands glided over her breasts, cupping them. Austin slid one hand down her stomach and found her clit, teasing it in light strokes.

"Oh, God, you two are driving me insane." Her words were barely coherent.

"I don't think she wants to dance anymore," Quinn said nonchalantly.

"I think you're right, buddy."

They rocked their hips against her in unison, Quinn's cock stroking her, driving her need higher.

"I want you both inside me," she insisted. "Please."

"I think she's begging for us to fuck her," Austin said.

"You're right. Do you think we should give her what she wants?" Quinn asked.

"If you don't . . ." She gasped for air when Austin flicked her clit. "I'm going to start without you."

Quinn's deep chuckle rumbled through her. "She means business."

Her whole body started to tremble. "I do," she squeaked.

Quinn's cock slid back, then she felt him position it against her back opening. Austin stepped back, holding her hands and bending her forward. Quinn pressed slowly against her, easing forward. Her passage opened reluctantly around him, but he coaxed it with a slow and steady pressure. When his cockhead finally pushed all the way inside, her canal hugged him tightly, and she rested her head against Austin's stomach.

Austin stroked her hair to one side and held it in his hand as Quinn pushed deeper into her.

"Damn, I love watching Quinn's cock push into your ass," he said.

She squeezed his hand, her head spinning at the intensity of the sensual onslaught of the thick shaft moving inside her tight passage. Finally, Quinn was all the way inside. Austin eased her up until she was standing. He moved closer with a smile, then his cockhead was pushing against her vagina. He slid inside easily, stroking up inside her next to Quinn's already embedded cock.

Both her passages were full of fat, hard cock. She squeezed, and both men groaned.

"Oh, God, somebody do something or I think I'll die," she groaned.

Both men took that as a cue and began to move. The thick shafts slid in and out, dragging along her sensitive passages. Triggering delightful sensations dancing through her entire body.

"Ohhh, yes." Pleasure pulsed through her with each slow, even stroke. She began to quiver, and her head spun.

They thrust a little faster, and she clung to Austin's shoulders as her heartbeat increased.

"Ohhh." Her moan was low and deep. "I'm going to come."

But just as she felt the orgasm start to blossom, rippling from deep inside, they slowed it down again. They pushed their big cocks deep inside her . . . stopped for a heartbeat . . . then pulled back again. She groaned as the thick cockheads stroked her insides.

"I . . . need you . . . to go . . . faster," she panted.

They sped up, and her body quivered at the exquisite pleasure, but as soon as she felt that delightful stirring deep inside, they slowed again.

She glanced up at Quinn's face through her haze of pleasure, and his grin told her they were doing this on purpose.

She squeezed them both tight, making *them* groan this time. And almost pushing her over the edge.

"Please, I beg of you, make me come," she pleaded.

Their arms slid around each other, holding her tightly between them. Then they sped up in earnest. She felt like a buoy bobbing on the water, simply riding the movements of the ocean waves. They pulsed deep, their hard cocks boring all the way in, then pulled back, triggering a swirling storm of delight within her.

"We want you to come, baby," Quinn said in a desire-roughened voice, then he kissed the top of her head.

Her body felt like it was shimmering, as if a magical spell had been cast on her and she was about to explode in a burst of stardust.

They pumped deeper and faster, and her whole body quaked as electricity surged through every cell of her body. She sucked in a breath as sparks flickered across her nerve endings. Then it happened. When they drove inside her, an orgasm swelled up and careened through her in a blazing wave of crackling flames.

She cried out as she was catapulted over the edge. The world dropped away as she floated in a total state of bliss, her body pulsing with pure joy.

She felt the men continue to pump into her, keeping her in this rapturous state. Then they both drove deep and groaned, releasing their seed into her at the same time. She moaned again, flung into a higher state of ecstasy.

They kept rocking their hips, keeping her in the delightful state of pleasure, but finally her moans diminished and she descended back to earth. She slumped in their arms, her eyelids fluttering closed.

"I think she fainted," Quinn said.

"Mmm. No," she murmured against his chest. "My knees just went weak."

Austin laughed and stepped back, his hands firmly around her waist, supporting her. Quinn scooped her up and carried her to the bed, then set her down.

"I think we could all use a rest right now," Quinn said as he climbed into bed and snuggled beside her, his arm around her waist.

Austin got in the other side and slid close to her, too.

"I love how our bride begs to be fucked," Quinn said.

Austin smiled. "And for us to make her come."

"Well, the two of you were torturing me."

Austin's eyebrow rose. "So we shouldn't do that again?"

She grinned. "Oh, I didn't say that."

Austin and Quinn both laughed, and she glanced from one to the other, delighted at the glow in both their eyes. How had she been so lucky as to wind up with both these wonderful men?

Her whole life, no one had ever cared about her, but now both Quinn and Austin were in love with her. They cared about her and what happened to her. They would protect her if she needed it. And she was sure they would support her in whatever she wanted to do.

"I love you both so much," she said softly. "I can't believe how lucky I am."

Quinn laughed, a joyous sound. "Austin and I went to Vegas to kick off our new life of leisure, each of us with hopes of finding the woman of our dreams, then you walked into my life again and turned everything upside down. I never would have believed we'd both fall in love with the same woman. And that it would be you, the woman I never stopped loving."

"Good thing you had me along," Austin said, "to make sure you didn't blow it."

She smiled and nodded. Then she yawned, feeling cozy and a bit sleepy nestled between their warm bodies.

"Now I'd like to have a little nap with my two strapping big husbands." She stroked down their taut stomachs and over their cocks, surprised to find them semi-erect. She giggled. "Then afterward, maybe we can find something fun to do."

"I'm all for that," Quinn said, tightening his embrace around her waist.

"Me, too." Austin nuzzled her neck as he rocked against her hand.

She wrapped her fingers around their thick shafts, and her eyelids fell closed. With a smile on her face, she drifted off to a deep slumber, content in the arms of the two men who loved her.

Acknowledgments

With fond thanks to my editor, Rose, who believed in me right from the beginning and gave me my first big break. Thanks to Eileen and Tiffany who have continued the journey with me. I appreciate all you've done to bring this book together. Also, thanks to Emily, my wonderful agent, who has been my guiding light for many years.

Acknowledgments

With fond thanks to my editor, Rose, who believed in me right from the beginning and gave me my first big break. Thanks to Eileen and Tiffany who have continued the journey with me. I appreciate all you've done to bring this book together. Also, thanks to Emily, my wonderful agent, who has been my guiding light for many years.